Praise for the Mackenzies series

"Heartrending, funny, honest, and true. . . . I want to marry the hero!"
　　　　—*New York Times* bestselling author Eloisa James

"I love the Mackenzies—every one of them."
　　　　—*New York Times* bestselling author Sarah MacLean

"Ashley writes the kinds of heroes I crave."
　　　　—*New York Times* bestselling author Elizabeth Hoyt

"A sexy, passion-filled romance that will keep you reading until dawn."
　　　　—*USA Today* bestselling author Julianne MacLean

"Skillfully nuanced characterization and an abundance of steamy sensuality."　　　　—*Chicago Tribune*

A Mackenzie Clan Christmas

JENNIFER ASHLEY

JOVE
New York

A JOVE BOOK
Published by Berkley
An imprint of Penguin Random House LLC
penguinrandomhouse.com

A Mackenzie Clan Gathering copyright © 2015 by Jennifer Ashley
A Mackenzie Yuletide copyright © 2019 by Jennifer Ashley
Penguin Random House supports copyright. Copyright fuels creativity, encourages
diverse voices, promotes free speech, and creates a vibrant culture. Thank you for buying
an authorized edition of this book and for complying with copyright laws by not
reproducing, scanning, or distributing any part of it in any form without permission.
You are supporting writers and allowing Penguin Random House to continue to
publish books for every reader.

A JOVE BOOK, BERKLEY, and the BERKLEY & B colophon
are registered trademarks of Penguin Random House LLC.

ISBN: 9781984805584

InterMix eBook edition of *A Mackenzie Clan Gathering* / November 2015
InterMix eBook edition of *A Mackenzie Yuletide* / October 2019

Printed in the United States of America
1   3   5   7   9   10   8   6   4   2

Cover art: *Image of castle* by Tadeas Skuhra / Shutterstock

Contents

A
Mackenzie
Clan Christmas

A
Mackenzie
Yuletide

Chapter 1

Mac Mackenzie paused, his paintbrush dripping, at the soft sound from the end of the corridor.

The skylights in his room at the top of Kilmorgan Castle, the vast Mackenzie manor house, were dark. Mac didn't remember night falling, but when he became deeply immersed in painting, time passed swiftly.

It was also cold, his fire having died to a glow of coals. Lamps glowed softly, which meant his valet, Bellamy, must have entered and lit them.

Mac pulled himself out of the painting of a Scottish landscape and restored himself to the here and now. It was mid-December, at two in the morning, and his wife and children were snugly asleep in the floors below. Mac's brothers and their families slept in their wings of the vast house, all awaiting the celebrations at Christmas and Hogmanay.

No one should be up near the studio at this hour, but that did not mean his son, Robert, hadn't climbed restlessly out of bed to roam the halls. Or that Robert and his cousins Jamie and Alec hadn't gathered for a stolen smoke or nip of whisky they didn't think their fathers knew about.

Mac wiped his brush and dropped it into his jar of oil of turpentine. He mopped at his hands, which never stayed clean, but didn't bother trying to scrub off his face. Nor did he remove the kerchief that kept his hair more or less free of paint. Once he found the source of the noise, he'd return and finish the shadowing that was challenging him.

He shrugged on his shirt, now noticing the cold. Painting with fervor heated his body, so he usually ended up in only his kilt and shoes.

Mac stepped into the cold, silent hall. It ran narrowly before him, ending in a T—one direction led to Ian's wing, the other to Cameron's. He saw a flutter of white in the shadows, heard again the quiet rustle that had cut through his painting haze.

"Iz?" Mac called softly.

He started down the corridor. If Isabella, his darling wife, had come up to entice him to bed, he'd play along. The studio had a wide, comfortable sofa, and he could build up the fire to keep them warm while they bared more skin . . .

Another flutter, then silence.

Mac began to grin. Isabella had a teasing streak, and when she turned playful, life became splendid. Mac's blood warmed, and he forgot all about painting.

"Izzy, love." He started after her, anticipation building. What game would she play this time? And how would Mac turn the tables, as he loved to do?

He reached the split in the corridor. Stairs led down from here to the floors below, or he could turn to one of his brothers' wings. Years ago, the sons and daughters of the Mackenzies had slept in nurseries on these top floors, but they had long since moved to larger bedchambers below.

That fact was in one way sad, but then again, the older

children would be marrying in a few short years, and nurseries would fill again. Mac's adopted daughter, Aimee, was nineteen now, and so beautiful.

Which was very worrying. Mac found himself snarling like a bear at gentlemen she danced with at the balls Isabella had carefully selected since Aimee's debut.

An icy draft poured over him as he tried to decide which way to turn. The wind cut, making him shiver. Who had left a blasted window open?

He thought the chill came from Cam's wing, and he quietly moved that direction. The short hall beyond was empty and dark.

"What the devil are you doing, love?" he said, a bit louder. "It's freezing. Let's go to the studio and make it cozy."

Another rustle. Mac followed the noise around the corner to the longer corridor. At its end was a flash of white, then nothing.

Mac gave up stealth and sprinted down the corridor. He'd catch Isabella and she'd laugh, then he'd carry her to where they could tear off what little clothing Mac wore and enjoy themselves.

A window lay at the end of the hall—open, Mac saw as he reached it. As he'd suspected. Mac slammed it closed.

He heard a whisper of sound and spun around. Behind him, where he'd just come from, stood a lady in white. A chance moonbeam caught on her red hair.

In that instant, Mac knew this wasn't Isabella. Different stance, different height, and Isabella was . . . alive.

Why he thought this woman wasn't, Mac didn't know. Maybe because the moonlight made her skin deathly pale, or because the white dress floated, though the draft had gone. Mac couldn't see every detail of her, but she seemed to have no hands or feet.

Mac's heart beat faster, but he felt no fear. Kilmorgan was an old place—this could be any lady, from any era.

"Good evening," he said softly. "I'm Mac. But you probably know that. What's *your* name, lass? Which one are you?"

The apparition was utterly silent. Mac took a step forward, wondering what would happen when he reached her. Could he walk straight through her? And would that be impolite?

He was halfway down the hall to the hovering lady when she vanished, abruptly and utterly.

Clouds slid over the moon. Mac was left in the freezing cold and dark, alone, disappointed, and suddenly tired.

He moved quickly back to his own wing, doused the lights in the studio, and fled downstairs to his bedchamber, which was warm and inviting. His wife was fast asleep in their bed, and never moved when Mac climbed in with her, spooning close to her in their heated nest.

～

"I saw a ghost last night," Mac announced at the breakfast table.

Ian Mackenzie took a moment to decide whether this declaration was interesting enough for him to look up from the letter and photographs that had arrived in the morning's post. Mac liked to spin yarns, and Ian had learned to ignore most of them.

He glanced at Mac, who slid into a place at the long table, his plate loaded with eggs, sausages, ham, and scones dripping with butter. A few rivulets of butter trickled over the edge of the plate to make perfect round pools on the tablecloth.

Their nephew Daniel laughed. "Did you, Uncle Mac?"

"I did," Mac answered without worry. "Vanished before my eyes."

Violet, Daniel's wife, made sure their seven-year-old daughter, Fleur, wasn't giving too many bits of toast to the dogs, and leaned forward eagerly. "Interesting. Where did you see it?"

"My wing. Then it floated to Cam's wing and disappeared." Mac shoved most of a scone into his mouth and chewed noisily.

Ian had difficulty knowing when Mac was teasing or serious. Hart and Cameron were straightforward with their speeches—sometimes loudly so—but Mac made up stories or played with words, bursting out laughing in the middle of them. Ian had learned to wait until Mac wound down to judge whether what he spoke was truth or exaggeration. He returned to his letter and let the others at the table play it out.

Breakfast at Kilmorgan was an informal meal, with food placed on the sideboard for all to enjoy. Some days the ladies indulged in breakfast in bed, but most mornings they made their way to the dining room to eat with the family. The younger Mackenzies were welcome—no banishment because they had not yet reached a specific age. The four brothers had made that decision years ago.

Ian liked the breakfast gatherings. He read his letters or newspapers while various Mackenzies chattered around him. At the house he shared with Beth and his three children, breakfast could be intimate or rowdy, the five of them crammed around the table.

As soon as Mac ceased speaking and began to eat, Ian's daughters, Belle and Megan, entered and helped themselves at the sideboard.

Megan finished filling her plate first and took a seat next to Ian. Megan was thirteen now, and becoming so beautiful. Ian lost himself in looking at her eyes, so like her mother's, and her hair that was glossy brown with a touch of red.

Belle, her plate heaped almost as much as Mac's, sat on the other side of her sister. Ian noted they kept to the placement that was usual at home—they knew he preferred it if everyone sat in the same seats day after day.

"Good morning, ladies," Daniel boomed at them. "Uncle Mac has seen a ghost at the top of Kilmorgan Castle.

What awful specter haunts our midst? A Highlander of old, calling to his clan? Great-great-great-grandfather Malcolm bellowing for his whisky? A lady waiting for her lover to return from one of our many rebellions?"

"Papa." Fleur shook her head at him. Like Violet, she was a skeptic.

Megan shivered. "I hope it's not the lonely lady."

Belle scoffed. "There are no ghosts. They are seen only by people who are drunk or mad." She caught Mac's grin and flushed. "Not that I mean you are mad, Uncle Mac. Or drunk. But it has been shown that oil of turpentine and the components of paints can make one's brain behave as though it is intoxicated. You might have breathed in too much last night."

Mac winked at her. "An excellent theory. Very scientific. I assure you, dear niece, I keep plenty of air flowing through my studio and avoid a buildup of fumes. I truly did see a ghost. Kilmorgan is quite haunted."

"Poppycock," Belle said, but Megan shivered again. "There has been absolutely no proven existence of ghosts and spirits," Belle went on. "Those who pretend to have gathered evidence are frauds. Oh, I beg your pardon, Cousin Violet."

"No need, sweetheart," Violet answered calmly. "I know all about frauds and hoaxes. Do not worry, Megan. Whatever your uncle Mac saw, it wasn't a ghost."

"If you say so," Mac said before he fell to devouring the rest of his breakfast.

Megan did not return the smile, from which Ian deduced she was not reassured. He reached over and squeezed her hand.

"There are no ghosts," he said firmly. "They do not exist."

"Quite right," Belle said on Megan's far side.

Belle looked for rational and scientific explanations for everything, from a flower pushing through the earth to how far away the stars were, to how rain clouds formed. Her inquisitive and eager mind had worked through most of the books in Ian's library, and she'd quickly absorbed everything her brother's tutors had taught them.

Jamie, Ian's oldest, had gone off to Harrow, leaving his sisters behind, but Ian had insisted they hire another tutor, one who could keep up with Belle's swift mind. She was determined to go to university, to study to be a doctor. Ian saw no reason why she should not—Belle was brilliant and ought to be allowed to do anything she wanted.

Beth tried to explain to Ian and Belle that education for a woman was very difficult, but Belle only furrowed her brow and said she'd do it. Ian knew she would, and he'd certainly use all his might as a Mackenzie to ensure that she found a university that would take her.

Megan was no less intelligent, but in a different way. She was highly imaginative, constructing entire worlds in her mind and acting them out with her dolls or the dogs. Where Belle made her way through scientific journals, Megan read fairy tales and lengthy novels. Megan was also quite musical, able, like Ian, to learn a piece of music by hearing others play it through once. Unlike Ian, though, Megan could play it back with feeling, often ending up sobbing by the close of the piece.

Megan was compassionate; Belle a force to be reckoned with. Beth expressed surprise that the two got along so well, but Belle was Megan's defender, and Megan's gentleness eased Belle when she grew frustrated and impatient.

"What is this talk of ghosts?" Isabella Mackenzie floated into the room, her red hair drawn up in the latest fashion, which Ian privately thought resembled a giant pincushion. Isabella changed her hair nearly every week.

Mac rose from the table, wiped his mouth, and kissed his wife soundly on the lips. "Saw one. Upstairs last night."

"How exciting." Isabella helped herself to toast and tea from the sideboard, sat down, and raised her cup to her lips. "Tell me all about it."

Mac launched into his tale once more, and Ian returned to his letter. He'd written to a man in London, asking for particulars on what was in the photographs and line drawings—an antique necklace with intricately worked loops of gold and hung with emeralds and lapis lazuli. It was ancient, Roman, and had purportedly been taken from the tomb of a Roman consul's wife. Somehow it had ended up in the treasury of a church in Norwich, and when the parish needed to raise money, they'd decided to sell it, as it was nonecclesiastical and had been hidden away for a rainy day.

They'd sold it to a small museum in London that hadn't really been able to afford it, and the necklace hadn't proved a great attraction, giant fossil bones being more interesting to the museum's patrons. The museum had quietly sold it on to a collector in Paris.

Ian had decided the necklace would look perfect on Beth, and wanted it for her Hogmanay present.

There was a problem, however. The necklace had disappeared after the sale, and no one knew where it was. Ian, with the determination Belle had inherited from him, set out to find it.

The letter, from a London acquaintance who'd photographed the piece when it had lain in the museum, confessed he did not know where the necklace had ended up. The Frenchman who'd purchased it claimed it had never reached his Parisian mansion. Somewhere between London and Paris, the necklace had vanished.

Ian read the words, studied the man's photographs and drawings of the necklace, and made up his mind that nothing would deter him.

"Excellent," Isabella said. "Once we trap it, we'll know whether it is a true ghost or someone playing tricks on poor, sleepless Mac."

Ian looked up. "Trap it?"

"Yes indeed." Isabella's green eyes sparkled as she gave Ian her wide smile. "We're off to catch a ghost."

"Poor thing," Megan said, her mouth turning down.

"It's only someone playing tricks," Belle said. "You'll see. We'll catch them and give them a good talking-to."

"Poor thing," Megan repeated.

Ian squeezed Megan's hand again and slid one of the photographs toward her. "I'm going to find this for your mama," he said. "Will you help me?"

Chapter 2

Jamie Mackenzie spent the miles on the train from London looking through the answers to his inquiries in disappointment.

He'd thought he could ask about the rare thing he wished to acquire for his parents' Hogmanay gift, write a few letters, and purchase it. He'd have to go through the Mackenzie man of business for the money and swear him to secrecy, but picturing the joy on his mother's face on Hogmanay morning was worth the trouble.

His father showed joy in a different way. Ian's face wouldn't change, but he'd go very still, absorbing every bit of information, and then he'd pull his son into a hard embrace. What Ian couldn't express through words came out in his very firm and thorough hugs.

But it seemed that buying an antique was more difficult than Jamie realized. Ian made it look easy, but then Dad had a calm stubbornness that made few refuse him. When Ian wanted a new bowl for his collection, no power on earth could stop him from obtaining it.

Jamie would have to be just as stubborn. He was his father's son, after all.

Curry likely could help. The man, a former thief, knew how to discover who had what and how to obtain it. Curry had taught Jamie many lessons over the years that his mother and father didn't know about.

Could Curry keep mum, though? He might not tell Ian, but Jamie wasn't so certain Curry could keep quiet around Jamie's mother. Beth Mackenzie was a wise woman, and Curry ate out of her hand. Jamie would have to find some way to keep Curry loyal to him for the duration of the hunt.

The door to the compartment burst open. A young woman in a fur-trimmed blue coat that covered her to her boots bounded in and slammed the door behind her. "I thought that was you! Jamie Mackenzie, the conquering hero, returns from Harrow."

Jamie blinked at his cousin Gavina, only daughter in Uncle Cameron and Aunt Ainsley's small brood.

"Never tell me they let you out of their sight," Jamie said, hiding his delight at seeing her. "Fifteen and not yet out—you can hardly travel alone on a *train*."

Gavina wrinkled her nose in an expression very like her mother's. "Of course not. Mum and Dad are in a compartment farther down the corridor. I became restless and wandered off. Dad gave his consent as long as I don't leave the car. Goodness knows what I'd get up to in the dining lounge. They'd let me stroll the length of the train if Stuart came with me, but he's asleep, the lump. Though he's far too young to defend my virtue. Not that he doesn't try."

She trailed off with a fond look. Stuart Mackenzie was very protective of his older sister.

"I'm old enough." Jamie jumped up. "I say we find the dining car. Or perhaps the end platform." He patted his jacket pocket, and Gavina brightened.

"Tsk, tsk." She twitched a finger at him with feigned disapproval. "You have whisky or cigars—or both. Do say you'll share."

"Of course. *And* defend your virtue." Jamie regarded her

critically, from the feathered bonnet on her red-gold hair to her slim boots. "You aren't supposed to know you *have* a virtue or why it needs defending."

Gavina rolled her gray eyes. "You cannot belong to this family and not know what the male and female of the sex get up to in the darkness of the night. Nor that there are terrible people out there for whom a young woman my age is a delectable morsel. But I have no fear, because I have a horde of cousins, not to mention a formidable father, who will never let me stray a step alone. Besides, I do know how to box, kick, and shoot a gun."

Jamie took a step away from her in mock worry. "Do you have a gun on your person?"

"Of course not. I don't need one with my father hovering over me every second. Now, lead on, Macduff," she misquoted. "I need coffee."

Jamie grinned and ushered her into the corridor. They walked down the train toward the dining car, waving at Uncle Cameron and Aunt Ainsley as they passed their compartment.

Ainsley rose, but instead of stepping out and calling them back, she simply nodded at them. Aunt Ainsley was a canny woman who knew when the young people needed a modicum of freedom.

Uncle Cameron was not always so understanding, but he, like Cousin Stuart, was fast asleep. The father and son sat facing each other at the window in identical positions— feet and arms crossed, heads slumped, snoring loudly. Aunt Ainsley would need to stuff cotton wool into her ears.

Jamie and Gavina moved through the dining car, scrounging mugs of coffee from waiters who looked smitten with Gavina, and strode through to the back platform of the train.

It was freezing outside, but the train blocked much of the wind. Jamie removed the whisky flask from his pocket and poured a dollop of Mackenzie malt into each of their cups. "For the chill. Ladies shouldn't drink spirits, you know."

Gavina sipped her doctored coffee and let out a sigh of satisfaction. "Ladies shouldn't do so very many things. I plan to be a spinster and shock people all the livelong day. Do say we'll have a fine time over the holidays. Next year, I shall be sent to finishing school. I am capitulating if Dad promises to send me to university, though everyone knows ladies go there only to catch husbands."

Jamie couldn't help laughing. Gavina's face fell at the prospect of finishing school, smoothed into happier lines when she spoke of university, and creased into a scowl when she spoke of snaring a husband. Jamie hoped he and Gavina ended up at Edinburgh together so he could watch her rebuff gentleman after gentleman.

"Out with it." Gavina fixed Jamie a shrewd look as he plucked a cigar from his pocket and lit it. "What were you looking so determined about when I sprang upon you?"

"Ah." Jamie took a pull of the cigar, enjoyed its flavor, and released the smoke. "I might just need your help. But this has to be a deep, dark secret."

Gavina crossed her heart and gave him her full attention. By the time Jamie finished explaining what he wanted to do, Gavina was leaning next to him, grinning out at the snowy fields.

"Excellent," she said. "You can count on me, Cousin. I'm your man."

~

"Did you really see a ghost?" Isabella Mackenzie wiped the last paintbrush she'd cleaned for her husband and set it in the jar with the others.

She enjoyed watching him paint and invented tasks as an excuse for joining him in the studio. Mac did need someone to keep things tidy up here, and he'd allow no maid or footman in to clean.

"I did indeed, my darling." Mac scraped his palette knife over brilliant yellow paint and used it to apply highlights to flowers in the foreground of his painting. He'd been doing more landscapes lately, beautiful things he shrugged about. "Nothing like Monsieur Monet," he'd say. "Or Cézanne. Man's a bloody genius."

"Belle is right that breathing in too many fumes can make a person see things," Isabella said.

Mac burst out laughing, and Isabella's heart turned over.

She'd been married to this man for years, and even now his smile, the sight of his muscles working as he turned to her in nothing but his kilt, had her hot as fire. She'd borne him two children who were nearly grown, but when he looked at her with his Mackenzie gold eyes, Isabella again became the debutante who'd tried and failed to scorn away the handsome young Highlander who'd crashed her come-out ball, danced her out to the terrace, and given her a kiss that changed her life.

There'd been plenty of turbulence those first years, but that turbulence had settled into intense, chaotic bliss.

"You cannae accuse me of being in a drunken stupor." Mac had not touched a drop of anything inebriating in many years. "Well, you could, but it would be a lie."

"I know, love."

Mac threw down his palette knife and advanced on her. "And when ye say *'love'* like that, ye know it undoes me."

Isabella lifted her face as paint-stained hands cupped it. Mac closed his eyes and kissed her, his mouth hard, experienced, calling up the heat he'd touched the night of her come-out ball. He'd kissed her, married her, and taken her to his bed in a matter of hours. Isabella had gone happily, and quite willingly.

A *bang* somewhere down the hall made them both jump. Isabella wanted to ignore it and continue reveling in her husband, but Mac brushed another kiss to her lips and made for the door, curiosity in every line of him.

Isabella, admitting curiosity herself, followed.

Mac led the way to Cam's wing of the house, where he said he'd seen the ghost. This corridor should have been quiet—Cam and Ainsley and family were still traveling to Kilmorgan—but plenty of noise echoed toward Isabella and Mac.

At the end of the hall, where a window overlooked the vast gardens of Kilmorgan, Isabella saw a flurry of activity. She heard Daniel's rumbling tones and the lighter ones of Violet, plus the youthful strains of the younger generation.

"What the devil are you all doing?" Mac asked the question before Isabella could.

Daniel busily tacked what looked like wires to the window, while Violet sprinkled powder on the floor. Fleur helped with that, flinging it happily about until Daniel sneezed. Belle assisted her aunt Eleanor to set up a tripod in the corner with a camera on it.

"Trapping ghosts," Daniel answered. "At least, trying to find evidence of one."

Belle looked up from securing the tripod's legs. "He means gathering evidence that it's a person up to no good."

"Oh." Mac sounded disappointed. "I would rather it be a real ghost. Like one of our ancestors Ian is always telling us about—Lady Mary or Celia or Josette from the old days. I'd love to have a good chin-wag with one of them."

"If she wanted a chat, she'd have stayed." Isabella slipped her hand through the crook of Mac's arm. "Likely you scared her, Mac. Maybe she thought you were your dad."

Mac shuddered. "Poor woman. I was hoping I could ask her a few things. Such as why Malcolm Mackenzie chose to punch an open hall all the way to the top of the stairs. Makes for a powerful draft."

"Draws the air," Daniel said. He hammered a nail into the window frame, which explained the banging. "An open tower with a cupola at the top lets air flow and not stagnate. Eighteenth-century engineering."

"Uncle Mac, there is no such thing as ghosts," Belle said impatiently. "This is what we will prove. Aunt Eleanor will take its photograph."

"Indeed." Eleanor, who had remained uncharacteristically silent as she adjusted the camera, beamed Mac and Isabella a smile. "I am rigging lines—well, with Daniel's help—that will open the camera's shutter when an unwitting person, or ghost, kicks them. Lighting is a bit tricky, because of course, we expect the ghost at night, but Daniel is rigging another device which will release flash powder at the same time and light the hall right up. Not only will the camera snap the photograph, but while the person is blinded, we can tackle him. It might not work at all, as so many things must happen in tandem, and we can't count on that, can we? But it is worth a try."

"Which is why I am coating the floor with powder." Violet straightened up and corked a now-empty glass jar. "The simplest way to prove it is a person and not a ghost is footprints. They'll walk through, never seeing the powder in the dark, and there is our evidence that she is a simple thief."

"The lady I saw had no feet," Mac pointed out. "Or hands."

"You *saw* no feet," Violet said. "In the dark, or faint light, like moonlight, white stands out well. If she wore black stockings and boots and black gloves, they'd fade into the darkness and create the illusion that she had no extremities."

Mac shook his head. "You lot are taking the romance out of it."

"If someone is breaking into the house, Hart will want to know," Eleanor countered. "If he loses his precious artwork again, he'll be most distraught. If we catch the intruder this way, we can give her a good talking-to and send her off to the police, thus sparing her Hart's wrath. You know how he is when he is upset."

Every head nodded. No one wanted Hart on a rampage.

"I am sure there is a good reason why the young woman entered the house," Eleanor went on. "I wonder what it is."

Daniel huffed a laugh. "The priceless paintings, Ming bowls, and plenty of jewels, silver, and sculpture we keep lying about. I am surprised there aren't a flood of thieves here every night."

"Our neighbors wouldn't dream of burgling us," Eleanor said. "Though thieves could always take the train from the cities and escape in a cart if they prepared well. Or find a place to stash the goods and sell them off a bit at a time while pretending to live virtuously in a nearby village."

Isabella gave Eleanor an amused look. "You have planned this well. How often have you thought of ways Kilmorgan Castle can be burgled?"

"Quite a lot. When I lived with my father and the money was tight, I remembered Kilmorgan's riches. I invented many ways I could relieve Hart of a treasure or two and use it to feed us through a winter. I justified it by telling myself that I deserved it after Hart tried to trick me into marrying him."

"Ye do deserve it," Mac agreed. "Though you did, after all, marry him, you poor woman."

"I did, didn't I? I suppose I will simply have to put up with him. I too would like to speak to this would-be burglar. Did Hart wrong her as well? Did she, like me, amuse herself while lying awake at night by planning the perfect heist?"

"She looked a bit young for Hart to have thrown her over," Mac said. "More Aimee's age. Hart hasn't looked at a woman since ye sprang back into his life like a comet. I doubt it's revenge she's after."

"Then it's the goods," Daniel said. He tugged at the wires he was affixing to the window. "These will ring a bell in our bedchamber, alerting us that the intruder has arrived. That way, we won't have to sit up all night in the cold."

"I hope she's a true ghost," Mac said, rubbing Isabella's hand. "Not only would she be interesting to talk to, but I could laugh at you all when your scientific machinations turned up nothing."

"That *would* be fun, wouldn't it?" Eleanor agreed. "I should adore talking with a ghost. So many questions. Could she even answer, I wonder? One needs breath to speak. And if she's from so very long ago, perhaps the wife or daughter of Old Dan Mackenzie, would we be able to understand her? Languages change through time."

Belle sent her a reproachful look. "I thought you didn't believe in ghosts, Aunt El. That's why you are helping us."

"Oh, I believe in all sorts of things." Eleanor smiled wisely. "The world is a far more interesting place than we realize. So many possibilities." She returned to adjusting the camera on the tripod, humming a little tune.

Belle looked perplexed, but Violet patted her shoulder. "It is a good idea you had to photograph it, Belle. All we can do is leave things in place, and hope Mac didn't frighten her off forever."

Mac grinned. "I was politeness itself. But we'll see, won't we?"

The atmosphere was optimistic, but when Daniel, Violet, and Belle raced back upstairs in the morning, the window remained closed, the powder undisturbed, and the camera in place, and no photographs taken of intruders, either ghost or human.

～

Beth had to smile at her daughter and husband sitting side by side in the main library at Kilmorgan, heads together. Newspapers and books lay strewn across the table, with Megan scratching notes in her careful handwriting.

"Jamie will be arriving soon," Beth said into the silence. Megan and Ian looked up with a start, Megan's alarm turning swiftly to guilt. She quickly covered her writing with her hand.

Ian, after his golden eyes widened a moment, recovered and assumed his usual calm. "Then we must meet him."

He closed all the books, one after the other, taking time to align them neatly. Megan looked as though she was about to eat her notes, and Beth felt both curiosity and amusement at her worry.

Christmas was coming, as was Hogmanay, and an air of secrecy always pervaded at this time. Ian and Megan were obviously scheming something to do with gifts.

Ian betrayed no concern but kissed Beth on the lips when he reached her. "Will you come with us, love?"

Beth shook her head. "You go. Eleanor is certain nothing will be done on time, so it's all hands to the pump."

Ian had long ceased trying to work out what Beth meant when she spoke in metaphors, though he might have a think on it and ask her later. He kissed her again.

Ian let the kiss turn long, never mind Megan standing nearby. This gave Megan a chance to hide what she'd been writing, which was likely Ian's intent. That and to keep Beth from asking questions.

"Keep your secrets," she whispered to him. "As long as the result is worth it."

Ian, for answer, kissed her again. Then he gave her his warmest smile, held his hand out for Megan, and led her away. Megan stuffed her papers deep into her pockets and skipped after her father, her lively step making the rosettes on the back of her sash bounce.

Chapter 3

Megan whooshed out a breath when Jamie lifted her from her feet in a crushing bear hug. She hugged him in return, always happy to see her brother, and pecked a kiss on his cheek. The cheek felt rough, and Megan saw with surprise that Jamie had whiskers, like their father, red and catching the light.

Growing up so fast, she thought fondly as Jamie released her. Aunt Ainsley embraced her next, and Uncle Cameron, whom she hadn't seen in a few months. Then Cousin Stuart, who was her exact same age, though he seemed to have grown a head taller than Megan in the intervening time.

Cousin Gavina sent Megan a smile and kissed her cheek, her beauty like a poem.

The adults headed for the carriage, but Megan hung back as Jamie and Gavina began to walk to Kilmorgan. Stuart, wanting to show he was as robust as his cousins, joined them. Megan knew she'd have to jog to keep up with the others, but she didn't want to go tamely home in the carriage without them.

Gavina kindly took her hand and slowed her pace, keeping Megan with her as the boys ran ahead and behind again, behaving like the unruly male creatures they were.

Megan had always been in awe of Gavina. Though only two years older than Megan, Gavina was radiant, poised, and not afraid to flirt with boys. Belle had confided to Megan that when Gavina made her come-out, she'd be what was called a diamond of the first water and likely showered with proposals.

Gavina, on the other hand, in spite of the flirting, had declared she had no intention of marrying at all. Megan would be interested to see what happened in a few years.

It didn't take long for Megan to realize that Gavina and Jamie were up to something. When she lagged behind a little, Stuart having run far ahead, Jamie fell into step with Gavina and began speaking quietly.

Megan had learned from her father that if she was silent and didn't draw attention to herself, she could find out very many things. She pretended her attention was elsewhere, but listened carefully.

"I'll hunt up Curry," Jamie was saying. "Do you think you can get in? The door will be locked."

"Oh, you just watch me." Gavina grinned at Jamie with confidence.

Gavina was smart, like Belle, but in a different way. Belle knew all kinds of facts from books, but Gavina could do things, like pick locks, discover secret passages, and figure out how to beat all the boys at hide-and-seek, tag, or any other game they'd played when they were children. Cunning and stealth, Gavina had always said, beat running and punching anytime.

Megan hoped they didn't plan to steal anything. Then Megan would have to tell, and she did not like tattling. However, if she knew nothing, she couldn't report it, could she?

"We have a ghost," she said in a loud voice as she caught up to them. "Uncle Mac saw it. Belle and Daniel and Violet tried to prove it was a person, but their traps caught nothing. So it must be a real ghost."

Both turned to her, their attention caught. Jamie expressed

derision and ran off to find Stuart, who had decided to climb a tree for some reason.

Gavina remained with Megan, gazing at her with avid interest. "A ghost? That's wonderful. Do tell."

~⌒

Ian, in his study, went over the telegraph messages he'd retrieved from the train station when he'd collected Jamie, frowning as he read them.

Lloyd Fellows, now a chief superintendent at Scotland Yard, had looked into the theft of the necklace—if it had been a theft—and had discovered nothing. Since Fellows was as dogged as Ian, Ian believed him when he said he'd turned over every stone.

The museum had reported no burglary. They claimed they'd wrapped up the necklace and sent it via courier to the man in Paris who'd bought it.

Interestingly, while the courier had agreed that his service had sent him to retrieve three packages from the museum and deliver them to various residences in Paris, he had not taken one to the gentleman who'd purchased the necklace.

The clerk in the museum, however, swore he'd wrapped it and left it for the courier.

Somewhere between the shelf in the museum storeroom and the courier's hands, the necklace had disappeared.

Fellows had thoroughly questioned the courier and concluded the man had not stolen the necklace himself. He'd worked for his firm for years and was one of their most trusted employees. No package he'd ever touched had gone astray.

Fellows then questioned the packers and clerks at the museum, but again, all were trusted men and one woman who had worked at the museum for some time.

Ian tossed down the telegraphs feeling old frustration work into his bones. It had been a long, long time since he'd had one of his "muddles." During one, he would become fixed, focused on one mundane task while his brain spun and tried to make sense of the world. Muddles distressed his family, he knew, and there had been no need for one for a very long time. Beth and his children steadied him now.

But occasionally Ian faced a problem he did not know how to confront. His wife, sisters-in-law, and brothers could sit and think through a conundrum or discuss it with others and come up with a solution.

Ian had difficulty voicing his thoughts and so tried to work through them on his own. But sometimes his focus would shift, and the equations would not balance.

A package could not simply disappear. Ian opened a notebook and took up a pen to try to reason it out.

The pages of the notebook were scribbled over with number sequences and codes Ian had invented. Beth enjoyed the codes, and they sent each other notes that only they could read. Ian liked that he could tell her exactly what he loved about her, including vivid, physical details that no one would understand but her.

Watching Beth decipher the notes, her color rising, her eyes sparkling, made him warm. Ian lingered now over one of the codes, his blood heating.

He forced his attention away. Even better if he could drape the lovely Roman gold over Beth's bare skin, but he had to find the necklace first.

If it had disappeared between being packed and the courier's arrival, there were several possible explanations. A: Whoever was supposed to pack the necklace had simply pocketed it and taken it home. B: The courier was lying and had taken the package, having worked all his life to engender trust. C: The museum still had it but had hidden it, hoping to keep the payment from the buyer and the necklace itself. In a few years, they could quietly sell it to someone else.

Ian jotted these notes in code, a new one he hadn't

taught Beth. He never hid his notebooks from her, but he wanted the necklace to be a secret for a time.

Another possibility—the necklace might have been stolen from its display at any time, and the museum had covered up the fact. Why they would, Ian couldn't fathom. If they did not report the theft, they'd collect no insurance.

Unless . . . Ian began to write, his pen flying. The museum might have sold the necklace covertly, for a greater price, some time ago, replacing it with a copy. Perhaps they'd sold the copy to the collector, then, realizing the man would know it was a fake, had contrived to have the necklace go missing.

Ian crossed a line through his notes. None of this was satisfying.

A thief could have simply broken into the museum, seen the package, realized it must contain something valuable, and absconded with it. Ian would ask Inspector Fellows where the package had been stored and how long it had lain there between being packed and the courier arriving.

He threw down his pen and ran his hands through his hair. Outside, people were shouting, drawing him from his concentration.

Ian went to the window. Below, in the snowy gardens, Mackenzie children, from Hart's youngest boy, eleven-year-old Malcolm, to the stately Aimee, were yelling, running, and pelting each other with snowballs. Even Aimee, a young lady now, alternately chased or ran from the others, screaming when a well-placed snowball slammed into her back.

Laughing, she scooped up snow and lobbed it at Jamie and Robbie with great skill.

Megan ran among them, managing to land a large glob of snow on her brother's back. Even Belle, who preferred to read rather than run wild, jumped up and down, cheering for Megan's hit. She then shrieked and ran when Jamie came after her.

They were all there, the children of Hart, Cameron, Mac, and Ian. In a few days, Fellows's three would arrive, completing the set.

Ian thought back to the days when he and his brothers struggled out from under the shadow of their father, battling loneliness and their own destruction. But now, with the help of their wives, Mac had conquered inebriation, Cameron had recovered from the crazed brutality of his first wife, and Hart had relaxed his need for absolute control and power—mostly.

Ian believed he'd come furthest of all. He could sleep without waking in terror, darkness no longer pressing him. He could meet the gazes of those he loved without fear he'd be trapped in them. He could stand at the window and gaze fondly at the younger Mackenzies, tangible evidence of the brothers' happiness, and become almost poetic. Beth would laugh.

The thought of his gentle wife, her blue eyes and sweet smile, made Ian turn from the window. The fact that all the children were outside in a snowball battle meant that the house was relatively empty, and he might find Beth alone . . .

Ian shoved his notebooks into his desk, locked it with the small key, and strode off to seek his wife.

Gavina Mackenzie slipped through the darkened upper corridors of Kilmorgan late in the night. The sun set early this close to the winter solstice, rendering the land deep black well before the family supper.

Inside Kilmorgan, however, lamps shone, chandeliers twinkled, fires burned high. The collected Mackenzies conversed, made music together, and told each other stories well into the wee hours. Tonight, Mac had been regaling the younger ones with the tale of his ghost.

Jamie, slipping off with Gavina to discuss strategy, had

looked superior. "And people say *my* father is mad. He's not daft enough to believe in ghosts. Has a good head on his shoulders, does my dad."

He spoke proudly, admiring Uncle Ian's ability to see a situation clearly, without clouds of assumption, supposition, and emotion getting in his way. If Uncle Ian didn't understand a thing, he'd research it from every angle and probably come up with mathematical formulas to explain it.

Gavina had seen as they'd grown up that Jamie had a similar ability. He was shrewd and clear-eyed, pondering every angle of a problem.

Gavina, on the other hand, dove right into a situation without worrying about the consequences. She came to grief from time to time, but she'd also done things none of her girlfriends would dream of—like going to the top of the Eiffel Tower by herself, getting herself locked into a library in London all night and reading the books young ladies weren't supposed to, and once riding in a point-to-point horse race. Well, no one had specifically *said* the race was "boys only."

Her parents were exasperated by and proud of her exploits. Gavina knew her mother had been quite the tear in her day—who did Jamie think had taught her to pick locks?

Gavina had the best father in the world, she thought as she silently entered Uncle Ian's study. She halted after she closed the door, waiting until her eyes adjusted to the faint light before proceeding. The sky was clear tonight, moon and stars providing beautiful illumination.

Cameron Mackenzie never scolded Gavina for riding in races or reading naughty books, and he never admonished her to act like a young lady. In his opinion, hiding the world from a young woman only made her vulnerable to blackguards and libertines. She should know what awaited her after her debut and how to stand her own ground.

Gavina wasn't certain her father would approve of her

burgling Uncle Ian's study, but in time he'd understand it was for a good cause.

Once she could see well enough, Gavina made her careful way to the desk. She daren't light a candle, for fear a diligent servant would see it. Curry, for instance. Uncle Ian's valet would recognize criminal activity when he saw it.

Ian's desk was a large, flat-topped affair with drawers on either side and a shallow one in the middle. No delicate secretary or davenport desks for Uncle Ian. He spent much time reading and researching his Ming pottery and other ancient artifacts, and he liked large surfaces on which to spread out his books. He was also writing a history of the Mackenzie family, drawing on papers and diaries he'd found in the attic.

Ian routinely locked all the drawers in his desk. Though no one came in here but family and trusted servants, Uncle Ian liked everything in an exact order, which he did not want disturbed.

Gavina took the thin wires out of her pocket and started on the desk drawers. Her mother had said that while a hairpin did well in a pinch, long, stiff wires were much better— one to hold the tumbler, the other to turn the lock.

Gavina had practiced diligently. At first she'd been amused by her mother's hobby, but she'd learned that it could be quite useful.

As it was now. In a few short moments, Gavina had all of Ian's desk drawers open, searching for the notebook Jamie had told her to look for.

She found it in the second drawer down, a leather-bound book filled with jottings and numbers plus folded pieces of paper. Within one of those papers was the picture Jamie wanted.

Gavina rose from her knees, hugging the notebook. Victory.

Her glee abruptly vanished when she heard footsteps outside the door.

Damn and blast. If Gavina were caught in the dark in Ian's study, desk drawers open, cradling Ian's notebook, she'd not easily talk her way out of it.

While her father stood by her with most of her escapades, even he wouldn't be happy with Gavina stealing from Uncle Ian. Drat Jamie and his fantastic ideas, and drat herself for leaping into the scheme with her usual enthusiasm.

Gavina darted across the room, using the lamplight from the corridor to find her swift way to the corner. Thank heavens for her Mackenzie cousins, who liked to explore every inch of this huge house and its secret passages. Because of them, Gavina knew there should be a small panel at the end of the bookcase—*yes*.

Gavina jabbed at the smooth panel until she found the depression that let it spring open, revealing a dark passageway. Gavina slipped inside, closing the panel as quietly as she could before she hurried through the tiny corridor.

The blackness here was complete. Gavina thanked heaven she wasn't an imaginative young woman or the darkness might terrify her. She only worried she'd trip and fall, because if she hurt herself, she'd have to call for help.

Gavina had wondered why this house had secret passages, as it had been carefully designed well after the need for priest holes and hiding places for Highlanders running from the Black Watch and the excisemen. Uncle Ian explained that Old Malcolm Mackenzie, who had designed the house, had put them in because he thought secret passages would be exciting.

Gavina blessed her ancestor for his whimsy as she moved through the passageway. She reached its end and pushed at the panel there until she stumbled out into another corridor—this one empty, thank goodness.

Voices sounded around the corner to the main hall.

Gavina hastened in the opposite direction, taking the back stairs and servants' halls to the top of the house.

Jamie waited in their appointed spot on the top floor of Ian Mackenzie's wing, in the nursery. His eyes widened when Gavina entered and stepped into the moonlight flooding the room.

"Good Lord," he gasped. "The ghost."

"Don't be daft," Gavina said impatiently. "It's me."

"No, I mean behind you."

Gavina swung around and saw a flutter of white that vanished into the blackness of the corridor. Thrusting the book at Jamie, she dashed out of the room in time to see the white apparition skim around the corner.

Gavina's skin prickled, superstitious fear wafting through her for the first time in her life.

Absolute nonsense, she told herself, and gave chase.

Chapter 4

Gavina followed the ghost around the corner, through Mac's wing, and on to Cameron's. It moved swiftly, and as Uncle Mac had claimed, glided seemingly without the use of feet.

Gavina sped onward, thrusting aside her tingle of foreboding. The only way to conquer fear was to face it. Her father had taught her that too.

At the end of the hall, where the large nursery she'd shared with her brother had been, the ghost disappeared.

Gavina halted with another shiver, but she squared her shoulders. This house was riddled with passageways, and the woman must have slipped inside one.

She heard Jamie pounding behind her, but she would not let her cousin laugh at her for being afraid of a ghost. Gavina sped her steps, making for where she'd seen the thing evaporate.

Something tripped her. Gavina fought for balance and took another step before a brilliant flash of light erupted in her face. She fell against the wall, half-blinded, cursing with more words than her father realized she knew.

Strong hands caught her, and Jamie pulled her to her feet. "You tripped the camera, ye daft lass."

Gavina pushed away from him, struggling for breath. "I realize that. Help me take out the plate, or Aunt Eleanor will know we were up here."

She groped for the camera, but Jamie reached it first. He pulled out the small photographic plate and put it into his pocket.

"I'll take care of this, never you mind. Why did you chase it?"

"Why?" Gavina turned to him in surprise. "To prove it's not a ghost. The question is, why did *I* trip the camera and she didn't?"

"Because she's a ghost," Jamie said, as though this were reasonable.

Gavina gave him a deprecating look. "Now who's the daftie? I thought you didn't believe in spirits."

"I didn't. Until I saw her." Jamie's face softened, his eyes golden in the moonlight. "She's a bonnie lass, isn't she?"

Gavina stared at him, lips parting. Jamie had never hidden the fact that comely females pleased him, but she'd never seen him wearing this besotted expression. He looked like a dreamy-eyed cow.

"Oh, for heaven's sake," she said in exasperation. "Let us go downstairs before someone comes to investigate. Daniel said he rigged up an alarm, and someone might have noticed the flash."

"Aye, well." Jamie gazed longingly at the spot where the ghost—or whoever she was—had disappeared. "She walks in beauty, does that poor lass."

Jamie only became poetic, and very Scottish, when he was going soft about something. He could wax lyrically over a brilliant sunset or a view over the water or a splendid horse running flat out. And now, it appeared, a beautiful woman.

"You are absurd, Jamie Mackenzie," Gavina said.

Jamie shrugged. "One day you will fall in love, dear cousin. On that day, I will smile."

Gavina glared at him as he sauntered down the hall, the Mackenzie blue and green kilt fluttering as he went.

As if Gavina would ever fall in love. At least, if she did, she vowed she'd not act like such a fool.

"For heaven's sake," she repeated in a mutter, and stomped after him.

~~~

Eleanor, Duchess of Kilmorgan, emerged from her dark-room the next morning with her mouth a flat line. She knew the young Mackenzies were mischievous—and no wonder, considering their fathers—but this was going a bit too far.

As she strode down the hall, the printed photographs in hand, she distractedly noted all that needed to be done before Christmas, and more importantly, Hogmanay. This year, they'd keep things simple—Hart had agreed to set aside the holidays for family and close friends, but that still meant a good many people. She and the housekeeper were hiring more staff to help with the decorating and the food.

Lloyd Fellows and Louisa with their children were already on their way. The McBride family would soon arrive as well—Ainsley's four brothers and their collective offspring. So would David Fleming and his wife and young son.

That made eleven families multiplied by two to three children each, though Ainsley's oldest brother, Patrick, and his wife had never had children of their own. The couple had raised Ainsley and her wild brothers and now were inundated with nieces and nephews.

Speaking of nephews—Eleanor pulled her swift thoughts back to the present.

She entered the dining room to find most of the family breakfasting. The din from myriad conversations assailed her, her husband's voice the loudest as he boomed something to Daniel.

Eleanor paused in the doorway. She never failed to delight in the scene of the four brothers, Daniel, their wives, and the younger Mackenzies gathered around in laughter and conversation. Her heart warmed most of all for Hart, seated at the head of the table, trying, and failing, to bring some order to the chaos.

Eleanor loved the chaos, and the thrum of energy the children brought. She'd spent much of her life alone, she and her father living by themselves in a run-down pile of a house. Her father had recently married a lady he'd hired to help him write his latest book, the two finding that they rubbed along perfectly. They too would be arriving in time for Christmas, taking their time over the cold journey from Aberdeen.

But to business.

"Robbie Mackenzie. Stuart Mackenzie." Eleanor bellowed into the crowd. "Please explain yourselves."

She turned around the photograph. Robbie, who'd taken a bite of porridge, began to cough. Stuart only sat still and became very red indeed.

The photograph showed two bare backsides caught in the brightness of a flash. They would have been anonymous rumps if both Robbie and Stuart hadn't glanced behind them to make certain the camera went off.

There was a collective hush as those around the table studied the photograph in amazement. And then a roar of laughter.

Ainsley and Isabella each tried to scold their respective sons, but they hid their mirth poorly. Ian looked slightly perplexed at the laughter, and Beth whispered into his ear, presumably explaining.

Hart's voice cut through them all. "For shame, lads," he thundered. "You've wasted your aunt's chemicals and no doubt upset her. I can imagine her shock when the photograph resolved."

He picked up a cup of steaming coffee and quickly drank it, lips twitching suspiciously.

"Hardly shocked," Eleanor said crisply. In a life with Hart, nothing much jolted her. "It was a joke, I suppose, on those adamant to find their ghost. But yes, you are very naughty."

Daniel broke in, not bothering to hide his grin. "You were hoping to see something *pale* and *glowing*, weren't you, Uncle Mac?"

Violet elbowed him, but Daniel only collapsed into laughter. Mac threw a piece of bannock at him.

Eleanor noted Gavina giving Jamie a long glance, and Jamie shaking his head ever so slightly. Eleanor's eyes narrowed. Now, what were *they* up to?

"Lads," Mac said to the still-red Robbie and Stuart. "Ye are very funny, but I can't let ye get away with it. Apologize to your auntie."

"Sorry, Aunt Eleanor," they both mumbled in overlapping syllables.

"They need to do more than that," Hart said.

"Never fear." Eleanor gave both boys a severe look. "I have plenty of ways they can make it up to me. Starting with cleaning up the darkroom and all the flash powder upstairs. Such a large amount of burned powder on the floor—it is not fair to have the maids sweep that up. You must have used too much, Daniel."

Again, Jamie and Gavina exchanged a glance. Eleanor would have to find the root of *that* later.

Daniel shook his head. "I swore I used just enough and no more. And no one tripped the alarm I rigged. Did the powder show any footprints?"

"It was such a mess, I could not tell," Eleanor said. "It will take some labor for it to be cleaned up."

She set the photograph facedown on the table as Robbie and Stuart looked even more dejected. Eleanor took her chair at the foot of the table, finished with the business. Two footmen sprang forward to serve her, the lads trying to stifle their own laughter.

Jamie went still, his gaze riveting to the door Eleanor

had left open. Eleanor turned in time to see a housemaid peek in and then retreat.

"Good Lord." Jamie sprang from his chair, shoving it back so hard he overturned it, and bolted from the room.

Mac, looking as stunned, followed him. Eleanor waved off the footmen and hurried out, wondering what on earth Jamie was on about now.

She found Jamie in the middle of the wide front hall, where footmen and maids on ladders wound garlands through the staircase. "Where did she go?" Jamie demanded of them.

One of the footmen frowned. "Who? Sir," he added quickly with a glance at Eleanor.

"That maid." Jamie rushed to the gallery that spanned the front of the house and scanned its length. "Didn't she come this way?"

"We didn't see," the footman answered. "We're looking up, not down. Um . . . sir."

The footmen at Kilmorgan often forgot to address Jamie with the honorific, as he was friendly with all the staff and, Eleanor knew, shared cigars and whisky with them.

"I saw her too," Mac said. "That was *her*."

"The ghost?" Isabella asked excitedly, coming up behind him. "Blast—I missed it."

Gavina had trailed after them. "Not a ghost," she said decidedly. "A housemaid."

"Indeed, we have been hiring extra help," Eleanor said. "Mac, if you and Jamie have frightened off a new maid, I'll be most unhappy. We need every pair of hands right now."

"That would explain things," Gavina said. "There's a new housemaid, and she was lost or simply exploring the place. Servants sleep in attics in most houses. She was likely looking for her room."

"Logical," Eleanor agreed.

Gavina looked satisfied, Isabella disappointed, Mac unconvinced. Jamie continued to frown, perplexed.

Simplest explanations were best, Eleanor always believed. She'd find the maid, soothe her, show Jamie and Mac that she was a real human being, and this ghost hunt would be over.

Not that Eleanor didn't wish they had a true ghost—one would be terribly interesting—but the holidays at Kilmorgan were *not* the most convenient time for them to appear.

～

Ian entered his study after breakfast to find Curry and a footman hastily restoring the room to rights. Papers littered the floor, drawers stood open, and a few books tumbled from shelves.

Ian paused in the doorway, hand on the handle. Curry, noticing him, carefully set down a stack of books and hurried to him.

"No harm done, guv. Just a prank. I think. Or the ghost. Evil spirits like to throw things about."

Ian knew no evil spirits had done this. Someone had broken into this room and rifled his desk.

Years ago, he would have become upset. Ian liked things to remain in a specific place, not only so he could easily find them, but because they felt *right* there. Now he was not so much interested in the mess as in the fact that his research for the necklace had been locked in his now-open desk.

"What was taken?" he asked sharply.

"Don't know, guv. Nothing, it looks like."

Ian scanned the room, his gaze coming to rest on the windows. He moved to one, but it was closed, locked, dust on the lock itself. This window hadn't been opened since autumn.

No one had come in that way, which meant the intruder had already been in the house.

Ian moved back to the desk. Curry had tucked his notebooks into the drawers once more, including, Ian was relieved to see, the one that contained his coded writing about the necklace.

Ian pulled that one out and flipped through it. The coded pages were intact, including the telegraph messages he'd received from the museum. One of the photographs of the necklace, however, was missing.

"Ah." Curry stooped and retrieved something from under the desk. "Where does this go, me lord?"

He held the photograph. Ian relaxed. He studied the picture of the shining necklace before he took it from Curry, slid it into the notebook, and carefully laid the notebook into its drawer.

"Thank you," he said sincerely.

"If a footman did this, I'll thrash him," Curry vowed.

Ian shook his head. "It wasn't a footman."

One of the footmen who was helping Curry clear up, shook his head fervently. "None would dare, sir. His Grace wouldn't have it."

Ian had meant that the footmen in this house were trustworthy, but true, Hart would never stand for theft.

Ian had different ideas about the identity of the culprit, though he wasn't certain, and this bothered him. The sooner he found and purchased the blasted necklace and gave it to Beth, the better.

He slid the drawer closed and locked it with his key, dropping the key into his pocket. Then he sat down at the desk, moved a clean sheet of paper into its exact center, and began to write out a message to Lloyd Fellows.

~

"Wise of you to ask me for help, young man."

Curry faced Jamie and Gavina in the old nursery in Cameron's wing later that afternoon. He took a notebook from his pocket and held it out to Jamie. "Next time you need to pick locks and search desks, you come to me first. Save us a lot of bother."

Chapter 5

Gavina reached for the notebook. "My fault," she said, her face heating with some chagrin. "I wanted to try my skills."

"And skilled you were." Curry gave her an admiring nod. "If you hadn't had to run and leave everything a mess, your uncle Ian would have never known. He came in when I was tidying."

"*Probably* wouldn't have known," Jamie said.

He looked a bit embarrassed under Curry's scrutiny, but fortunately said nothing about Gavina muffing it because she was a girl. She'd have had to punch Jamie, in that case.

When Jamie had consulted with Curry this morning before breakfast, Curry had expressed great alarm and made Jamie give him back the notebook and photographs Gavina had managed to purloin. Curry agreed to help them, but if Ian found anything missing from his desk, he'd take apart the house until he found it. Then explanations would have to be made and the secret would come out.

Wiser to let Curry replace the notebook and then retrieve it again, quietly, when Ian was busy at the distillery.

Next Christmas I will simply buy everyone pretty cards, Gavina thought. But no, though the adventure was proving not to be as easy as she'd hoped, Gavina was so far enjoying it.

"Now, then, how are you going to read all these notes and make sense of them?" Curry asked. "His lordship likes a good cipher."

Gavina had already looked through the codes and found them hopeless but intriguing. She would have to ask Uncle Ian to teach her about them.

"The telegrams weren't in code," Gavina said. "I read those. They said the necklace has disappeared, stolen, most like, but included names."

"Of people who might have taken it, you mean?" Jamie asked her. "Or know where it is?" He switched his focus to Curry. "Do you think you can locate it?"

Curry nodded without worry. "I'll put me ear to the ground. The chief super don't hear what I can." He gave Jamie a shrewd look. "Might be very expensive, though. Why not just let your father buy it for your mum?"

Jamie lifted his chin. "Because I want to surprise him. And Mother."

His eyes flickered, betraying his unease. Gavina thought she understood—Jamie wanted to prove he was as clever as his father. Jamie would never say that, but Gavina knew her cousin well.

Jamie took his position as the oldest of the young Mackenzie males seriously, but he felt a bit in the shadow of his father and uncles. He wanted to be like the men of the family—fearless, smart, and formidable. People in London moved out of the way when Uncle Hart descended from a carriage or strode through the park, and Jamie, Gavina sensed, envied that power.

Finding a gift for Aunt Beth before Ian could would make Uncle Ian proud, earn his praise, and even make Ian happy, something Jamie tried to go out of his way to do.

Watching Jamie, Gavina decided a few things.

Curry and Jamie spoke awhile longer, then Curry departed

to begin his hunt. Gavina lingered, memories of the nursery surrounding her—she and her cousins laughing and playing as children, the room full of noise. Nanny Westlock, now retired, had kept them under control with her wisdom and no-nonsense ways.

Through it all—their play, quarrels, celebrations, rivalries, friendships—they'd been loved. Their parents had fought through strife, grief, and heartbreak to come together, and they loved their children fiercely.

We love them back just as fiercely, Gavina realized. *Though we might act like ungrateful wretches and not show it.* Jamie was trying to give to his father what Uncle Ian and Aunt Beth had given him. It was touching.

Gavina shook herself. She'd grow positively maudlin if she went on at this rate.

"Jamie," she said as he pored over the notes they'd copied out of Ian's book. "You told my brother and Robbie to point their bums at that camera, didn't you? So the triggered flash and exposed plate would be explained."

Jamie nodded in a matter-of-fact way. "You didn't want Aunt Eleanor to develop a photograph of you looking pop-eyed and guilty, did you? I exposed the plate you triggered to full light so it would wash out the image, then put another one in the camera and rigged up the flash again. I asked Robbie and Stuart to set it off, to play a trick on the ghost hunters, and smeared the flash powder around to hide everyone's footprints." He let out an aggrieved sigh. "I never told them how to pose."

"Aunt Eleanor will have them working like dogs the whole holiday because of it."

Jamie flashed her a grin. "They're being punished for acting like hellions. If they'd just made faces or something, they'd have gotten away with it. Their own fault."

"I suppose." The explanation made Gavina feel a tad less guilty. Her brother, Stuart, had a mischievous streak a mile wide. "What do we do now?"

"Wait for Curry to report. Thank you, Gav. You were right that I needed your help."

Gavina tried not to feel pleased. Jamie was a smooth-tongued devil, well she knew, Mackenzie to the core. But it was nice to be appreciated.

She left him, wrapped up well, and went out to the paddock. Her father, the giant Cameron Mackenzie, swung down from a horse, his man and closest friend, Angelo, taking the reins. Gavina greeted them both but waited until Angelo led the horse away before she launched herself at Cameron.

"I love you, Papa," she said, wrapping her arms around him.

Cameron started then enfolded Gavina in his embrace as she dug her face into the folds of his coat. He smelled of horse and peat smoke, the scents she'd always associated with her father—scents that assured her he was well, and she was protected.

Cameron's voice vibrated through her. "I love you too, lass."

Gavina squeezed again, then rubbed the tears from her eyes as she kissed him on the cheek. She released him and ran for the house, leaving her father looking grateful if slightly perplexed.

～

Beth went tiredly to her bedchamber that night, having spent the entire day helping Eleanor with preparations for the coming celebrations. While she loved being with her sisters-in-law, she was happy to escape the frenzy, see her children to bed, and retreat to her own sanctuary.

She found Ian waiting for her, a kilt draped around his nightshirted body. In the summer, he'd be wrapped in only the kilt, but in the deep Scottish winter, even Ian Macken-zie grew cold.

He lounged on the cushioned settee at the foot of the

bed, his favorite place to sit and read or write in his note-book or simply stare into space and contemplate whatever he'd found important that day.

Beth took a moment to run her gaze over his long legs, stretched out and crossed at the ankles, black slippers on his large feet. He focused on a point next to the fireplace, his golden eyes still, his hands quiet on his knees.

Riding, chasing his children, and striding over the rugged Scottish land had kept Ian's body strong and fit. Where other men at four and forty might be softening toward middle age, Ian was as robust and hard as he'd been at twenty-seven, when Beth had first met him.

When he heard her step, Ian turned his head and looked at her.

He had whole worlds inside him, and they shone out through his eyes. No wonder he'd avoided looking directly at anyone when he was younger. Hart Mackenzie could pin a person with his hard stare, but Ian could transfix them for life.

Ian didn't rise when Beth entered—he saw no reason to be formal with her. She sank down on the settee beside him, snuggling into his warmth. Ian's arm went around her, and his lips brushed her hair.

"Deep thoughts, my love?" she murmured.

"Mmm." The rumble of his voice made Beth nestle closer. "Will you tell me, my Beth . . . Why is a photograph of naked buttocks funny?"

He gazed down at her, a pucker between his brows. He truly wanted to know, had likely been trying to puzzle it out all day.

"Honestly, I don't know," Beth said. "I suppose because it's unexpected and a bit rude."

"I am rude," Ian said without worry. "That's what m'brothers and Curry tell me. They don't laugh—they explain why I'm rude. Or try to."

"Not the same thing." Beth groped for the right words.

"It's naughty, and it's a shock. I think that's what brings the laughter. But Stuart and Robbie were really quite bad. We shouldn't laugh—we should scold them, lest they be tempted to do it again."

Ian nodded, as though agreeing with her, but Beth knew the gesture was to make her happy, not an indication he understood.

"I like when you laugh." Ian's voice darkened, his eyes softening with heat. He lifted a blunt finger and touched her lips. "It makes your face glow, and your body shake."

"Does it?" Beth lost the thread of the conversation, mesmerized by his gaze, his voice.

"Aye, love." Ian cupped her face, drawing her up to him. "Your beauty, it shines in your laughter."

"Ian Mackenzie," she whispered. "That is most poetic."

Beth knew Ian didn't give a damn about being poetic—he never said a thing unless he thoroughly meant it.

Ian's kiss parted her lips and filled her with fire. Beth ran her fingers through his thick red-brown hair, and surrendered herself to his magic.

The settee was soft, the kilt warm. The Scottish winter receded as Ian's touch, kisses, and body on hers washed everything cold away.

～

Lloyd Fellows yawned, covering his mouth at the last minute as he sat facing his half brother Ian in Ian's study the following morning. The room was still dark—the sun rose late at this time of year, and if the sky clouded over, sometimes there was no light at all.

Ian's rooms were always cozy, warmed with fires and lamplight. Kilmorgan was too far from any gasworks to have gas laid in, but the kerosene lamps and candles created a soft glow.

"Took the night train," Fellows explained as he stifled another yawn. "I never sleep well on trains."

"It is the fastest way from London." Ian didn't make polite conversation, Fellows knew. He stated a fact.

"I realize that. But just as I settle in, the train hits a curve or swerves over points and I'm jarred awake again. My wife, on the other hand, sleeps like a baby."

Fellows let a smile come as he thought of his wife, Louisa, lying on the opposite bed in the compartment, her eyes closed, face serene. She was as beautiful in sleep as she was in everything she did. Had the space been less cramped and their three children unlikely to pop in at any moment, Fellows would have used the bunks for something more interesting than slumber.

Ian waited patiently until Fellows had run through this speech. Ian had grown quieter over the years, Fellows observed. He remembered the terrified and furious young man who'd tried to attack him in the Tuileries gardens in Paris, and how Fellows had been convinced that Ian was not only mad but a murderer.

He was glad now that he'd been proved wrong. Ian was a unique person with a brilliant mind, and Fellows had come to enjoy getting to know him.

"You have news," Ian stated.

Not a guess—Fellows would not have asked for this early meeting after a mostly sleepless night on a train if he had nothing to report.

"I have found no evidence of any theft at the museum," Fellows announced, "except the obvious fact that the Roman necklace has vanished."

Ian said nothing, eyes unworried.

Fellows continued. "There is a man called Cornelius Pemberton. He is a scholar, of the sort who has much money, travels everywhere, and takes what he likes. The problem is, he'd prefer to acquire items for his collection without paying the market price." He lifted his hands. "I have no proof he is responsible. My suspicion comes from long experience, instinct, and knowing far too many villains in both the criminal and upper classes."

Ian did not nod, but Fellows watched Ian think it through, processing the information like one of Pascal's adding machines.

"As I say, there is no evidence," Fellows went on. "Pemberton is a thorough villain, but always manages to keep his hands clean. Any person caught thieving for him never gives him up."

"He must pay them well." Ian rose, restless, and paced to the window. On the shelf below it lay a Ming bowl in a case—one was often on display here, switched out every week with another in his priceless collection. Ian understood collection mania, but he always bought his bowls fairly, giving over exactly what they were worth.

"I assume so," Fellows said. "We've tried to bring him up on charges, but they never stick. Mr. Pemberton has excellent solicitors, and he'd be able to afford the best defense barristers if we ever got him to court."

Ian studied the Ming bowl. "You believe he has the necklace."

"I'm fairly certain he does. It's the sort of thing he goes in for—solid gold, ancient, with history attached. Pemberton is also a frequent visitor to that museum. He'd know who was who inside the building, and possibly recruited someone to take it for him. But again, I have no thief to put my hands on, no sighting of the necklace anywhere in Pemberton's possession, nothing."

Ian folded his arms. With his solid stance, the kilt wrapping his hips, he looked like a fierce Highland warrior from the bad old days, like his ancestor, Old Dan Mackenzie, reputed to be a crazed fighter.

My ancestor too, Fellows reminded himself. *Old Dan Mackenzie's stubborn ferocity is just as much inside me.*

"You would not have come up to Scotland on the night

train if you were not certain," Ian said. "You would have sent another telegraph and traveled at your leisure. You did not want to put your suspicion on paper, but wanted me to know."

"Yes."

Fellows could dance around it all he liked, but Ian was right. Long habit of saying nothing that couldn't be proved had kept him from simply telegraphing: *Cornelius Pemberton has it.*

Fellows rose and faced Ian. "Now you know. What do you want to do about it?"

Ian's brows flicked upward, slight surprise at the question. He'd already made up his mind, Fellows could see.

"We go see Mr. Pemberton and take it away from him," Ian said.

~~~

Ian traveled to Mr. Pemberton's large house outside Nottingham in the company of Lloyd Fellows and Megan.

Ian hadn't intended to bring Megan. He and Fellows had walked to the station at Kilmorgan Halt the next morning, after Fellows had gotten a good night's sleep and persuaded his wife he and Ian needed to run this errand.

It was the twentieth of December. Ian wanted to be back tomorrow, for the night of the solstice, the Longest Night, which he and Beth traditionally spent together. Christmas would follow soon on its heels, and then Hogmanay.

Ian calculated he'd need a day to travel to Pemberton and wrest the necklace from him, which would put him back in plenty of time for the Mackenzie festivities. Mac was planning games he'd think were uproariously funny, and the cooks had brought in plenty for feasts, but Ian wanted only to immerse himself in his family and absorb their warmth.

He and Fellows had stepped onto the train when a breathless voice had sounded behind them.

"Papa! Wait!"

Ian turned to see his younger daughter rushing through the gate to the platform, the stationmaster in vain trying to stop her. A satchel, strapped around her shoulder, slapped her side as she raced toward Ian.

The train began to move. Fellows was already in the compartment, Ian just stepping in.

Ian had only a second or two to ponder. He could wave Megan off and tell her to go home to her mother, shouting at the stationmaster to convey her there safely.

Or he could take Megan with him, pay the fee on the train, and telegraph Beth at the next station so she wouldn't worry.

Ian was heading to confront a villain who got away with his crimes by being wealthy and well connected. It was no place for a child.

The stricken look on Megan's face decided things. Ian stretched out an arm to her. "Run!" he called.

Megan's sunny smile blossomed. She sprinted for the train, Ian catching her up as it chugged down the platform. He swung her into the carriage, then fell inside himself and slammed the door.

Fellows was on his feet in surprise and consternation, but he gallantly gestured Megan to a seat. Megan, out of breath, plopped down, beaming at her father and uncle.

"I'm to be helping you, Papa," she declared. She patted the satchel at her side. "I've found out so very many things."

Chapter 6

Mr. Pemberton lived five miles outside Nottingham in a mansion built in what Ian's brother Cameron called "Bastardized Scottish Jumble."

Turrets and crenellations rose around a whitewashed stone house flanked by four round towers. A road snaked to this house through a snow-covered meadow, ending in a stone bridge over a tiny, now-frozen stream. A door built to look like a drawbridge appeared to be the only entrance to the house.

Ian took in the design and calculated that the house could not be more than thirty years old.

They'd reached Nottingham after dark and stayed overnight at the station hotel. Megan had been delighted to eat at the restaurant with her father and uncle, and she'd slept in a trundle bed in Ian's chamber.

In the morning, the coach Fellows had hired slowed as they crossed the bridge, wheels thumping hollowly over stones. The bridge was solid and well engineered, another modern convenience built to look old.

Ian descended when the coach halted and handed out his daughter. She had revealed several interesting things about the necklace and its provenance last night.

The front door was a slab of very old wood, which possibly had been a true drawbridge at one time. It was immense, and a smaller opening had been cut through it to lead into the house.

A footman admitted them and led them into a hall that was very much in the Scottish baronial style—whitewashed walls and huge beams like the ribs of a ship holding up a dark wooden ceiling.

From what Ian had pieced together from old drawings and plans, the hall of the original Kilmorgan Castle had looked a bit like this. When Old Malcolm had built the new house, however, he'd left castle architecture well in the past, embracing the most modern materials and designs the mid-eighteenth century had.

Ian and his party were not expected. Fellows told the footman to announce that Lord Ian Mackenzie and Miss Mackenzie had come to call upon Mr. Pemberton. Ian noticed that Fellows omitted his name and the fact that he was a chief superintendent of Scotland Yard.

The footman coolly took Ian's card and ascended the large staircase at the end of the hall, leaving them alone.

"He's snooty because you're Scots," Fellows said. "Never mind the 'lord' tacked to your first name and the fact that his master lives in a pretend Scots castle."

Ian hadn't noticed the footman's disdain, and he did not much care about it. Megan, likewise, seemed taken with the many antique weapons hanging on the walls, unworried about their reception.

"That is a rapier from seventeenth-century France," Megan said, pointing. "From the time of Louis the Thirteenth. That is a broadsword from the fourteenth century, probably from Germany."

Fellows studied the swords with interest. "How do you know so much about weapons, young lady?"

Megan gave him a look of surprise. "Books. I'm very interested in antiques and history, and swords always come up in adventure stories. That is a basket-hilted claymore, and that is a Roman short sword."

Ian's pride soared as he watched thirteen-year-old Megan twist her face into a very adult expression as she rattled off the information. She, like Ian, remembered almost everything she read.

Megan would be grown up soon. In five years she'd be making her come-out and looking to be married.

Time. It went by so fast. Before Ian had met Beth, every hour had stretched as though bathed in treacle. Now days were liquid, flowing smoothly along. Nights moved even more swiftly, and were joyful when he was wrapped in Beth.

The stiff-backed footman returned and told them coolly to follow them upstairs. Ian took Megan's hand and led her after him. He did not necessarily want to bring Megan into contact with Mr. Pemberton, but still less did he wish to leave her alone in this strange house.

Ian glanced around in distaste as they ascended. He knew people believed that his zeal about Ming bowls was a part of his madness, but at least he focused on one type of object and displayed them in an orderly fashion.

This house was a jumble of different bits and pieces from many centuries and countries, from an elephant saddle from India to Meissen porcelain to a shield from fifteenth-century Venice. The clutter of Mr. Pemberton's collection mania littered every surface, including the floor.

The footman led them to a double door, which was carved with a scene of medieval soldiers hacking each other to bits. Some wore plaid great kilts, which made Ian cringe. Scotsmen hadn't begun wearing kilts until the sixteenth century.

The footman opened the door, which swung back in silence. The room beyond was cavernous. Carpets overlapped one another on the floor, and every space was

covered with shelves, cases, and tables with paths around
them, rather like a library or museum.

At the end of this room was a clearer space before a fireplace, a carved mantelpiece taking up an entire wall. Before
this sat a group of furniture—a carved bishop's chair from
whatever cathedral had been ransacked surrounded by several modern and comfortable-looking chairs.

The man who rose from the bishop's chair was a stranger
to Ian. White-haired and upright, he wore a long dressing
gown and a fez used as a smoking cap, though he held no
pipe or cigar.

He had visitors, two of them. They sprang up in conster-
nation from the wing chairs and turned to Ian in dismay.
Ian knew these two very well—one was Curry, his valet.
The other was his son.

"Dad!" Jamie blurted, then he deflated. "Aye, well, 'twas
to be expected, I suppose. Meant to surprise you, sir. But
perhaps you can join me in persuading Mr. Pemberton to
let go of the piece?"

~~~~~

Jamie breathlessly resumed his seat, his face hot, aware of
his father's scrutiny. He had tried most of his life to please
his dad, which was difficult with a father who could out-
think him at every turn.

Ian said nothing, however, only moved to a chair as
Pemberton, seemingly pleased that even more people had
come to accuse him of theft, waved at them all to sit.

Jamie kept his face blank, but he clenched his hands. He
ought to have known his father was too canny, too quick to
figure out what he and Curry had learned—that Mr. Pemberton had hired a man to steal the necklace for him.

Curry had discovered this by contacting his old friends
and asking for gossip. One had admitted that a mutual acquaintance, a chap known as "Old Joe," had gained

employment at a museum, minded his manners for a year, and then purloined a necklace as it was being packaged to send to a French geezer.

Joe had simply put the package into his pocket and walked out the back door. He'd delivered it to Pemberton, who had arranged for his employment at the museum in the first place, and Pemberton had paid Joe a hundred pounds.

Jamie had been incredulous. "The bloke handed over a necklace worth tens of thousands of guineas for *a hundred quid*?"

Curry had shrugged. "As far as Joe were concerned, it were a bird in the 'and. Better take the ready money than try to sell it on his own. Pieces like that are hard to fence, lad."

'Struth, Jamie had said to himself.

Ian settled into his usual nonchalance as Pemberton surveyed them all in delight. Wasn't no one more coolheaded than Dad when it came to fencing with other collectors, Jamie thought with some pride. If Ian Mackenzie wanted a thing, he obtained it. Even men like Pemberton were no match for him.

"Gentlemen. And young lady. Welcome." Mr. Pemberton sat down again in the bishop's chair, a little smile hovering around his mouth. That smile worried Jamie more than his father's steady gaze or Uncle Lloyd scowling as though itching to make an arrest.

Megan, Jamie's sweet little sister, watched the scene avidly from Ian's side. She had a canny way of obtaining vast amounts of information by simply observing.

Ian studied the Biedermeier chair Pemberton had pointed him to, looking over its green and gold striped seat, thin scrolled back, and delicate arms—probably wondering which stately home in Austria it had been stolen from. After he'd looked it over carefully, Ian sat down, booted feet planted on the floor.

He said nothing as he glanced at his large, gloved hand

resting on the chair's arm, looked Pemberton in the chest, and then flicked his eyes to Jamie.

Waiting for Jamie to continue the interrupted conversation. Jamie shivered inside, both in excitement and trepidation.

He cleared his throat. "Mr. Pemberton. We all know you acquired the Roman necklace—*how* you did so is immaterial to us. We only wish to purchase it. At a reasonable price." Jamie darted his father a quick look, but Ian didn't move. He'd returned his gaze to the V where Pemberton's dressing gown closed over his stiff white shirt.

Jamie steepled his fingers, exactly as he'd seen Uncle Hart do, but maintained a slight frown, like Uncle Cameron when he negotiated over the price of a horse.

"Reasonable to whom?" Pemberton asked in an interested tone.

"To all concerned," Jamie answered. "After our transaction, we would have the necklace, and you would have a price and our silence."

Pemberton listened with grave attention, then sank back into his wooden seat and chuckled. "My dear young man, are you offering to purchase an artifact you believe stolen in the presence of a chief superintendent of Scotland Yard?" He gave Uncle Lloyd a beatific smile.

That was exactly what Jamie was doing. *Damnation.*

If one of Jamie's uncles had marched in here and demanded the necklace, it would even now be in the Mackenzies' possession. Uncle Hart would have coolly told Pemberton to hand the necklace over, and Pemberton would have scrambled to fetch it, apologizing all the way.

What Dad would do, Jamie wasn't certain. But he'd never be sitting as Jamie was now, squirming in shame and worry. Jamie was out of his depth, and Pemberton knew it.

Dad and Uncle Lloyd weren't coming to his aid. Curry had relapsed into silence as well, an old habit, Jamie knew, when he was around a beak. No matter how close Uncle Lloyd had become to the family, he was still a policeman.

Into the heavy and awkward silence came the light voice of Megan.

"We only want the necklace to give to our mum on Hogmanay. Did you know it was made for Empress Pompeia Plotina by an artisan who wanted to impress her? She rewarded him with a villa in Roman Britain, which is where this necklace was found. Only, archaeologists are unconvinced it is the correct necklace. There is speculation that it is a medieval replica, copied from documents left in the jewelers' home."

Pemberton's assured expression slipped. "Is that so, young lady?" He sounded no less pompous, but Jamie caught a quaver in his voice.

"Oh yes." Megan patted her satchel, which was half her size. "I have done ever so much reading. It's fascinating, really, how the jeweler fell in love with the empress. Though he knew he'd never be with her, he could make her beautiful gifts. But it is now believed the original necklace was lost, possibly buried with its maker, or destroyed by Emperor Trajan in his jealousy."

"Or sold by him," Pemberton said. "The Roman emperors weren't known for their moderation." He resumed his superior smile. "Even if the story is true, it makes the necklace no less valuable. Medieval jewels can be just as precious."

Megan gave him a frown. "No matter what, it was very bad of you to steal it. What you ought to do is return it to the museum, and then we will purchase it from the man who was supposed to have bought it from them in the first place."

Pemberton gazed at her in perplexity, then at Ian, who remained a silent statue. Jamie was flushed with embarrassment, but he couldn't help admiring Megan.

"Out of the mouths of babes," Pemberton said softly.

He sat up, folding his hands on his lap, his patronizing

smile returning. "Alas and alack, my friends. Perhaps before you stormed my little castle and postulated your theories, you should have ascertained whether I still had the necklace. It has indeed been stolen—from *me*. I no longer have the thing. Not that you will prove I ever had it, so put away the frown that says you'll drag me off to jail, Chief Superintendent Fellows, there's a good chap."

Chapter 7

Ian sprang to his feet, his patience at an end. "Who does have it?" he demanded.

Pemberton also rose, slowly, but Ian knew the man wasn't as calm as he pretended to be. "If I knew that, do you not think I'd have sent someone after him? To drag him back . . . And give him up to the police, of course." He made a short bow to Fellows.

Ian scowled. Pemberton was exactly the sort of man he disliked—overly clever and pleased with himself, certain he was smarter than anyone he knew.

Ian briefly wondered whether Pemberton had encouraged the thief to steal the necklace, knowing inquiries were being made about it. Ian hadn't exactly hidden his interest.

"You do know," Ian said. "Tell me."

He noticed Jamie watching the drama closely. The question of why Jamie was here distracted Ian, which made his frustration rise. But he knew that if he crossed the room and shook Pemberton as he wished to, Fellows would stop him.

Megan remained in her seat, clutching the arms of the chair, another Biedermeier piece, very fine. She said nothing, waiting for Ian to fix the situation.

He wished he could. Ian had wanted to make the world perfect since the day Jamie had been born. That determination renewed itself when Belle and then Megan had come along. Ian knew he never could make the world right for them, though Beth said she loved him for trying.

Jamie climbed to his feet. "Please, Mr. Pemberton," he said with an odd tremor in his voice. "It's Christmas."

Ian began to frown. Jamie had never been sentimental about Christmas before—he saved his revelry for Hogmanay.

Megan's lip began to quiver, her blue eyes widening. She said nothing, only clutched her satchel and looked pathetic.

Out of the corner of his eye, Ian saw Curry grin and turn away.

Pemberton stared at both children in exasperation. "Oh, very well," he said with a sigh. "It was taken by, of all people, an archaeologist. I highly suspect so, anyway. The man dug up a Roman barracks near here and found nothing but pots, so I suppose he wanted a bit of gold for his trouble. I noticed my necklace was missing after he'd paid me a visit to view my Roman artifacts. My necklace looks remarkably like one at that museum in London."

He let his eyes go wide, pretended innocence.

"Where is this man now?" Ian asked.

"Oh, who knows." Pemberton shrugged. "He was quite upset when he saw my necklace, went on about keeping artifacts in their own countries, returning the Rosetta stone to Egypt, and all that nonsense. I said things were much safer here in jolly old England, and besides, my necklace came from a dig in East Anglia. Or so I've been told."

Damnation. Had this well-meaning archaeologist already taken the necklace to whatever ruin it had come out of and thrown it back in?

Ian tried to ask another question, but only a growl came from his throat. Fellows smoothly took over. "The name of the archaeologist?"

"Richard Magill," Pemberton answered readily. "Not of

the British Museum or anything, or any university I've heard of. From whatever dig will employ him, I suspect. I didn't think much of him."

Again, the perfect man to push the necklace onto if Pemberton needed to be rid of it. There were so many objects in this room worth fortunes that Pemberton could stand to lose one gold necklace if it meant keeping himself out of Newgate.

Ian gave Pemberton a final glare, then he gestured for his children to accompany him and stalked from the room.

He saw no reason for cordiality or formal leave-taking. They'd cornered a thief and obtained the name of the man who likely had the necklace. Ian had no reason to remain after that.

He heard Fellows murmuring something to Pemberton and Curry's voice chiming in, but Ian was no longer interested in Cornelius Pemberton.

The footman who'd admitted them rushed to open the doors, or tried to. Ian, with his long stride, beat him downstairs to the front door and slapped it open.

The carriage they'd hired waited. Ian opened its door, lifted Megan in, and waited for Jamie to join them.

Jamie hung back. "We have our own transport, sir. Curry and me, I mean."

"Dismiss it," Ian rumbled. "Inside, Jamie. Curry," he called as Curry emerged from the house.

Curry sighed. "I'll see to it. Go with your father, lad."

"Meet us on the train," Ian told Curry, and climbed into the coach.

"Yes, sir. Of course, sir," Curry said with exaggerated patience. "Shall I also prepare you a large meal and polish your boots at the same time?"

Ian ignored him and took his seat in the coach, facing Megan, Jamie beside her. Fellows climbed inside and landed next to Ian. Curry slammed the door, made an ironic bow, and hurried off.

"Damn Pemberton," Fellows said as the carriage started, his scowl very like the ones Hart could produce. "Er, beg pardon, Megan. But he's a slippery cove. I want to arrest him for *something*."

"Send your inspectors to ransack the house," Ian suggested.

"On what charge? We do have rules—we can't search a man's private home for no good reason."

"There is plenty of good reason." Ian met Fellows's hazel eyes with equanimity. "The Biedermeier chairs in that room came from a villa near Budapest that was robbed of almost everything last year. Hart and I stayed in the villa when he was the guest of a former Hungarian ambassador. I remember the chair because there was a small gouge on the arm in the shape of a bird's beak. I sat in the same chair just now. If Pemberton doesn't have a bill of sale from the ambassador, you can nick him."

He turned to look out the window as Fellows gave him a sudden and pleased grin, and the carriage swayed onto the road, leaving the false castle behind.

Curry did catch up to them on the train, entering the first-class compartment with a tray of tea and plenty of cakes. Jamie and Megan fell upon the cakes, and Fellows gratefully accepted a cup of tea. Ian took nothing, resting his hands on his knees as he watched Jamie and Megan eat with enthusiasm.

Curry, who had learned not to wait for Ian's command either to leave them or join them, sank onto the seat next to Jamie and plucked up a tea cake.

"Your face, lad," Curry said cheerfully. "When you said, *'Please, Mr. Pemberton. It's Christmas,'* I thought I'd split me sides. You should be in a theatrical, Master Jamie."

Jamie grinned. "Megan played her part. She can make her lip tremble on command."

"I didn't lie," Megan said hotly. "I do want to find the necklace for Mama. Even if it's medieval, not Roman. It's pretty."

Ian agreed. He didn't give a damn about the necklace's provenance, only the delight it would give Beth.

"What do you want to do now?" Fellows broke in. "Hunt up this archaeologist?" He took a slurp of tea. "That means more messages, more train travel. You can explain to my wife about my constant absence. I doubt it will go well for you."

True. While she was a quiet, soft-spoken woman, Louisa Fellows had a backbone of steel.

"David Fleming," Ian said. He swept up a cup of tea from the rattling tray.

Jamie frowned. "Uncle David? Do you think he'll know where to find the man?"

Ian already knew why he'd corner David, Hart's closest and oldest friend, but he'd learned from experience that others wanted to hear everything that went on in his head.

"Fleming helped excavate a British Roman villa in Shropshire about five years ago, for Dr. Pierson, his friend and mentor," Ian said.

Four nods, all rather impatient. But Ian had no way of knowing *which* part of the explanation they wanted, so he simply related everything.

"They employed an archaeologist to help them," Ian continued. "Dr. Howard Gaspar. He might know Mr. Magill or of him. So I will ask Fleming."

Fellows gave him a nod. "Sound thinking."

Megan took on a dreamy look. "That excavation was where Uncle David met Aunt Sophie."

Jamie snorted. "Yes, very romantic. Uncle David told us about falling in the mud and making a huge fool of himself before she'd even look at him."

Curry chuckled. "Aye, that's the way of it, lad. As you'll find out soon enough."

Megan continued to look sentimental, Jamie confused.

Ian nodded. "A man is always a fool when he falls in love. Your mother has plenty of stories about my idiocy. But you must not let that stop you."

"What if the young lady has no use for you at all?" Jamie muttered.

"Eh?" Curry asked with interest. "Is there already a young lady?"

"No," Jamie said quickly, but his face had gone crimson.

Curry laughed and clapped him on the shoulder. "You're almost grown, lad. It was bound to happen."

Megan licked crumbs from her fingers. "Jamie's in love with our ghost."

"I am *not*!"

Jamie sounded ten years old then, winding himself up for an argument with his sisters.

"He thinks she's beautiful," Megan went on serenely.

Jamie growled. "She's not even a real woman."

"Why did you go to Pemberton?" Ian asked Jamie abruptly. Everyone stared at Ian, as they were apt to when he suddenly changed the subject. But it was important, and Jamie looked horribly embarrassed under his sister's teasing.

"Sir?" Jamie asked, eyes widening.

Ian did not repeat the question, only waited.

Jamie deflated. "Because I wanted the necklace. I knew you were trying to buy it for Mother, and I wanted to find it first and give it to you both. For Hogmanay."

Ian gazed at him in true puzzlement. "Why? Did you think I wouldn't find it?"

"No." Jamie grew flustered. "I just . . . To save you the bother. No . . . Maybe to prove I could find it. I don't know. I wanted to do something wonderful for you and Mother. To please you."

"As a surprise," Megan put in. "So you'd be happy on Hogmanay."

"And, I suppose," Jamie said in a small voice, "to make you proud of me."

Ian was extremely proud of Jamie already, his tall, robust son who had inherited none of Ian's difficulties. Jamie had a free and easy way about him, coupled with Mackenzie determination, and most people liked him at once.

Ian loved Jamie with a love he'd not known he possessed. The same went for Belle and Megan, two daughters who shared their mother's beauty.

This love had come upon him naturally, out of the blue, when he'd beheld Jamie's tiny face peeking from the bundle in Beth's arms sixteen years ago. The love had blossomed again for Belle, and again for frailer Megan, whom they'd worried over the first year or so of her life.

Both his children watched him now in worry, Megan with eyes of deep blue. Beth's eyes.

Ian launched himself from his seat and caught the startled Jamie in a rough embrace.

Jamie's return embrace told Ian that no more words needed to be said. Ian pressed his son, his precious son, to his heart.

They released each other at the same time, Jamie surreptitiously wiping his eyes. Ian then caught Megan for her share of the hugging.

My lad and lass, Ian thought. There was another lass waiting at home, along with Beth, his light, his love. *Can any man be as blessed as I am?*

Daniel Mackenzie thought himself equally blessed. He not only had the most beautiful wife a man could find, but that beautiful wife knew her way about a combustion engine.

She'd also given him a blue-eyed mite called Fleur, now seven years old and hopefully sound asleep in a nap. While Daniel kept Fleur from the more dangerous aspects of his machines, the dear girl could already competently steer a motorcar from the safety of her mother's lap.

At the moment, in the snowy yard Daniel had adapted

into a space for working on his motorcars, Violet adjusted a nut on the motorized cycle she and Daniel had built, her hand competent on the spanner.

Daniel had kept a close eye on the motor-bicycles that European manufacturers were creating from regular bicycles. The Peugeot company in France was doing wonderful things with them, but Violet had proposed they build their own and improve on the design.

Thus, the Mackenzie prototype was born. The cycle had thick tires, a hard steel body, a bicycle-like steering bar, and a belt drive adapted from Daniel's motorcar constructions.

"That should do it," Violet said, lifting her spanner away. The engine had rattled ominously and the cycle had refused to slide into gear on their first try this morning. "Flywheel was canted."

"Well then, my lady." Daniel patted the seat. "Your steed awaits."

He knew Violet would never politely beg off and tell Daniel to be the first to ride the cycle. She grinned at him, tossed aside the spanner, and swung her leg over the seat.

"Mount up," she said. "And hang on."

"If we're too banged up for supper, Aunt Eleanor will not be pleased," Daniel said as he scrambled aboard behind her.

"I'll be careful, fusspot." Violet pulled her leather helmet over her head and adjusted her goggles. Daniel did the same, never failing to think how adorable Violet looked in her riding gear. "Off we go."

The cycle's back wheel slid in the mud as the vehicle leapt forward. Daniel clutched Violet—not a bad handhold— as she swung them through the open gate, held by a grinning stable boy.

The cycle didn't have much power, but with the engine rumbling beneath him, the wheel churning up earth, and the ground gliding by so close to his feet, Daniel swore they were flying.

Kilmorgan was crisscrossed with tracks and riding paths, kept debris-free so the many Mackenzies could walk, ride, or bicycle without mishap. Violet took advantage of these paths to zoom the cycle across the snow-covered park and out onto the road.

The cycle jounced and bumped, roared and belched. Daniel saw many days of fine-tuning ahead, but he didn't mind. Violet would be working alongside him, her slender hands affixing a nut or splicing a wire.

Afterward they could hurry to the house to bathe, perhaps sponge each other off in the privacy of their suite . . .

Daniel emerged from this heady fantasy to find Violet turning the cycle to a narrower, winding road that led straight into the hills.

"Not sure the wheels will take it!" he bellowed into her ear.

Violet must not have heard him, because she leaned over the handlebars and urged the vehicle into more speed. The cycle slipped and slid, the road climbing to dizzying heights.

On the one hand, Daniel was elated. A cycle could go where a motorcar or a carriage, or even a bicycle, could not—the freedom was amazing.

On the other, it was downright terrifying. The cycle wove close to the edge of the path, from which tumbled a razor-steep drop. This lane was accessible only by horseback, and farther on, had to be traversed by foot.

The short winter day was ending. Darkness would soon enshroud them, and the cycle was not yet equipped with lamps.

"Darling," Daniel said into her ear. "Vi, love."

Violet braked, skidding them sideways before the cycle halted inches from the precipice. She yanked up her goggles.

Instead of answering, Violet pointed to the heights above them. "Whatever is that?"

Daniel sighted along her gloved finger. This path led to a high clifftop, where Daniel's grandfather had built a picturesque ruin, back in the days when such things were the rage.

A light flickered on the clifftop. The beam moved to and fro, a ghostly signal in the gathering gloom.

"Uncle Mac likes to paint up there," Daniel said over the rumble of the cycle. "He's daft like that. Aunt Isabella might have met him for a liaison, away from the crowded household."

"On a dark December afternoon?" Violet glanced back at him, eyes glinting. "Isabella would never let herself freeze like that."

"Trespassers, then," Daniel said. "Perhaps we should offer them shelter."

"Or our ghost."

Daniel had already considered that, but he liked more earthly explanations. "Maybe. Shall we find out?"

"I intend to." Violet set her goggles in place with a determined jerk.

"Wait, love—do ye think the cycle can make the . . . *Oop!*" Daniel yelped as the cycle bounced forward hard, nearly unseating him.

Daniel clung to his wife as she ascended the path. Violet was a fearless driver, which was why Daniel's cars won the time trials in France every year. He'd long ago learned to let her take the wheel, and then to close his eyes and hang on.

In the end, the cycle proved it could not make it to the top. Violet halted when a slab of rock rose like a stair step on the far side of a bend. From here, they'd have to continue on foot.

They dismounted and Violet stopped the engine and laid down the cycle. Daniel hoped, as they made their way upward in the dying light, that they'd be able to start it again.

They climbed in silence, both knowing the way from scrambling up and down this hill for the last eight years, in all weathers. As the pillars of the folly came into view, the false ruin eerie in the winter twilight, Daniel stopped and tugged Violet to his side.

"I know you're courageous, love, but we don't know who's here," he said. "A desperate man, armed? Or a sad, lost traveler? Let me go first."

Violet hesitated, as though she'd argue, then she nodded and stepped aside so Daniel could lead.

The folly was a square stone building laden with ivy and moss. From its porch, on a clear day, a viewer could see misty hills, sharp mountains, and the sea.

A lantern lay on its side at the foot of the lowest step. The candle still flickered inside as Daniel set it upright.

"Someone has been living here," Violet said.

She stood in the doorway that led into the folly. The interior consisted of one wide room, where Mac came to paint, or Eleanor and Hart sometimes fled to for privacy.

But Aunt Eleanor, though raised in brutal Scottish winters, drew the line at frolicking with Uncle Hart outside in the dead of December. Daniel also doubted Eleanor would leave behind a pile of blankets and the remains of a loaf of bread and bottle of wine.

Daniel lifted the bottle, examining it by the lantern's light. "From Uncle Hart's cellar."

Violet gazed about in excitement. "So she *was* in the house. Probably went to steal more food or blankets when Mac nearly caught her."

"You think the lady in white and whoever is staying here are one and the same?" Daniel swept his light over the blankets, food basket, and a camp chair that reposed in the corner.

"I do, indeed," Violet said. "No male vagrant would be this neat—not that I believe she is a vagrant. No tattered belongings, no odor of unwashed body. She took what she needed from us and nothing more."

"Including a bottle of Hart's very expensive French wine." Daniel hefted it, noting that half the contents were still present.

"What else could she drink to keep herself warm?" Violet asked. "She is using a glass." She pointed to a crystal goblet that had been placed neatly on a square of cloth next to the bread. "And partaking of it slowly."

"Hmm." Daniel set the bottle down. "We must have frightened her off with the cycle. I will have to make the engine quieter."

Violet turned to him, her smile wide with triumph. "I do believe we've found our ghost."

"And lost her again." Daniel gestured at the empty folly.

"Not necessarily. I can guess where she's gone. I believe we need to ask Eleanor to present the newly hired housemaid to Mac, and then find out why she's been wiling her way into Kilmorgan."

Daniel agreed. Violet continued to smile at him, her face so beautiful, her adventurous yet warm nature shining out, that he could not help taking her into his arms and kissing her.

Chapter 8

That evening, Eleanor asked the housekeeper to send the new housemaid to her sitting room.

"Do not alarm her," Eleanor told the housekeeper. "Simply state that I wish to ask her a question—I have no complaint with her work."

The maid arrived at seven o'clock as instructed. Mac was there with Isabella, ostensibly having tea, with Jamie, who'd returned not an hour ago with Ian, stuffing himself with scones.

The maid was a pleasant-looking young woman with red hair and a freckled face, her smile ready but not insolent. Her family had recently moved into a cottage in the village, the maid taking employment here to help her mother and father.

She curtsied as she entered. "You sent for me, Your Grace?"

"Yes, indeed. Lachina, isn't it?"

The maid curtsied again. "Yes, Your Grace." She looked grateful Eleanor hadn't made her take a generic name like Mary or Jane as many employers did.

Mac and Jamie stared at the young woman, but neither

clutched their hair or shouted, *That's her!* They looked, if anything, puzzled.

Eleanor kept her voice kind. "I only wanted to tell you that I am pleased with your work. After the holidays, I will speak with you about keeping you on permanently. That is, if you'd like."

Another curtsy, the young lady flushing. "Yes, Your Grace. I would like that very much."

"Good, good. Well, run along. Mrs. Mayhew will no doubt be put out with me for interrupting your schedule."

Lachina dimpled with good-natured acquiescence. "Yes, Your Grace. Good evening." She spun on her heel and breezed away, pinafore strings flying.

Eleanor shut the door once Lachina had gone. "Well?"

Jamie was already shaking his head, and Mac joined him. "Not her," Mac said. "Similar coloring, but not the lady I saw in the attic. Or in the hall the other morning."

"Agreed," Jamie said. "The maid we saw was different. More . . ."

"Ethereal," Mac said.

"I suppose," Jamie supplied, sounding disappointed.

Isabella sipped tea serenely. "Maybe it really was a ghost. That would be far more interesting, wouldn't it?"

"Daniel and Violet were most positive a true human being was sleeping in the folly," Eleanor pointed out.

"Perhaps," Isabella said. "But that does not necessarily mean the ghost Mac and Jamie saw and the visitor to the folly are the same person."

"True," Eleanor had to concede. She sat down and poured herself a fresh cup of tea. "Well, we shall just have to find out who is using the folly. I can rig up a camera there—if we can all keep our mischievous sons from it."

Jamie grunted. "Daniel and Vi probably scared away whoever it was. We'll never solve this."

He'd been downcast since they'd returned from Nottinghamshire. Eleanor had not pried about the errand—everyone needed secrets at Yuletide—but the journey seemed to have been an unsuccessful one.

"Nonsense, Jamie. You help me with the camera, and I guarantee, we'll have our ghost by Christmas. Whoever it is can join us for Hogmanay and help us welcome in the first-footer."

Eleanor lifted her cup, hoping to salve the disappointment, but Jamie remained morose, Mac frowning in deep thought.

"He's here," David Fleming said as he abruptly entered Ian's Ming room two days after the solstice. "You can cease sending me blasted telegrams."

Ian and Megan had been going over Ian's collection, deciding which bowls would be taken to their own house when they traveled there after Hogmanay. Ian liked to switch out a half dozen to admire at home, a different six every time.

Ian quickly closed the case he'd opened, and Megan slammed the logbook, leaping to her feet.

Once an avowed bachelor and the man Hart had recruited to do his dirtiest deeds, David now had a beautiful wife and a four-year-old son who was perpetually determined to climb him like a tree. Wife and son were not with him at the moment, but neither was an archaeologist lurking behind him.

Ian had sent David the first message from the station in Nottingham, not a quarter of an hour after they'd left Pemberton's, and subsequent ones all the way to Scotland. Once he'd reached home, he'd spent a memorable night in Beth's arms—their traditional celebration of the solstice—and resumed telegraphing the next morning.

David had soon replied that he'd heard of Magill, who was a colleague of Dr. Gaspar, a man who'd worked on

Pierson's dig. Magill wasn't thought much of in archaeologists' circles, David warned.

No matter. Ian had telegraphed back: *Bring him to Kilmorgan.*

Now, Ian swept past David and strode from the room, Megan following. David, with a noise of exasperation, came behind.

The man who must be Mr. Magill waited in the lower hall. He gazed in fascination at the soaring walls and the immense staircase covered with footmen hanging garlands and ribbons.

Beth was there, welcoming Magill to Kilmorgan.

No. Ian raced down the stairs and halted next to her. "My Beth," he said. "David will see to him."

Beth gave him a little sideways look, then went back to her conversation with Magill. "An archaeologist, you say, Mr. Magill? That is quite fascinating. I look forward to speaking with you about it. Our housekeeper will show you to your chamber, where you can refresh yourself."

"How kind." Magill bowed to Beth, a somewhat fatuous smile on his face. He was a portly man with a white beard and puffy side whiskers, dressed in a thick coat as though prepared to face a winter storm. "I admit, I did not know what to expect from Highlanders."

Beth kept her smile fixed. "If you need anything, you must only ring."

Ian regarded the man stonily. He could not demand that Magill hand over the necklace while Beth stood next to him, and he worried that the man would start blurting out questions about it.

"Come with me to my Ming room," Ian said to him abruptly. "I will show you my collection."

Beth gave Ian a gentle look. "Poor Mr. Magill has traveled all the way from London, he has told me. Let him at least sit down for a moment."

Ian preferred to shake Magill upside down until the necklace fell from his pockets. "When you are rested, come to the Ming room. Ask a footman the way."

Beth sent Magill a hapless smile, but at least Mrs. May-hew took him in hand and led him away before Beth could ask him more questions.

Beth then turned to Ian, as though to begin an interrogation, but Ian quickly ran back up the stairs.

"Mama's going to guess," Megan whispered as she hurried after him.

"We must keep her away," he said. "Can you do that?"

Megan flashed him a grin. "I will do my best." She threw her arms around her father in an impulsive hug.

For a moment, as Ian drew Megan into his embrace, he forgot all about Magill and the necklace, the long journey to visit the sneering Pemberton, and his worries that Beth would discover the secret.

He only knew the love of his daughter, and astonishment that he'd been given such a gift.

Ian's eyes were wet when Megan drew away. She gave him a quick kiss on the cheek and then ran off, unaware of how much she touched her father's heart.

❧

Because David tried to persuade her not to, Beth decided to accompany Mr. Magill to the Ming room a half hour later. Mr. Magill was eager to see the antiquities, not minding at all that he'd barely taken time to remove his coat and wash the train's soot from his face.

David met them on the first-floor landing and did his best to suggest that Beth show his wife, Sophie, around Hart's great house.

Sophie had already seen Hart's great house, when she'd first married David. Beth watched David narrowly—Mr. Magill was an unlikely friend for him, and there was little reason he'd insisted on bringing the man to Kilmorgan.

David Fleming was up to something, and usually that meant no good.

David finally gave up dissuading her and simply led the way across the house.

"We're not alone," David said to Ian as they entered.

Ian stood impatiently in the center of the carpet, his annoyance when he saw Beth plain.

David and Ian had brought Mr. Magill to Kilmorgan for a covert purpose, Beth surmised, and that purpose was not benign, at least not for Mr. Magill. The two regarded him exactly as hunters might a bear they'd lured into a trap.

"Ian," Beth said. "Please tell me why Mr. Magill is here."

Ian only looked at her, and Beth knew she would learn nothing from him. Ian had difficulty with lies, which he got around by saying nothing at all.

David took on his smooth look, the exact one he assumed when trying to butter up one of Hart's political opponents.

"Do not try your charms on me, David," she said severely. "I believe I will remain for your conference, whatever it is about."

"Dear lady." Mr. Magill turned an excited face to her. "I was summoned to speak about Roman antiquities, on which I am an expert."

"Are you?" Beth looked him up and down. Mr. Magill was the soft sort of Englishman who looked as though he had much fondness for port and ale and summoned others to do anything difficult for him. "We do not have Roman antiquities at Kilmorgan."

This did not seem to bother Mr. Magill. "I am honored to have been asked to share my knowledge with such a man as Lord Ian Mackenzie. He is highly regarded as the foremost expert in Ming pottery."

"He is indeed." Beth folded her arms. "Why, I wonder, do my husband and Mr. Fleming wish to ask you about antiquities?"

David broke in. "For *his* expertise, of course." He softened his voice, a sure sign he was changing tactics. "Do you know, little Lucas talked of nothing the entire journey but seeing his Auntie Beth again. He is up in the nursery, probably already getting into mischief."

"Surrounded by Mackenzie children who are already smitten with him," Beth returned. "Do not try to shunt me aside, David. I am not leaving."

David gave her a resigned look. "Ah, the stubbornness of the female of the species."

"Indeed," Mr. Magill said. "But why should she not remain if she is Lord Ian's confidante? What pieces did you wish me to assess, my lord?" He turned to Ian in anticipation.

Ian took a paper from his coat, stepped between Beth and Mr. Magill, and unfolded the page. As Ian's body was in the way, Beth could not see what was on it, but Mr. Magill's eyes widened.

The archaeologist's pink face drained of color, and panic entered his eyes. He stared at the paper for a moment, lips parting, and then he tried to run.

Chapter 9

David tackled him. Mr. Magill yelped as he went down and struggled to free himself, but David was far too strong.

Ian reached down and yanked Magill to his feet.

As he did so, the paper he'd held fluttered to the floor. Beth immediately picked it up.

It was a pencil drawing, in detailed color, of a necklace. Fine gold links held droplets of blue and emerald, the setting beautiful and appearing ancient.

"Ian?"

"Damnation." Ian tried to hold Magill and reach for the paper at the same time, and it was David who plucked the sheet from Beth's grasp.

"I am trying to buy this piece," David said smoothly. "Mr. Magill knows where I can obtain it. That is what Mr. Pemberton told us."

Ian's mouth was set in a grim line, and Magill only spluttered.

Beth gave David a glare. "Cease your lies, please, and tell me what is going on."

David heaved a sigh. "Nothing for it, Ian. Your wife, if it is possible, seems to be even more stubborn than mine."

He turned to Beth. "It was meant as a surprise for you. But it is proving to be more trouble than it's worth."

"Shut your gob, Fleming," Ian growled.

"For heaven's sake, the pair of you." Beth took the drawing from David. "This is a Christmas gift for *me*?" Her heart softened. "Oh, Ian."

"Hogmanay," Ian said. "Not Christmas."

"It is quite beautiful." Beth touched the paper, the glory of the necklace incredible. "But I hardly need such a thing. You've already given me plenty." She looked up to see Magill's worried gaze on the drawing. "And you both must tell my why this necklace upsets Mr. Magill so much."

"He stole it," Ian rumbled. "It was already stolen, I mean, but Magill took it again. I want him to tell me where it is."

"Good heavens." Beth stared at the picture, then at the three men. Ian was adamant, Magill terrified, David hovering between amusement and shame.

"This man is a thief?" Beth asked, assessing Mr. Magill once more. "He hardly looks like a criminal."

"I am not!" Magill protested. "Dear lady, you are correct. I am no villain."

"Yet you took this piece from Pemberton," David said. "So Ian tells me. Popped it in a box and absconded. The look on your face screams your guilt."

"Of course I took it from Pemberton!" Magill shouted. "The man is a philistine. This piece was taken illegally from a dig, dropped in a museum far from its home, and sold off to the first collector who bid for it. And then Pemberton sends in a wily thief to bring it to him. The necklace belongs to none of them." Magill drew himself up. "It should go to a museum in East Anglia, properly labeled as to where it came from and when. It is invaluable for the information it provides, a window to the past. But collectors care nothing for that. They only want a pretty trinket to put on a shelf, or in this case, to hang around a wife's neck." His face went still more red. "Begging your pardon, your ladyship."

"Brave words from a thief," David began.

Beth held up her hand. "No, no, he makes a good point. Mr. Magill, please enjoy our hospitality. There is a bad storm coming, and you will likely be here over Christmas. Being snowed in at Kilmorgan is no terrible thing, I assure you. I will be interested in conversing with you. I am so fascinated by archaeology."

She felt Ian's grim stare on her, but he did not contradict her. Ian had long ago learned to let Beth handle people and confusing situations, while he dealt with *things*.

"David," Beth continued, "will you please show Mr. Magill the house? The duke has many fine paintings and sculptures to enjoy—all purchased legitimately, I assure you."

David did not trust the man, Beth could see, but David knew when it was time to make an exit. He gave Beth a gallant bow.

"Of course, my lady. Mr. Magill, wonders await you."

Mr. Magill, who had wound himself up to defend his actions, looked a little bewildered. He allowed David to usher him out, babbling thanks to Beth and continuing to protest his innocence. David winked at Beth as he closed the door behind him.

Beth knew Ian would explode the moment they were alone, and she held up her hand to forestall him. "David dragged the poor man here in the middle of darkest winter. The least we can do is give him a meal and a bed."

Ian started for the door, but halted before he reached it. "We must take the necklace from him. David doesn't believe him, and David is usually right."

"Perhaps, but we can argue about it later. A heavy snow is coming, and it's Christmas. I agree with Mr. Magill's sentiment anyway—something this beautiful should be given back to the museum from which it came, put on display to anyone interested."

Ian turned, his golden eyes filled with the intense light she'd come to love. "I wanted it for you, my Beth." He moved to her, one solid step at a time, until he stood before her, tall and hard-bodied, his kilt brushing her gown. "It will look beautiful on you." He traced her bodice over her collarbone, where the necklace would lie.

Beth's heart beat faster as Ian's touch ignited all kinds of fires inside her. "It is a kind thought, Ian, but I'd be just as happy to see it displayed in a case along with other antiquities."

"The museum couldn't afford it." Ian's voice softened, his gaze following his fingers. "That is why they sold it."

"I believe you." Beth's thoughts began to scatter as Ian moved still closer. "I have it—we can give the museum an endowment to keep this necklace and all the things found with it. They can call it the Ian Mackenzie Collection."

Ian leaned to her, his warmth as enticing as the desire in his eyes. "The *Beth* Mackenzie Collection."

Beth's heart fluttered. "Would a museum put a woman's name on an archaeological collection?" She asked it half in jest, not really caring at the moment.

"They will if they want the endowment."

"Mmm." Beth laced her arms around her husband's neck. "Perhaps we could speak of this later."

"Aye," Ian whispered. His lips went to her neck, her mouth, his kisses heated.

The carpet in the Ming room was very soft, as Beth had come to know. It cradled her now as Ian took her down to it, his eyes a golden light in the gathering darkness.

~

Snow stung the windows of David Fleming's suite of rooms, the usual ones he was given when he stayed at Kilmorgan. So many years he'd been coming here, he thought as he opened the door to warmth. But the last five had been far different.

The reason was the lovely dark-haired woman with green eyes who turned as he entered.

Sophie Tierney, now Sophie Fleming, had saved David's life. The day he'd opened his eyes in a hungover stupor and seen her measuring gaze, he'd been reborn.

Sophie touched a finger to her lips as David entered, gesturing to the door that led from sitting room to bedroom. "I finally persuaded him to nap," she said softly, and let out a relieved sigh. "I should not wonder at his persistence. Lucas is *your* son."

"And yours." David came to Sophie, touched her cheek, and brushed a kiss to her lips. "Stubborn as his mother."

Sophie widened her eyes. "Good heavens, then we are both doomed."

"We are indeed." David kissed her again, the taste of her filling his soul. "Magill was almost as stubborn. I had to lead him all over the house up and down before he finally grew tired and adjourned to his bedchamber. Wore myself to the bone."

David had a good idea how he'd like to take his rest from his labors, and kissed Sophie again. He slid his hand beneath her hair and let the kiss turn deep.

Sophie rested her hands on David's chest. "Love?" she whispered. "You did find out what Mr. Magill did with the necklace, didn't you?"

David brushed the corner of her mouth, letting her green eyes fill his vision. "We'll let him sleep the sleep of the just for now and pry it out of him tomorrow. It turns out that his motives are pure if his methods are questionable. Beth will let him return it to the museum and be a hero."

At the moment, David was more interested in Sophie's taste, her heat, and the empty bedchamber through the door opposite the one their son lay behind.

"Oh dear." Sophie pushed at his chest, and David straightened, his need turning to trepidation.

"*'Oh dear'* what?"

"Did you not speak with Uncle Lucas about Mr. Magill? I thought he told you all about him."

"We sent telegrams. I did not have time to travel to see your uncle's estimable self."

When Ian had demanded David's help, David had contacted Dr. Pierson, his mentor and uncle of the beautiful woman in his arms. Pierson had known Magill and told David where to put his hands on him.

Magill hadn't proved a very practiced criminal. He'd been exactly where Pierson had said he'd be—in the Reading Room of the British Museum.

Sophie had been busy preparing for the journey here, which included quite a lot of shopping. The overnight train, during which they mostly made certain young Lucas did not open every door including one into the foggy darkness, did not leave them much time to chat.

Magill had shut himself into his compartment and slept. David had made sure he did not come out during the journey, which again, had not left him time to be with his wife.

Now David was weary, snappish, and ready to curl up around her in bed.

Sophie eyed him with uneasiness. "I was certain Uncle Lucas would have told you. Mr. Magill has done this sort of thing before. 'Rescued' antiquities from ruthless collectors, I mean."

"Indeed. He seems adamant." David's foreboding rose. "But you look very worried, which worries *me*, because you are no fool."

Sophie drew a breath. "He rescues the things, yes, proclaiming that he is saving them for research and for the public to enjoy. And often he does. Other times . . ."

"Other times? My love, you are filling me with dread. Pray, douse me with the horrible news at once."

"The things disappear, and Mr. Magill seems to be flush with money. He has quite a lot, you see, and then suddenly has nothing at all. Uncle Lucas believes he bets on the horse races, but isn't certain. He's asked him, but Magill always has an evasive answer."

David groaned. "You mean our virtuous archaeologist lifts a few choice antiquities and sells them to pay off his gambling debts? Scheming little toad. I didn't quite believe him when he came all over pious to Beth."

"He doesn't sell them all the time," Sophie said. "Many of the things he takes from collectors he really does give to museums. That is why I say we need to find the necklace and lock it up if he has it with him. In case."

Snow slapped at the windows, and a glance that way showed David that the panes were white, with little visible in the stygian darkness of late afternoon beyond.

This chamber was cozy and warm, a fire crackling. David's son slept in peace, and Sophie was soft against him.

"The man is going nowhere in this gale, love," David said, leaning down to nip her earlobe. "I will procure the necklace from him in the morning. I'll go through his bags if I have to."

Sophie looked indecisive, but she nodded. "He did look exhausted. As do you." She traced his cheek.

David's thoughts fled at her touch, at least the ones that weren't decadent. "Is our bedchamber as warm as this one?" he murmured as he pressed a kiss to her temple, inhaling her scent.

"I believe so."

"Then let us adjourn to our bower, my love."

Sophie's answering smile made his heart turn over, and as always filled him with astonishment that he was actually married to her.

David clasped her hands, pressed a long kiss to her lips, and allowed her to lead him to their empty chamber, and so to bed.

~~~

That night in Jamie's bedchamber, Gavina and Jamie regaled Gavina's cousin Andrew McBride with the story of the ghost and the hunt for the necklace—Jamie including all the pranks he and his cousins had played on the ghost hunters.

Andrew laughed with enjoyment. Gavina was a bit smug that Andrew, quite grown-up and at university, conceded that the "children" had a good story to tell. He clapped Jamie on the back, and said he was sorry he'd missed the excitement.

They sat in a circle of lamplight. A fire flickered at one end of the chamber, and the shadows outside the reach of the candlelight were deep.

"We still haven't found the ghost," Gavina said. "Daniel and Violet looked over the camp at the folly, but she didn't return." She glanced at the window, which shook from the wind, and shivered. "I hope whoever it is isn't out in this."

"I don't think she is, lass." Jamie's voice became hushed.

Andrew, who sat facing the fire, drew a sharp breath, and Gavina swung around to see what had startled them.

In the corner near the fireplace, a woman in a white dress floated. Uncle Mac had been right about her having no hands or feet, because none showed as she hovered there, the gossamer white of her gown fluttering in a sudden draft.

Jamie and Andrew sat transfixed. They looked like gaping fish, Gavina thought.

It could not be a ghost, she told herself. Whoever had been living in the folly was flesh and blood, needing food, drink, and blankets.

Gavina sprang to her feet. The draft, she realized, came from the panel that had opened near the fireplace.

The woman's eyes widened as Gavina ran at her, pools of black that resolved into the eyes of a living, breathing woman. Her feet were covered by folds of her sweeping skirt, her hands by black gloves and the too-long sleeves of her gown.

Gavina seized her. Warm limbs moved under her grasp,

and Gavina's elation soared. She'd been right. She'd been *right*.

The young woman had a lovely oval face and a quantity of red hair that tumbled from beneath a battered hat. She collapsed into Gavina, her lips pale with cold.

"Please, you must help," she declared in a flat accent Gavina couldn't place. "He'll die out there. You must help him."

Chapter 10

Mac Mackenzie responded to the pounding on the studio door with ill grace. He did not often have a chance to paint these days, what with Eleanor recruiting him to help with her mad decorating or to make certain the younger children did not destroy said decorations or themselves.

Isabella, reposing on the chaise in diaphanous draperies, quickly snatched up her dressing gown.

Mac hadn't had much time to enjoy *her* either. He yanked open the door, his paintbrush dripping on the scrubbed floor.

When he saw what awaited him, he took a few steps back, nearly slipping on the paint.

The ghost stood before him. At least—the ghost transformed into a frightened-looking young woman with a dust-streaked face and wide hazel eyes. She was flanked by Jamie, Gavina, and Andrew McBride.

"Uncle Mac," Jamie said breathlessly. "You're the only one awake."

"I already wish I weren't. What the devil?"

Isabella was next to Mac in an instant, gazing at the young woman with great interest. "Good heavens. Is this your ghost?"

"Yes," Mac and Jamie answered at the same time.

"Her name is Magdala," Gavina said swiftly. "But we'll tell you about her later. She says the archaeologist fellow has run off into the night, straight into the storm."

"With Mum's necklace!" Jamie said in anguish.

The wind echoed Jamie's wail. Mac had barely met the little bearded fellow David had brought with him before he'd been whisked away to Ian. Mac wasn't quite certain why the man was here—to consult with Ian about Ming whatnots, Mac had assumed.

"He rushed out in *this*?" Mac demanded as the wind continued shrieking and snow battered the panes behind him. "Where does he hope to go? The train doesn't run until morning even on the sunniest days."

"If he's unfamiliar with Scotland, he might not know this," Isabella said. "We'd better go after him."

Mac's attention remained on the young woman hovering behind Jamie and Gavina. "What the devil were *you* doing, rushing around up here in the dark? What were you doing in the house at all?"

"Perhaps we should interrogate her later, Mac," Isabella said sliding her hand to his arm.

"I don't think the man will last long in this weather," Magdala said. Her accent was curious—flat but with a bit of a lilt and a full stop of consonants. Almost Irish, but that wasn't quite right.

Mac snapped from his speculations to the present. Anyone outside right now would freeze to death.

"You are right, love," Mac said. "Jamie, wake Bellamy and have him rouse the house. Once we find Magill and drag him home safe and sound, we will all have a long talk."

~~~

Ian pulled on his greatcoat, readying himself with Daniel, his brothers, and Mackenzie retainers to rush into a storm to save a thief.

The men arrayed around him looked grim. Storms in the Highlands were no joke. A man could die quickly if he did not know how to find shelter, or he could blunder into the loch or off a cliff.

The ladies hovered nearby, ready to shove their menfolk outside to rescue a complete stranger. Beth helped Ian button his coat and don thick gloves. Though Ian did not need the help, he didn't mind Beth's touch, or her whispered, "Be careful."

He kissed her, absorbing her warmth. He'd go out, find Magill, bring him home and lock him in his chamber, and then take Beth to bed, where he'd been lying in great contentment before Curry had banged on the door.

Curry elected to stay behind to coordinate a wider search if needed. Violet, on the other hand, bundled up to accompany Daniel. She donned her helmet as she argued with Daniel as to who would drive the motorized cycle.

Ian kissed Beth once more. He wanted nothing more than to return to their chamber with her, but he had no intention of leaving Magill to die in the storm.

"You know I am a much better rider," Violet continued, though Ian sensed she'd already won the argument. "You can keep a lookout."

Daniel heaved an aggrieved sigh and prepared to follow her out, but Ian put a hand on Daniel's shoulder. "Let me ride with Violet."

Daniel stared at him, perplexed. "Are you sure, Uncle? The cycle isn't the most stable of vehicles."

"I know where to look for Magill," Ian said. "And Violet knows how to drive the cycle better than anyone."

Violet was already fastening her goggles. "Give him your helmet, Daniel."

Daniel thrust it at Ian, resigned. "If ye come to grief, Uncle Ian, I'm fleeing to the Continent and *not* breaking the news to Aunt Beth."

Ian mounted the cycle. He managed to slide the leather

helmet over his head and adjust the goggles before Daniel
cranked the engine to life. Violet, already aboard, played
with the throttle, the engine sputtering and coughing in the
cold.

"Ready, Uncle Ian?" Violet shouted.

Ian was not at all, but he clutched Violet around the
waist as the cycle leapt forward and bumped down the track
toward the woods.

The cycle could not go as fast as Daniel's best motorcar
or even a running horse, but it was much more maneuver-
able than the motorcars, Ian could see. Violet turned it
sharply and rode up a hill, snow slapping their faces. Ian
was uncomfortable in the close-fitting helmet and the goggles that squeezed his head, but he saw the sense in them.

The roads through and around Kilmorgan had been flat-
tened and in some places paved with stones, instigated by
Daniel so he could run his motorcars around the estate and
down to the village. The road Violet took, however, bumped
and jounced, jarring Ian's bones.

The darkness pressed them. Thick clouds blotted out all
illumination from moon or stars, and soon even the lights
of Kilmorgan fell behind.

Violet knew these hills, but she went slowly, peering
ahead, while Ian scanned for any sign of Magill.

"Where would he go?" Violet shouted behind her.

Ian had already pondered this. Their nearest neighbor
was miles away. The village was too, and it would be shut
for the storm. The road south to Inverness would soon be
impassible.

That left the distillery, which Magill likely didn't know
about. Even if he stumbled across it, the steward and his
family who lived there would have held on to him and sent
word to the main house.

The mysterious woman had seen him, had pointed the
direction he'd been heading.

"The folly," Ian yelled to Violet. Magill might have

spied the young woman's lights or watched her descend from the hill if she'd decided to look for refuge in the house.

Violet nodded and swung the cycle sharply to ride up the next hill.

Magill would freeze to death out here. Even if he hid inside the folly, out of the wind, the cold would be absolute. The cold had driven young Magdala, who had been living in the folly for some time, to the house to seek warmth.

Whoever she was, she certainly was robust if she'd survived out here in December, only sneaking into Kilmorgan for supplies. But she was a mystery to be solved once Ian put his hands on Magill and wrested the whereabouts of the necklace from him. He hoped Magill hadn't lost the bloody thing.

No, the man would more likely hang on to the necklace after all the trouble he'd gone to obtain it. He must have brought it to Kilmorgan with him, one more reason to flee.

Ian leaned into Violet as she struggled to guide the cycle up the hill. The road was steep but passable—Daniel and Violet had come this way only a few days before.

Neither Ian nor Violet saw the snowbank until it was too late. Ian reasoned with detachment that the wall of snow must have come down from the cliff above, loosened by the weight of the storm and pushed by the wind.

Violet swerved. The wheels skidded out from under them, and the cycle threw off its riders, who went tumbling and falling, straight into the frozen bank of snow.

~

Beth and the other Mackenzie wives prevented Magdala from bolting once the men had started the search. The young woman had tried to slip away, but Beth saw her and called out, then ran after her as Magdala charged down the ground-floor gallery, heading for the door to the garden.

Magdala put on a burst of speed, but Eleanor stepped

from a side hall in front of her, and Magdala stumbled to an abrupt halt.

"Enough of that, young woman," Eleanor said. "It is far too cold for you to run off, and we do not need to be hunting for yet another person tonight."

Magdala gazed at Eleanor in stubborn fury. She drew a sharp breath as though ready to argue, but then she wilted. "Yes, ma'am," she said in a subdued voice.

Beth remained suspicious of her sudden capitulation, but Magdala allowed the ladies to guide her into a ground-floor sitting room warmed by a blazing fire. Curry trotted in with a tray of coffee and plenty of cakes, the man knowing exactly how to comfort worried members of the Mackenzie family.

Ainsley plunged into the questioning while Eleanor and the others were still sorting out the coffee and tucking into the cake. Ainsley had taken a very large slice for herself, one slathered in custard.

"You'd better explain yourself," Ainsley said to Magdala. "Gavina is quite frustrated with her male relatives who believe you're a ghost. Tell us why you are haunting Kilmorgan."

Isabella studied Magdala sharply, as did Eleanor, Eleanor with unblinking blue intensity.

"I believe I know why," Isabella ventured.

"You wanted to find out what we'd be like," Eleanor finished for her. "Before you decided whether to announce yourself."

"You ought to let her speak," Beth said. "What is your name, child? Besides Magdala, I mean?"

All four Mackenzie wives turned to Magdala, who clutched her coffee and returned a look of defiance.

"Mackenzie," she said, lifting her chin. "My name is Magdala Mackenzie. Or it ought to be."

Chapter 11

Magdala found herself pinned by four gazes—two blue, one green, and one gray. The ladies were not as astounded as Magdala assumed they'd be, nor were they angry. They only looked at her.

"Yes, I thought so," the duchess said. The duchess worried Magdala most. She could seem vague and babble about nothing but her shrewdness was unnerving.

"Who are your parents?" Beth, the one married to Lord Ian, asked gently.

"My father is dead." Magdala swallowed, that sorrow never far away, though he'd been gone since she was eight years old. "My mother is descended from Lord Will Mackenzie, the brother of Lord Malcolm who became Duke of Kilmorgan in 1747."

All four looked thoughtful. "Lord Will and Josette," Beth said. "Ian would know about his descendants. He has been researching the family," she told Magdala.

"So your mother is the link?" the duchess asked with interest. She poured more coffee into Magdala's cup, though Magdala had taken only the barest sip.

"She is." Magdala spoke with confidence, though even she admitted the story sounded far-fetched. But Mum had told her for years that they were descended from dukes, though their branch put them a long way from inheriting anything. No male heirs were left on their side anyway.

"Where is your mother now?" Isabella asked. She was a fiery redhead and looked Scottish, though Magdala knew she was wholly English, the daughter of an earl of very old lineage. Magdala had found out everything she could about the Mackenzie family.

She tried to keep her voice neutral. "In St. John's. I was raised there. My mother recently married a man."

A pious, pompous wretch who didn't approve of Magdala or her reprobate father. Magdala was of age and should be married, so this man thought. *Out of the way*, Magdala knew he wanted to say.

"Not someone to your taste?" the duchess asked with astuteness.

Magdala shook her head. "I hope she comes to her senses. But as I was at a loose end, I decided to find out where my mother's people had come from."

"You traveled alone?" Beth asked, eyes widening. "Across the ocean?"

Magdala's lips twitched. "There are liners now that make the crossing in a remarkably short time. I saved money, but still didn't have enough for a ticket, so I took a job on a liner and then chucked it when we reached Southampton. I journeyed from there by train."

"Very resourceful." The one called Ainsley, Lord Cameron's wife, nodded with approval. "And here you are."

"I was a maid," Magdala said defiantly. "Where I come from, it isn't shameful to work for a living."

"Of course it isn't, dear," the duchess said. "Nor is hiding out in the folly and stealing food and drink while you spied on us. Only foolish. You could easily have written a letter from wherever this St. John's place is. We would have invited you for a visit, and probably paid for your transport so you wouldn't have had to labor for it."

"How could I know that?" Magdala demanded. "I'm a stranger, a nobody. Why should you believe me?"

"Well, we would have learned all about you first," Eleanor said in a reasonable tone. "We still will, but it is Christmas, this storm is fierce, and we are Scots—if Isabella and Beth aren't by birth, they are at heart. We will extend all our hospitality. Besides, you helped us by telling us about the fleeing archaeologist."

Magdala frowned. "He looked so odd. Up to no good, I'm certain, but he'll die out there. And now you are all being kind." She didn't know how to respond to such kindness. Breaking down and weeping came to mind, but Magdala didn't want to look as weak as she felt.

Beth took her hand. "That is what we do, my dear. You are welcome here, Magdala, whoever you happen to be."

She squeezed Magdala's hand and gave her a heart-warming smile, which tore through Magdala's defenses all the more.

Tears trickled from her eyes, and the moment they did, Magdala found herself in Beth's embrace, learning how easy it was to let the sobs come on her soft shoulder.

～～

Hours went by. One by one, the men and boys returned, in need of warmth and rest.

None had found Mr. Magill. And, to Beth's consternation, none of those returning were Ian and Violet.

Daniel arrived with Cameron and two of the many dogs, and when Beth told Daniel she'd heard nothing of Violet and Ian, Daniel's tiredness turned to alarm.

"Where the devil are they?" he demanded of the searchers.

But none had seen Ian or Violet, nor any sign of the cycle, nor had they heard its unmistakable roar in a long while.

"Newfoundland."

Ian sat up, frozen to the bone, pushing snow from his body.

"Wha—?" A body stirred next to him, one buried in almost as much snow.

"Her accent," Ian said. "From Newfoundland. A large island off the coast of Canada."

"Whose accent?" Violet croaked.

Ian didn't bother to answer. Magdala, who looked enough like a Mackenzie to be one, spoke with a lilt he now recognized. He knew a collector of Ming pottery who was originally from St. John's, and though the man had lived in England some time, he retained the unmistakable accent of a Newfoundlander.

Ian reflected in nearly the same moment that the snow had saved their lives. Not only had they landed in its softness, but it had buried them, keeping out the deathly chill of the wind.

He climbed stiffly to his feet, chunks of snow cascading from him. The motorized cycle lay a few yards from them, mangled and silent.

Ian helped Violet to stand. Snow fell thickly, and the wind was fierce.

Violet took in the cycle with dismay, lifting her goggles to stare at it. "Oh dear, Daniel will not be happy."

"Up," was Ian's answer as he pointed to the top of the hill.

The folly was much closer than the house and would provide some shelter. When daylight came, they could pick their way down the trail and back home.

Violet nodded. She slid her goggles back on, as did Ian—they were difficult to see through but would keep the ice from their eyes.

Ian led the way, moving snow with his boots or breaking

icy patches so Violet wouldn't slip. She sensibly stayed close behind him, holding on to his coat when they climbed a particularly treacherous stretch.

After about twenty minutes of struggle, they reached the outcropping of rock that held the folly. Ian made for the dim outline of the building, knowing to stick to the cliff wall on his left to avoid going over the edge. Even so, he tripped on the first step of the porch, falling again into snow.

Violet tugged him up. Ian gained his feet and climbed the steps, finding the folly's door by touch.

It was not locked, to his relief. Ian had been prepared to break the door open, but he was just as glad he did not have to.

He tripped once more as he entered the folly, this time over something that wasn't snow. Ian landed on hands and knees, his face an inch from a human body.

Light flared. Violet had struck a match, which she now touched to a candle in a lantern. She bent down, flashing the light over the body lying prone under Ian's bulk.

"Your archaeologist, I presume?" she asked.

Ian turned the man over. He was indeed Magill with his white hair and side whiskers, now unconscious and very cold. Ian rose, grasped Magill under the arms, and dragged him to the fireplace.

"Is he alive?" Violet had shut the door, and now unwound the long scarf from her neck.

Ian found Magill's heartbeat and heard his wheezing breath. "He is."

The fireplace had never been lit in Ian's memory, and they had no wood here in any case. Violet looked about in futility—there was nothing but a few old sticks of furniture along with the supplies Magdala had left. She lit a second lantern and unfolded the blankets she'd found.

Ian had no compunction about breaking the furniture and stuffing the pieces into the fireplace. The chairs had been brought here by his father long ago, and were brittle, rotted from the wet Scottish air.

With Violet's matches—she'd found a whole cache Magdala had hoarded—Ian had the broken sticks of furniture lit like kindling, the pile of it slowly catching.

"Will nae last," he announced.

"I hadn't planned to settle in for the winter." Violet held her hands out to the meager fire. "This is better than some places I've stayed in my life, I am sorry to say."

From the stories Violet had told him, Ian believed her.

He hauled Magill closer to the fire. The man didn't wake, only grunted and broke into a snore.

Ian patted down Magill's coat, and then reached into his pocket and drew out a handkerchief-wrapped bulge.

Inside the folds of the cloth lay an intricate gold necklace glinting with lapis lazuli and emeralds, the piece as whole and beautiful as the day it was made.

Found.

<hr>

The night grew colder. Magill slept on, remarkably relaxed. Ian and Violet sat on either side of him, the three of them close enough to share heat, while the feeble fire burned to embers.

"You are good to take care of him," Violet remarked.

Ian shrugged. "I wanted the necklace. When we return home, I'll give him to Fellows."

"I know, but you could have left him to rot in the storm and taken the necklace off his frozen body in the morning."

Ian had considered this. He knew a man like Pemberton would have let Magill freeze to death, no matter how cruel such an act might be. But Ian recognized that although he was as mad a collector as Pemberton, he would never be such a monster.

"Hart could have left *me* to die," Ian reflected. "In the asylum when I was a boy. When Hart became duke, he did not have to bother with me. But he came for me. Took me home."

"Uncle Hart is a good man," Violet agreed. "No matter how much he tries to hide it."

"Aye. I was grateful, even if I couldn't speak to tell him so."

Ian felt Violet studying him as they sat in brief silence. "I could have been left to die too," she said. "But Daniel didn't let that happen." She went quiet, and finally, Ian had to turn his head to look at her. Violet's eyes were filled with love. "Daniel brought me home with him, gave me a family of my own."

Hart had done that for Ian years ago. Ian hadn't been able to do much more at first than eat, sleep, and wonder at this turn of fate, but he knew now that his gratitude to Hart, Mac, and Cam had run deep. Not to mention to Curry, always at his side.

"Beth gave me even more family," he said out loud. "The best family."

Violet's smile held warmth. "Your wee ones are turning out well. Jamie is amazing, Belle smarter than anyone I know, and Megan so gentle and sweet. But she's not feeble. I think Megan will rule the roost wherever she goes."

Megan did have a large heart and a quiet strength. Others would underestimate her . . . to their peril.

"My bairns are the best in the world."

Ian stated it as a fact. There were no more perfect people in existence than his three children, except of course for Beth, their mother.

Violet surprised Ian with laughter. "The pride in you is astonishing, Uncle Ian. Or perhaps not so astonishing. Do your brothers know you hold your children above theirs? The rest of them are remarkable as well. Particularly our Fleur." Her eyes went soft as she spoke her daughter's name. "And I think Gavina will become an astounding woman."

"My brothers know," Ian said. "And understand."

Violet's laughter continued, though Ian wasn't certain what was amusing.

"At daybreak, we'll go back," he said. "I will wake Magill then. I'll not carry him down the hill."

"Neither will I," Violet said decidedly.

"Then the four of us will descend." Ian leaned his head back on the bricks of the fireplace and closed his eyes. It was not comfortable, but at least this corner had warmed a bit.

"The four of us?" Violet's voice held a strange note. "You, me, and Mr. Magill make three."

Ian opened his eyes and stared at her. Violet held his gaze a moment and then turned scarlet, which Ian had learned from Beth meant a person felt flustered, or caught in a lie or secret.

"How did you know?" she asked in a whisper.

Ian resumed reclining against the wall. "You are sick in the mornings and then eat quite a lot. I have seen you come out of the nursery looking furtive, and you fuss over the youngest members of the household. Beth was much the same with our children."

"Damnation, Uncle Ian. Does everyone know?"

Ian looked at her again. "I don't know. Have you told Daniel?"

"Not yet." She smiled. "I was saving it as a Christmas gift."

Ian considered this, thinking of Daniel, the wild, impetuous boy who'd grown into . . . well, a wild, impetuous man. "A good idea."

"You'll keep this our secret then?"

Ian nodded. "But you must not ride the cycle anymore. You could have hurt yourself. You must be very careful."

"I *was* being careful. I'm a much better driver than Daniel. A snowbank fell on us. It doesn't matter now anyway— the cycle is a wreck. Daniel will be heartbroken."

Ian gazed at her a long time, daring to meet her eyes. "No," he said calmly. "He will not."

Violet and he shared another long look, and Violet nodded. "I agree."

Ian gave her a smile, then he leaned his head back again and let himself doze off. All would be well; he knew this in his heart.

───◡

Morning light blazed, cutting through the darkness to stab into Ian's brain. He opened his eyes, ready to growl at Curry for letting the bedchamber grow so cold, and then he groaned.

He sat on a thin blanket on a cold stone floor, a fire burned to ash behind him. Violet Mackenzie, moving as stiffly as Ian felt, yawned and rubbed her eyes. Between them, Magill let out a series of inelegant snorts and woke with a gasp.

The light that had woken Ian came from the open door, along with cold wind. A silhouette blocked the light, one of a large Scotsman, who was already roaring in his loud way.

"Ian!"

Ian struggled up, but before he could make it to his feet, Hart reached down and hauled him the rest of the way up. Ian found himself immediately crushed in an embrace, his oldest brother as powerful as ever.

Ian rested his hands on Hart's shoulders. "It's all right," he said into Hart's intense eyes. "You found me."

"I know." Hart's fingers dug into Ian's arms, the man shaking a little. "Now, let's go home."

Chapter 12

Breakfast was a lively meal in spite of the late night, with the searchers, the rescuers, and Magill safely back home.

Beth couldn't leave Ian's side. Ian had shoved poor Mr. Magill into the house but released him into Lloyd Fellows's custody. Magill's near-death in the frozen night had subdued him, and he'd gone off to bed with a hasty mumbled apology. Beth forbade Fellows from taking the man to jail or back to London until after Christmas. Yuletide was for family, and forgiveness.

The ladies had found Magdala some clothes to replace the secondhand and too-large gown she'd been wearing, and Beth bade her tell her tale as the family feasted on bannocks and porridge, eggs and bacon.

Jamie gazed at the young woman in some dismay. "So you're my cousin?"

"I am indeed, lad," Magdala answered. "At least, I believe so."

Jamie looked crestfallen, and Gavina laughed at him. "You've broken his heart," she said to Magdala. "He was smitten with our ghost."

Jamie flushed, though he was always one to admit the

truth. "I was, aye. But it was not meant to be, I see. I don't believe in cousins marrying. No matter what the eugenics people try to prove, breeding too close to the bloodline is a disaster. Especially when it comes to human beings."

Magdala raised her brows at him. "You are a bit young for me, in any case, Jamie. I have reached my twenty-first year."

That brought more laughter, and Jamie again conceded graciously.

"On the other hand," the deep voice of Andrew McBride echoed down the table, "you're not *my* cousin."

At twenty-one, Andrew was taller than his father, Sinclair, and he had the McBride handsomeness—fair hair, strong face, intense gray eyes. Magdala lifted her chin and gazed a challenge at him, but her cheeks were pink and her bravado faltered under his wide smile.

Hmm, Beth thought to herself.

She switched her gaze to Violet, who was sitting very close to Daniel. Violet looked weary, and a bit pale, but also very happy.

Well, well, well. They had been waiting for more children to come, and now it seemed they had managed it.

The year was ending satisfactorily, in Beth's opinion.

After breakfast, Ian headed for their bedchamber and much-needed sleep, but Beth followed him determinedly. *Not quite yet, Ian Mackenzie.*

When she reached their chamber, Ian was unwrapping himself from his kilt, his coat already on the floor. Curry was not there to pick up after him—Beth had sent the man to bed, as he'd been up all night like the rest of them.

Beth closed the door, getting lost in the sight of her husband's fine body appearing as he shed his clothes. He glanced at her and his tired eyes softened.

"Shall we to bed, my Beth?"

His voice, low and vibrant, weakened her at the knees, but Beth made herself remain upright.

"All's well that ends well?" she asked. "Is that what you mean? Nothing more to say?"

Ian continued to disrobe, his under-drawers falling away so that he stood naked before her.

"Nothing." His golden eyes glinted as he walked toward her.

Beth held up her hands, and Ian paused, but the light in his eyes did not dim. "I suppose you retrieved the necklace."

Ian turned away without answering. He lifted his coat, rummaged in the pocket, and drew out the necklace, all gold and blue and green.

He brought it to Beth and lifted it to rest against her bodice.

Beth caught the necklace in her hand, the metal holding the warmth of Ian's pocket. The piece was beautiful, the links intricately worked by some unknown jeweler nearly two thousand years ago.

"I wanted to give it to you for Hogmanay," Ian said softly. "But it will do for Christmas Eve."

Beth gazed at it in reverence. "It's beautiful. But I still want it to go to a museum."

Ian regarded her in silence a moment, then gave her a nod. "It is yours. Do what you will."

"Don't be offended. It's just that I think more people ought to be able to enjoy it. It's a treasure."

Ian's glance told her he thought she was mad, but he wouldn't argue with her daft ideas. He took her hand, lifting it to his lips.

He was dissolving Beth's attention again. Ian licked her finger, then drew it into his mouth, closing his eyes to suckle it.

"You really didn't need to give me such an extravagant present," Beth began, but she trailed off, her breath deserting her.

Ian kissed her fingertip, then lightly nibbled it. "I want to show you what you mean to me."

Beth's heart fluttered, and every part of her began to heat. "You've already given me the best gift."

Ian's brows rose. "Do you mean last Hogmanay? It was only a painting of the dogs, and Mac did that."

"I don't mean that. Although I love it." The painting was very small, made to stand on her writing table, where she could see the doggie smiles of their current crop of pets, who would most likely be sleeping on her feet under the desk.

"What then?" Ian returned to kissing her fingers, the backs of them this time. Then he turned her hand over and pressed his lips to the inside of her wrist.

Beth could barely continue. "You gave me you, ye daft Highlander. And Jamie. Belle. Megan." Her heart filled as she spoke the names of her beloved children. "Ian, you took me in when I had no one. Now I'm surrounded by this wonderful family, and I have you, all to myself. I am the luckiest woman on earth."

Ian lifted his head again. His eyes filled with desire, Ian no longer interested in conversation.

He snaked one arm around Beth and drew her against his delightful body.

"*You* are lucky? I am the one who is lucky, my Beth. I saw you in at the theatre, I sat next to you, I *met* you. I told you exactly what I wanted, and instead of running away, you gave me your beautiful smile. I thought an angel had come to rescue me from all that was darkness. And you did. So wear the damned necklace."

Ian rarely spoke so heatedly, or made such a long speech. Beth couldn't stop her smile, the same one she couldn't hold back when he'd told her bluntly that faraway day that he wanted to marry her so he could bed her.

"I love you, Ian Mackenzie," she said. "All the words in the world can't convey how much."

Ian cupped her cheek and brushed a lingering kiss to her lips. "You'll wear it, then?"

"And I love your stubborn single-mindedness. Yes, I'll wear the necklace. Until after Hogmanay, when it goes back to the museum."

Ian never gloated when he won. He only gave her a triumphant smile and lifted Beth into his arms, cradling her while he carried her across the chamber.

He laid her down on the bed where they'd spent so many nights and had conceived at least one of their children. Beth helped Ian with her many buttons, letting him pull—and tear—her clothes away. A night on the clifftop hadn't diminished his strength.

Ian showed her his single-mindedness again when he clicked the necklace around her throat. He leaned to kiss her breasts, his mouth warming the jewels and her skin.

When he lifted his head, all his love shone in his golden eyes, brighter than the Christmas sunshine.

"I love you, my Beth. You are the greatest gift the world has given me. I can only try to thank you like this." He touched the necklace, the priceless thing that he'd gone to such trouble to find.

Beth touched his face. Every year, her love for this man grew in strength, until she wasn't sure her heart could bear it. "You don't know your own worth, Ian, but I do." She drew him to her. "I do."

Ian touched her lips. "No more words. Happy Christmas, my Beth. My love."

"Happy Christmas, Ian."

Beth surrendered to his kiss, nothing more she needed to say. Ian slid inside her, completing her as he always did, while the midday sun slid through the window to surround them with brilliance.

A
Mackenzie Clan
Gathering

Chapter 1

Something woke Ian Mackenzie deep in the night. He lay motionlessly, on his side, eyes open and staring at darkness.

A dozen years ago, awakening to total darkness would have sent Ian into a crazed panic, ending up with him on his feet, roaring at the top of his voice in English, Gaelic, and French. Servants would have rushed in, restoring lights some foolish footman had put out, to find Ian standing up beside his bed, swearing in rage and fear.

Now, he lay calmly, absorbing the soft quiet of the darkness.

The reason for his calm lay behind him on the bed—his Beth, curled against him in a nest of warmth.

Whatever change in the huge house had alerted Ian had been too subtle to wake Beth. She slept on, her breathing even, one hand soft against his bare back.

Ian's mind rapidly churned through possibilities of what had dragged him from his dreams. His children—Jamie, Belle, and Megan—were fast asleep in their nursery. Ian knew whenever one of them was wakeful, knew it in his bones. They were shut behind the door of the large nursery at the end of the hall. Safe.

He let his senses expand to every tiny sound of the night. This was Scotland in the autumn, and winds flowed down the mountains to swirl around Kilmorgan with the shrieking of a dozen banshees.

The vast house itself, built a century and a half ago, was usually alive with noise. Creaking of pipes Hart had installed to bring running water to the bedchambers. The crackle of Daniel's electrics experiments, the tinny sounds of the interior telephone system nephew Daniel had also created. ·

At the moment, all those noises, except the wind, were silenced. All except the *snick* of a window somewhere in the darkness of the house.

Ian and Beth were the only residents at Kilmorgan Castle, the vast mansion that stood north of Inverness. Hart, the Duke of Kilmorgan and master of the house, was in Edinburgh with Eleanor and his two children—they'd be here in the next day or so. His other brothers, Mac and Cameron, were at their respective country homes with their families, not due to arrive at Kilmorgan until a few days after Hart.

Ian knew the exact location of each house of his brothers, and how long it would take the families to travel to Kilmorgan to celebrate Hart's birthday next week. None of them could have arrived early, in the middle of this night, without Ian knowing about it.

Kilmorgan was quite empty for now, except for Ian's family, the skeleton staff needed to run the place, and three of the dogs.

Dogs . . . They were in the stables, guarding the prize racehorses. They weren't barking or making a fuss.

But Ian knew, without understanding how he knew, that someone who shouldn't be there was inside the house.

He slid out of bed, moving smoothly enough not to wake Beth. He stood a moment at the bedside, strong toes curling on the soft carpet, cool air brushing his bare skin. His valet, Curry, had dropped a nightshirt over Ian's head as Ian had headed to bed, but later, when Beth had joined him, the nightshirt had been quickly tossed away.

Ian moved past the shirt, a pale smudge on the carpet, to reach for the long folds of plaid Curry had laid across a chair to warm before the fire. Ian wrapped the kilt around his large frame, tucking the excess folds in around his waist. He then moved to the chest of drawers, opened the top one, and slid out a Webley pistol.

Ian never kept loaded guns in the house. Far too dangerous with children around. All shotguns were locked into cabinets in the steward's house near the stables; any personal handguns were kept unloaded, ammunition locked away in a separate place. Ian had made this a firm rule, and Hart had agreed.

Ian moved from the bedroom to his connecting dressing room, unlocked a cubbyhole within a cabinet, and pulled bullets from a box there. He lined up six in a perfect row, returned the box and locked the cabinet, and slid the bullets into their chambers with precision.

He left the dressing room through the door that led to the corridor, paused long enough to click the pistol's barrel into place, and strode swiftly and silently down the hall toward the gallery at the end.

Clouds covered the moon tonight, but a gaslight near the staircase illuminated a long stretch of corridor lined with windows. This was the front of the house, overlooking the drive that led to Kilmorgan. From the outside, the row of floor-to-ceiling windows was part of the grand façade created by Malcolm Mackenzie, the ancestor who'd first turned Kilmorgan from a cold castle into a home.

Ian saw no one in the upper hall, no furtive movement in the shadows, nothing out of place. He crept toward the staircase, his bare feet making no noise on the carpet.

Lights on the landings were kept burning all night, so that members of the household who wandered about wouldn't fall headlong down the stairs. Tonight, no one but Ian was in sight as he quickly descended.

Not until he turned along the ground-floor gallery that ran toward Hart's wing of the house did Ian find anything wrong.

A flurry of movement at the far end of the gallery caught his eye. Ian took in what he saw, assessed it all quickly, then pushed the conclusions to the back of his mind as he sprinted toward the half-dozen men in dark clothes trying to exit through the garden door.

Ian could move swiftly and in silence, and he was upon them before they realized. He heard muffled curses in several languages, saw the bulk of bodies and what they carried. Several of the men made it out before Ian wordlessly landed amongst them.

The man Ian caught by the back of the neck expertly broke from him, swung around, and jammed a short cudgel toward Ian's stomach. Ian, who'd learned about dirty fighting both from his brothers and on the streets of Paris, avoided the cudgel and grabbed the arm that wielded it.

He swung the man around and into another, then Ian shoved his pistol into the second man's face.

In the next moment, both men crashed themselves into Ian, fighting for the gun. One man got his hand around it, but Ian yanked hard, and the pistol fell, skittering across the floor into darkness, out of sight, out of reach.

The toughs were good, but so was Ian. They had layers of clothes hampering them, while he fought like his ancestors, in kilt and bare feet.

The first man grunted as Ian ripped the cudgel out of his hand and bashed it into his abdomen. The second man's fist came at Ian's face. Ian caught the fist with his big hand, then the second man punched Ian right in the gut.

Ian spun away, fighting pain. The man he'd cudgeled

was doubled over, and Ian spun back to the second man, battling until he got him into a headlock.

The first man, holding his stomach, went for the pistol. A growl escaped Ian's throat. He slammed the second man away from him and went after the first.

The second man dashed out the garden door, but Ian didn't care. The first man, seeming to recover at every step, ran to where the pistol had fallen and scooped it up. Instead of turning to shoot Ian, he raced along the gallery toward the main stairs.

Ian went ice-cold. Beth was up there. Ian had heard the echo of their bedroom door closing as he'd fought—the galleries and staircase let sound carry in an almost magical way. He knew Beth would have made her way to the stairs and started down, as Ian had, to see what was going on.

This thug with a pistol was running directly toward her.

Ian sprinted after him, kilt flying up over his thighs as he put on a burst of speed. Ian knew this gallery, and the thug didn't—where the bare spaces between carpets lay, where tables had been placed in the middle of the floor so a piece of sculpture could be viewed from all sides. Ian dodged these and leapt from rug to rug, gaining on the man before he reached the stairs.

Ian tackled him. He heard Beth give a sharp scream as the thug went down under Ian's body.

Ian felt the cold pistol touch his ribs. In the next second, he'd be dead.

He used that second to roll, grab, and twist. The pistol came away from the man's hand and went off, the bullet striking somewhere in the vast ceiling.

Beth's scream came again, and then her shouts for help.

Ian hauled the thug around and punched him full in the face. The thug, instead of fighting back, wrenched himself out of Ian's grip, charged for the front door, yanked it open, and ran out into the darkness. Ian heard the man's boots crunching on gravel, and then nothing.

Ian dashed out after him, but the tough was gone, swallowed by night and swirling mists. Dogs were barking now, and men carrying lanterns were hurrying from the stables.

Ian closed the door. The thugs didn't matter anymore. The safety of Beth and his children was all to him.

Beth ran down the stairs, her dressing gown floating behind her. "Ian, are you all right? *Ian?*"

Ian caught her as she came off the staircase. He lifted her from her feet and crushed her to him. The feeling of her soft body came to him, the vibrancy that was the woman he loved.

If the man had reached Beth . . . The thug was the sort to grab a woman and use her as a shield, and then shoot her when she was no longer useful.

If Ian had been a few seconds too slow . . .

He buried his face in Beth's neck, inhaling the warm scent of her. She was beautiful, and well, and in his arms. Safe.

People brushed past him—the household servants coming see what was wrong. Lights flickered and grew brighter. Men came into the house through the front and garden doors, exclaiming, making sounds of disbelief and dismay.

Ian wanted them to go away, to leave him with Beth alone in this bubble of peace he found in her arms, a place where the world couldn't touch him.

But it wasn't to be. His valet, Curry, once a London street villain, clattered down the stairs on swift feet. "*Bleedin'* 'ell!"

Beth tried to lift away. "Ian—love—I'm all right. We must see what is happening."

She was correct, of course. Ian had learned in this first decade of his marriage—ten beautiful, sparkling years— that he could not withdraw from the world. Once in a while, yes, with Beth and privacy, and maybe a lick of honey, but not always. He'd grown used to facing immediate situations without panic, without having to bolt.

Letting out a long breath, Ian raised his head. Beth gave him a little smile and tucked his kilt, which had come awry while he'd chased the thug, more securely around his waist.

The little gesture made Ian's heart beat swiftly. To hell with facing the world. Ian would take Beth back upstairs and let her unwrap him, so she could enjoy whatever she found in whichever way she wanted to enjoy it.

Beth, catching the look in his eyes, let her smile grow wider, but she shook her head. *Not yet*, she meant. *But later . . .*

Ian would be sure to take her up on the unspoken promise. Resolved, he twined his fingers though Beth's and let her lead him the rest of the way down the stairs.

The entire gallery glowed with light. The servants had turned up every lamp in the place.

Beth gasped in shock. Ian had seen and noted everything out of place as he'd run past in the dark, but he'd pushed the vision aside so it wouldn't distract him in his pursuit of the intruders. Now he faced the gallery and the truth of what he'd observed.

Most of the tables that had held sculptures were empty, and almost every painting from the garden end of the gallery was gone. These pictures had been painted by famous artists through the centuries, plus a precious handful by Ian's brother Mac. Only those that had been hung high, out of easy reach, remained. A few paintings lay piled on the floor, half-ripped from frames, the frames broken. Ruined.

Hart Mackenzie's priceless art collection had just been ravaged and stolen, the thieves fleeing with the loot into the night.

Chapter 2

"It isn't your fault, Ian," Beth said for the dozenth time.

She watched worriedly as Ian paced the drawing room. He'd donned a shirt, belted his kilt around his waist, and put on shoes, but only because Curry had chivvied him into them. The police would be there in no time, Curry had argued. He couldn't have his master seen by the bloody Peelers with his backside hanging half out of his kilt.

The children had been sleeping quietly in the nursery when Ian and Beth had gone upstairs to check on them. They left without waking them. The three would be vastly disappointed in the morning to have missed all the excitement, but Ian's relief that they hadn't been hurt or upset was profound, and Beth shared it.

Now Ian strode back and forth under the twenty-foot-high ceiling adorned with pointed corbels, and refused to sit down. His restlessness told Beth he wanted to be out chasing the criminals. The only reason he was still in the house was because he did not know where to begin looking.

Eleven years ago Ian might not have answered Beth at all. Since then, Ian had taught himself to respond to people, even if the question or declaration, in his opinion, merited no answer.

He turned his head and fixed Beth with his golden stare. "Hart isnae here."

Beth, for her part, had learned to, as she put it, *speak Ian.* What he said might not seem to answer the question, but would be one or two steps beyond it. Sometimes seven or eight steps. Ian saw no reason to fill in the gaps for people, wasn't aware he needed to.

Hart isnae here meant that Ian felt responsible for the whole house and what went on inside it in Hart's absence.

"Lack of better door locks are to blame," Beth said, annoyed with Hart for not supplying them, or guards for his priceless collection. "You are entitled to go to bed of nights."

She warmed, remembering how, earlier this night, when she'd finished writing her letters and had finally climbed into bed, Ian had come awake. His nightshirt and her nightgown had fallen to the floor, and Ian had slid over her, his mouth and hands banishing her tiredness.

Ian was a determined and passionate lover. Beth had been happy, satisfied, and sleepier than ever when he'd rolled onto his side and spooned her against him.

Ian caught her blush now, and heat warmed his eyes. He was never shy about physical love. While learning to show emotion was difficult for him, he'd never seen a reason to be embarrassed about desire.

I always want you, my Beth. Why pretend I don't?

Beth sent him a little smile and was rewarded by another flicker of Ian's eyes.

"It is Hart's fault," Ian concluded.

"Exactly." Beth rose and went to him. "If he insists on displaying costly works of art in his downstairs gallery without stationing guards everywhere, then he cannot be surprised when someone tries to steal them."

Ian listened, his gaze steadily on hers. He enjoyed look-ing into her eyes now—sometimes wouldn't look away for a long time. "Hart will blame *me*," Ian declared. "But we will tell him he is wrong."

"That we will." Beth took his hand. "Shall we go talk to the police sergeant? The poor man is terrified."

Ian closed his fingers firmly around hers. "I will send a telegram," he said as they left the room together.

"Do you mean to Hart?" she asked. "No—you mean to Inspector Fellows, to Lloyd. The sergeant will no doubt do that, love. He'll have to report it to Scotland Yard."

"But it won't be a telegram from *me*," Ian said.

Beth decided to concede this, and continued downstairs with him.

~~~

"Ye were done over proper, me lord." The sergeant was originally from Glasgow but had been assigned this post in the north. Highlanders made him nervous, Beth had seen, and the Mackenzies made him more nervous than most.

The sergeant was rocking on his heels in the middle of the ravaged gallery. The constable by his side, a local lad, had brought out a pencil and tiny notebook to take down the particulars.

"Professionals, I'd say," the sergeant went on. "In and out, never raising an alarm. You'd have lost more if ye hadn't been wakeful, sir."

The sergeant rocked again as he spoke, not comfortable with the way Ian gave him a swift glance then wouldn't look at him again while Beth described what had happened.

As she spoke to the sergeant and constable, Ian turned on his heel, walked past them, and headed out the garden door, which was a glass single French door. Beth gave the sergeant a reassuring smile and hurried after Ian.

She found her husband at the bottom of the steps outside the door. The stairs led to a path that guests used for strolling from the art gallery around the house to Kilmorgan's famous gardens.

Ian took in the trampled grass and the scuff marks on the marble steps, then walked a little way down the path and peered up at the trees that grew near the house. While Beth and the two men watched, mystified, Ian moved back up the steps and ran his hands along the garden door's frame. He opened and closed the door a few times, then bent down to examine the lock.

Ian walked into the house again, past the worried sergeant and to the front door, which he also went over. Beth followed him closely, not because she was concerned, but because whatever Ian did was certain to be interesting.

"They had a key," he announced.

Beth blinked. "A key? How could they?"

Ian shut the front door and ran his hand along the bolting mechanism. "This was unbolted when the last man ran out. He didn't have to stop and fumble with it. The thieves came in through the garden door and unlocked the front door from the inside in case they needed to leave through it."

"So they had a key to the garden door?" she asked.

Ian kept tracing the heavy iron bolt. "The lock on the garden door was nae picked. Or forced. Nor was this one." He glanced at Beth, saw her trying to comprehend, and touched the keyhole. "No scratches. No nicks where the door meets the frame."

"Who on earth would have a key to Kilmorgan Castle?"

"Me," Ian answered readily. "Mac, Cam, Hart, Daniel, you, Eleanor, the majordomo, Mrs.—"

"Yes, yes, I know." Beth put her hand on his wrist. "I mean, who outside the family or staff?"

"No one," Ian said at once.

"Precisely. Oh dear."

Ian didn't shake off her hold, but he didn't answer either.

"That means," Beth went on, "that the key must have

been stolen from one of us at some point. A copy made. The thieves must have been planning this for some time."

Ian said nothing. Whether he agreed with her, Beth didn't know. He would tell her at some point, but it might be tomorrow before he did, or next week.

The sergeant approached them. "Well, me lord, if ye don't mind me saying so, how they got in here is no' so important. They did it, and that's that. What ye need to do now is decide what they took and make a list. We can circulate it, and if the pieces turn up, we'll know they're His Grace's."

Ian's gaze went down the mostly empty walls. "Three Ramsays, a Turner, three of Mac's landscapes—not his best work—a Giorgione, a Velázquez, a Delacroix, six of the Norwich School, a portrait by Édouard Manet and studies by him and his colleagues, three landscapes by Cézanne, a Canova sculpture, two ancient Asian bronzes, five wax figurines Degas gave Mac, and a Raphael."

Ian closed his mouth. The sergeant stared, but the constable busily scribbled in his notebook. "Sayz-anne, Sez—" The lad looked up in perplexity. "How are you spelling that, me lord?"

Beth enlightened him. The constable nodded and carefully wrote it down.

"Well, be sure, me lord," the sergeant said. "If you remember any more, send word down to the station and let us know."

"There is no more," Ian said.

Beth smiled at the sergeant. "Do you need anything else here tonight? We are rather tired."

The sergeant gave her a patient look. "Aye, me lady, that'll be all. We've had a look for finger marks and footprints, and we've talked to the rest of your servants."

"Then we can say good night." Beth, playing gracious hostess, saw the two to the garden door and out. She closed the door, acknowledging the sergeant's admonition to be sure she locked it.

"Like closing the barn door after the horses are gone," Beth said, turning her key in the lock and removing it. "There's a thought. Did they bother with the horses? Cam's new colts would be worth a lot of money. Not to mention all the Kilmorgan jewels upstairs."

"They had a key," Ian said. "No one sleeps on the ground floor."

"I know." Beth deflated. "The artworks in the gallery were the easiest to take. I cannot imagine why Hart doesn't keep the house better fortified."

Ian shrugged. "He is Hart."

Beth knew what he meant. Hart had a belief that no one would be foolish enough to steal from the Duke of Kilmorgan, and in most circumstances, he would be correct. These thieves must not understand Hart's power, or they did not care about it, which was a frightening thought.

Beth sighed. "And now we have to break the news to him. And Mac—he loved those figurines. Not to mention his own paintings."

"He didn't love his paintings," Ian said as they climbed the stairs. "Mac gave them to Hart because he doesn't like them and didn't want to see them in his own house."

Knowing Mac, this was no doubt true. "Even so," Beth answered. "A Raphael, for heaven's sake."

"The Raphael," Ian said. "It's ... . wrong."

Beth could imagine art experts the world over swooning at his dismissal. But she understood what Ian meant. The Madonna and child in the painting Hart owned had been idealized, and Ian preferred art that was very realistic—he liked the Dutch and Flemish painters, and Velázquez, for instance, and he liked still lifes most of all. Still lifes were about real things, he said. While Beth found the work of Cézanne stunningly beautiful, Ian said the proportions

disturbed him. That was why Ian loved his Ming bowls—
each one was a small, exquisite, perfect form.

Cold rushed through Beth at her last thought. "Ian—
your bowls. We haven't checked that any were taken."

Ian maintained a room at Kilmorgan that housed the
bulk of his collection. Each bowl had its own shelf, and was
labeled, numbered, in order. Ian also kept a few bowls in
the house he shared with Beth ten miles north of Kilmorgan, swapping them out every so often with bowls here,
depending on what he decided he wanted to look at that
week.

Instead of rushing up the stairs in consternation, Ian
shook his head. "You and I and Curry have the key to *that*
room. No one else."

"But if the thieves stole the key to the house . . ."

Ian kept on shaking his head. "No one else."

"Still, we ought to make sure."

Ian's look told her he thought her worry unnecessary.
But he took her hand and walked with her down the wide
hall at the top of the stairs to his collection room.

Beth turned up the lights as they entered, but she saw
that Ian had been correct. Every bowl was in its place, except the three that had been taken to their house after their
last visit.

Ian drew Beth into the circle of his arm and kissed the
top of her head. "Don't worry, my Beth. You and our children weren't hurt. The paintings are just paint."

Another shudder had just gone through the art world,
but Beth understood. For Ian, the people in his life—his
wife and children, his brothers and their families—were far
more important than artwork and paintings, things that
only represented the real. And for Ian, the real would always triumph over the imaginary.

"I love you," Beth said, her heart warming.

Ian frowned, puzzled by her response. Then his face lost

its drawn, concentrated look, and his eyes softened. "I love *you*, my Beth. Love you, love you, love you."

He liked saying it.

~~~~~

The nursery was in an uproar in the morning. Ian ran to it when he heard the shouting, and found his son Jamie standing in his nightshirt in the middle of the room, demanding to know why he'd not been woken when the thieves had broken in.

Jamie was nearly eleven years old now, growing taller and sturdier each year. He had the dark red hair of the Mackenzies, his mother's blue eyes, and an arrogant manner worthy of his uncle Hart.

Jamie considered himself the leader of the band of younger cousins, being the oldest of the children. The only cousin he deferred to was Cam's son, Daniel, but that was because Daniel was a grown-up, fifteen years or so older than Jamie.

"Dad!" Jamie yelled as Ian came in. He insisted on calling Ian *Dad*, when the girls liked to refer to him as *Papa*. "Why didn't you fetch me? We'd have caught 'em!"

Ian didn't bother to wonder how Jamie knew about the night's adventure. Curry and the rest of the staff would have readily told the three children the tale.

"No," Ian said. "They would have hurt you."

"I'd have laid into 'em," Jamie insisted. "Daniel and Bellamy have been teaching me how to fight." Bellamy was Mac's valet, a former prizefighting pugilist.

"No," Ian repeated. He found he had to say this word many times to Jamie before its meaning penetrated. "They were strong and violent. One almost shot me. I would have died if he had."

The nanny, a very proper woman, gave Ian a severe look. "Sir, you'll upset the young ladies."

Megan and Belle, both in dressing gowns at the nursery table, were listening avidly.

"I'm not upset," Belle said. "Papa is only trying to explain to Jamie that running off half-cocked after a violent criminal is dangerous."

Jamie gave his sister, a year younger than he was, a deprecating look. "'Tis my duty to look after ye."

"No," Ian said again. "He would have killed you too, lad. These were hard men. They did not care."

Megan, the youngest at seven years old, left her chair and came to Ian. She laid her hand on his. "Then we are glad you are well, Papa. You are well, are you not?"

At her touch, Ian forgot all about the missing paintings, the man turning the gun on him, his terrible fear when the thug had run for the stairs.

He was now with the most precious things in his life, which were far more important than Hart's artwork or the Ming bowls. Ian had run right past the Ming room to the nursery last night to make certain the children were safe. He hadn't thought about the bloody bowls at all until Beth had mentioned them.

Ian lifted Megan into his arms, kissed her hair, and lost himself in the sweetness he'd never realized fatherhood would bring.

~

By the end of the day, a flurry of telegrams had gone back and forth through the train station at Kilmorgan—to Scotland Yard, Hart, the rest of Ian's brothers. Ian went to the train station himself to send and pick up the replies, too impatient to wait for servants to do it for him.

He let Jamie accompany him on the errand, and they walked back together, Jamie carrying all the telegrams after his father had read them. Ian was opening the last two.

In Edinburgh. Arrive tonight. Fellows.

Ian folded the missive and handed it to Jamie. The next

one was addressed to *Lady Ian Mackenzie* and was an anomaly among the correspondence today.

Arrive 8 A.M. on the 7th. John Ackerley.

Ian folded the telegram but tucked it into his own pocket instead of giving it to Jamie.

Fellows was Chief Inspector Fellows of Scotland Yard and Ian's half brother.

John Ackerley was the brother of Beth's deceased husband, and was a missionary who'd been absent from England for more than a dozen years. He'd arrive at Kilmorgan tomorrow morning.

Ian walked in silence while Jamie made observations on everything they passed with his usual verve. Ian wasn't certain what he felt about John Ackerley's arrival, but the telegram burned inside his coat, very hot indeed.

Chapter 3

Chief Inspector Lloyd Fellows never arrived at Kilmorgan Castle without mixed feelings.

On the one hand, Fellows no longer entered the house in trepidation tinged with rage. He'd made his peace with the dead father who'd refused to acknowledge him, and reconciled with his half siblings.

He was invited to—no, expected to—attend all major celebrations at the ducal seat, including this one to acknowledge Hart's upcoming birthday. Fellows could run into and out of the house anytime he wanted, Hart had told him. Make himself at home. Thus far, Hart had kept his word.

On the other hand, Hart and his brothers had been raised to luxury and splendor, even if their father had been a brutal bully. While they'd lived in terror of the man, they'd had every physical comfort provided, been given the best education, and had piles of cash settled on them.

Fellows had grown up in the gutter, raised by a barmaid mother who loved him, and loved him still. Fellows and his mother had worked fingers to the bone for every scrap of food they'd ever eaten. Even now, the lofty title of chief inspector carried only a modest salary that let him live in the middle-class area of Pimlico with his wife, daughter, and two sons.

The question of where his boys would go to school was starting to become an argument. They were four and six, respectively. When William, the oldest, turned eight, he would be expected to leave his tutors and go to a school.

Hart had already promised a place for him at Harrow, to be educated alongside the other Mackenzie lads. Fees paid, of course. Hart was anxious to close the chasm their mutual father had created, to give Fellows everything he'd have been entitled to had he been legitimate.

Fellows, proud man that he was, wanted to send his children to a school he could afford, to be raised with young men of their own class. Fellows would never inherit what Hart or his brothers would, and he did not want to imply that his sons stood a chance to either. The laws of England would never let them.

Louisa, his wife, was the daughter of an earl. Fellows had assumed Louisa would take Hart's side—aristocrats together—but Louisa saw the sense of Fellows's argument and was standing with him.

There it lay. Fellows knew Hart would begin the debate again this visit, but Fellows would stand firm.

Then had come the telegram from Ian that Kilmorgan had been robbed. Hard on its heels had come the message from the sergeant in Kilmorgan's village to Scotland Yard about the robbery. Fellows had demanded to be given the case and had taken the first train north.

Louisa, who insisted she needed far more time than that to pack, would travel there with her sister and family in a few days, as planned. She'd kissed Fellows and sent him off.

It was very late when the coach that had been sent to fetch Fellows let him out at the castle. He stepped down from the carriage without waiting to be helped and strode for the front door.

It was called Kilmorgan Castle, but it was a huge house rather than a crenellated fortress, built in the Palladian style in the middle of the eighteenth century. The original castle from the 1300s was now a ruin, a tumble of blocks on a hill that overlooked the valley. A hundred and fifty years ago, the English army had burned the castle, and later pulled it down. Many of its stones had been incorporated into the new house.

Malcolm Mackenzie, the current Mackenzies' illustrious ancestor, had designed the house, including the many wings to contain the large number of children each duke seemed to sire. The house and gardens had been the envy of aristocrats both English and Scottish, which had been the point.

The man who met Fellows at the massive front door and reached for his luggage was Ian's valet, Curry.

"It weren't me, Inspector," Curry said immediately. "I 'ad nothin' to do with it. I was asleep in me room, dreaming peaceful dreams."

Fellows swept off his short-crowned hat. "I haven't started rounding up suspects yet, Curry."

"I know. It's 'abit of mine, the minute I see a copper, to say it weren't me, don't matter what's 'appened. In this case, it's a pile of artwork been nicked. I wouldn't know 'ow to sell that on, would I? Even if I would steal from 'is nibs, which I wouldn't."

Curry had been an excellent thief in his time, Fellows had heard. All in the past, Curry would hasten to say. He'd reformed. It was true that since he'd begun working for Ian Mackenzie, Curry had kept to the straight and narrow.

"You wouldn't be such a fool as to rob Hart," Fellows said. "Don't worry. You're safe from me."

Curry blew out his breath. "Well, that's a relief. I'll take these up to your usual. The scene of the crime is down there."

Curry pointed down the long gallery that was well lit even this late, and scurried up the stairs with Fellows's one bag. A footman took Fellows's hat and coat, and left him to wander down the gallery, taking in the damage.

"Good Lord," Fellows said under his breath.

The villains had done a thorough job. They'd taken what they could carry out quickly, abandoning the rest when Ian had set upon them. Some famous paintings had hung in here. It was a bloody shame.

Fellows examined the door at the end and saw that it was as Ian had said in his telegrams—the lock had not been picked nor forced.

A stolen or copied key, Ian had speculated. Or an inside man, Fellows added silently. Someone promised a great reward if he left the door open.

A neutral investigator would not discard the idea that Hart himself had organized the crime. Many an art collector robbed himself for the insurance money in times of need. Sometimes the paintings had already been quietly sold over the years and replaced with copies. A robbery got rid of the damning fakes, and the unlucky insurers paid out.

Hart didn't need the money and had no reason for this fraud, but a good detective would check Hart's financials and then decide. If Fellows were to conduct the investigation correctly, he'd need to do such things. All must be aboveboard. He knew full well the state of Hart's finances, however, because Hart hid nothing from him these days. Even if there were a question, Ian would know the answer. Ian carried the all the figures from the entire estate's accounting ledgers in his head.

Fellows removed a small camera from his coat. Hart's wife, Eleanor, had given it to him, for use in Fellows's detective work. Eleanor loved photography and was quite good at it, and she enjoyed trying out every brand-new photographic gadget invented.

This camera was quite small, but had a special attachment that would hold several plates at once. The plates then could be developed in a darkroom, which of course Eleanor had set up here.

The photographs turned out sharper when the photographer used bright, electric lights, which the gallery did not have, but Fellows turned up the gaslights to full illumination and clicked away with the camera. He took pictures of every blank spot, of the damaged frames and canvases, the door, the lock, the dirty boot prints on the carpet. Hopefully some of the footprints were the villains' and not simply the local constable's.

As Fellows lifted the camera from the last shot, he turned to find Ian standing a foot away.

Fellows had learned not to jump at Ian's sudden appearances. His half brother could move quietly for a man so large.

"Ian," Fellows said, tucking the camera back into its case. "Thank you for the telegrams. Your assessment was helpful."

Ian neither acknowledged this nor modestly waved it away. "Can you catch them?"

Fellows gazed up at the blank walls. "I'm going to have a bloody good try."

Ian gave him a nod, as though he approved. "I'll show you what I found," he said, and walked away, assuming Fellows would follow.

Fellows, having learned that Ian was a more thorough investigator than all his sergeants and inspectors put together, did.

~~~~

The next morning, Beth wanted to go to the station herself to retrieve her first husband's brother, but there had been too much to do at the house. She hadn't wanted to neglect Lloyd Fellows, who'd so quickly come to help, so she'd asked the majordomo to send the carriage.

The man who stepped from the coach upon its return so resembled Beth's late husband, the vicar Thomas Ackerley, that she paused on the stairs for a heartbeat of astonishment.

Once the man raised his head, however, after the footman took his hat and his battered satchel, the exact likeness faded. John was slightly leaner than Thomas, more tanned, a bit taller, and had more of a toughness about him. Beth's first husband had been quite strong in mind—his parish had been in a rougher part of Bethnal Green—but he'd always been soft of face and body.

Beth had met John Ackerley exactly twice. The first time had been when she'd married Thomas. John had been the admiring younger brother, happy that Thomas had found a wife. The two brothers had been kindness itself, something the very young Beth had been starved for.

After Thomas's death, John had traveled to London from his missionary station in Africa to help erect a stone to his brother and make sure Beth was all right. By that time, Beth had been established as a companion to the wealthy woman who was to eventually leave Beth her fortune. John had been married, eager to return to his mission, and satisfied that Beth would be well.

John had written a few years ago of his wife's death from a heart ailment, and then again recently when he'd decided to retire and return to England.

I have moved about the world a good deal as you know, he'd written, *and learned many things, some of which might interest you. I would like to visit your husband and your good self, if I may, not to impose my company, but to ensure myself that you are well, and to see if I can do anything to assist you and his lordship.*

Beth had read the letter out to Ian. She'd thought Ian would not like the idea, but to her surprise, Ian had shrugged and said of course John should come. He was of Beth's family, and there was no reason not to see him.

Beth had penned a reply, John had said he'd be in England by August, and Beth had invited him to the family gathering in September.

Now, here he was.

"John," Beth said as she stepped off the stairs. She caught the hand he held out to her.

John smiled, making him look more like Thomas again. "Dear little Beth. My, how good life has been to you. I suppose I must call you Lady Ian now."

"Not at all, John. You're family."

"I confess I can think of you only as Thomas's gentle Beth. I am happy to find you in better circumstances, my dear. And I am looking forward to meeting the brilliant Lord Ian Mackenzie."

"Who is about somewhere," Beth said, waving her hand. "I sometimes lose him in this vast place. Our own house up the road is smaller and more cozy."

"Ah, but this is a fine house." John looked around in admiration. A huge pedestal table stood in the center of the staircase hall, the stairs rising around it. Eleanor always ensured that a giant vase of fresh flowers was kept on this table, no matter what the season.

The walls rose with the staircase, high into the house. Paintings lined the way, beautiful ones by Mac and other artists, many of them family portraits. Beth was glad Ian had stopped the thieves before they'd reached the stairs.

Noise erupted at the front door, and Ian Mackenzie himself strode in. He was surrounded by men who worked for him at the distillery, and they were all, including Ian, arguing loudly about something.

When Ian lost his inhibitions, he could shout at the top of his Scots' voice as well as any of his brothers. Right now he was in full volume, turning to face the man who managed the Mackenzie distillery.

"Do it *now*, man! Before ye lose another forty barrels of the bloody stuff. Shite and fucking hell."

Ian's face was red, golden eyes glittering with rage. Two dogs circled at his feet, peering anxiously up at their master.

Beth hurried to him. "Ian, whatever is the matter?"

Ian could curse like a sailor, especially when his shyness

deserted him and fury took over. He was seldom enraged anymore, growing angry only at threats to his children or Beth, or the Mackenzie family in general, but it occasionally still happened.

"Ian?" Beth tried again. "We have a guest."

Ian didn't see John behind Beth—or if he did, the man was of no consequence to Ian at the moment.

"Forty barrels, ruined from rot that nobody bothered t' notice," he snapped. "*I* didn't notice. How the bloody hell could I not have? I notice everything." Ian's face had gone scarlet, his jaw tight. He brought up his hands and started scrubbing them through his hair. "Everything," he repeated. *"Everything."*

Oh dear. Ian couldn't go into what he called a *muddle* now—not in front of John Ackerley.

In a muddle, Ian would fixate, either repeating a phrase or doing a task over and over again, as though he were an automaton stuck on one setting. He didn't go into muddles much anymore, having learned to stop and breathe before emotions overwhelmed him.

Beth reached up and took his hands, closing her fingers over his. She looked into his intense golden eyes. "Ian. *Think.*"

The touch broke Ian from wherever he'd been about to go. He clamped down on Beth's hands, took a long breath, and fixed his gaze on hers. For a moment, he was aware of only Beth, his rock in the swirling storms of his life.

After a few tense moments, Ian leaned down to nuzzle Beth's cheek, and she felt his lips.

When he straightened up, his face had returned to a normal color, though the anger in his eyes still sparked as he looked down at her.

"If I did not notice the barrels gone bad," he said in a firm voice, "then they must not have been bad. I would have remembered."

"Aye," his steward said, sounding relieved the shouting was over. "Ye do have a way of seeing all things, me lord."

Ian didn't look away from Beth, directing his words to her and her alone. "Someone did it deliberately. Forty barrels of Mackenzie malt, down the spout."

"Deliberately?" Beth asked, perplexed. "How could someone do it deliberately?"

The steward answered. "Or there are many ways, me lady. Insects, certain oils or acids—one man can ruin another's trade if they set about it right."

"But who would?" Beth knew that Scotsmen who dealt in whisky could be competitive, but she couldn't imagine the boisterous men she'd met from other distilleries destroying another's yield on purpose. They wanted to best one another, but fairly.

Ian shook his head, kept shaking it. "I don't know."

"Do you think the thieves did this?" Beth asked. "Or their colleagues? They steal the paintings while another group of them spoils the whisky?"

Ian stopped. She saw the wheels inside his brain begin to move, the anger fade as fascination with the problem took over.

He lifted Beth's hands to his lips and kissed them, but absently. Ian was already at work in his mind, on the search for the culprit. "Love, I need to—"

Ian broke off as his gaze came to rest on John, who was standing quietly at the foot of the staircase. Ian stared at him, becoming more and more focused as he noted every detail about the man.

"Ian, this is John Ackerley," Beth said quickly. "My brother-in-law. John, Ian Mackenzie."

"Delighted to meet you." John stepped forward and held out his hand. "I've heard so much about you, my lord. I am very grateful to you for allowing me into your house."

Chapter 4

Ian didn't like him.

He didn't know why he instinctively did not like John Ackerley, but as the man held out his hand, the last thing Ian wanted to do was shake it.

When Ian had told Mac about the letter John had sent Beth about his impending visit, Mac had given him a wise look.

"The trouble with taking a beautiful woman to wife," Mac had said, rubbing one of his brushes with a rag. They'd been in Mac's studio, in London, high up in his house, where Ian had gone for refuge. "Is that we constantly believe all other men in the world want to take our ladies away from us. We're usually right, but we can't let on that it worries us."

As always, Ian thought what Mac said was daft, except the part about all men wanting their beautiful wives. All men should want Beth.

Ian didn't truly believe Beth would run after John Ackerley. The man was a missionary, had been in love with his wife, and by his photograph, was a somewhat rotund gentleman with graying hair and beard. On the other hand, Ackerley wasn't mad. Not obviously anyway.

"What you do," Mac had advised, "is treat Beth like a queen. Let her know she is the center of your world. But don't hover too closely—this can make a woman's awe of you turn to amusement and even irritation. Give her enough attention that you charm her but not so much she wants to see the back of you. 'Tis a very fine line to walk."

"Beth already knows she's the center of my world," Ian pointed out.

"Aye, but you need to *show* her that once in a while. Show her you can give her what no other man can."

Ian didn't understand the relationship between Mac and Isabella—it was turbulent, the two thinking nothing of loud arguments that rattled the house. The next moment, they'd be madly loving again. Mac threw wild parties with wild people, which Isabella took with aplomb, and then the next day, they'd shut the door to the world, retreating into quiet coziness with their children.

Ian hadn't sought his brother for guidance so much as to calm his troubled mind. Mac's studio, filled with the scent of paint and oil of turpentine could relax him. Even watching Mac paint, his brother clad in his usual kilt with red kerchief on his head, was soothing. As much as Ian didn't understand the fuss about art, he enjoyed watching Mac's brush sliding paint smoothly across the canvas, creating objects in only a few strokes, bringing a whole world to life from nothing.

"Go home and take Beth to bed," Mac said. "That will make you feel better, if nothing else."

At last, a bit of advice Ian could agree with. He'd put action to word.

As Ian stared now at John Ackerley's outstretched hand, he recalled every last nuance of the conversation with Mac and every detail of its aftermath with Beth.

Beth hovered next to him, her tension palpable. She was

afraid Ian would do something odd, such as walk away without speaking or return to his worry about the distillery and ignore John utterly.

Ian wanted to walk away. As a younger man, he'd often turned and run from a crowd, especially when all eyes were upon him. He hadn't known what to do with that unnerving focus on him, how to respond. Removing himself from the situation had been the best solution.

Ian had learned to stand his ground, had learned how to calm himself. He could now at least *pretend* to react in the correct way.

Ian reached out, clasped Ackerley's hand, and gave it one brief, hard shake. The other man's eyes widened at Ian's powerful grip, and he flexed his fingers when they withdrew.

"Is there somewhere we can speak together, my lord?" John asked as he rubbed his hand. "I have been so long away from home that I am eager to catch up with my old friends."

Ian and John were not old friends—Ian had just met the man—but he admitted a strong curiosity about this gentleman who'd known Beth long ago. Ian nodded and gestured up the stairs. "Our sitting room."

"I'm sure you'd rather refresh yourself and rest after your journey," Beth said quickly. "I've had a room prepared for you in the guest wing, John. An entire set of rooms, actually, all to yourself. Shall I show you to them?"

Both Ian and John turned to stare at her. Beth was being a polite hostess, ready to offer comfort to the weary traveler. However, John made no sign he wanted to rest and change his clothes. He wanted to talk to Ian. Ian wanted to talk to him, so he made the gesture up the stairs again.

Beth held up her hands. "Very well. I will withdraw. I will have your things put in your suite, John, to be there when you need them. You and my husband speak as long as you like."

She understood. Ian's heart warmed.

Without further word, Ian led Ackerley up the stairs to his wing of the house.

As they passed the Ming room, Ackerley glanced inside. "I say, do you mind if I . . . ?" He trailed off.

Ian waited to hear the rest of his sentence, but Ackerley obviously wasn't going to finish. Ackerley seemed to pause for a response—what, Ian had no idea—then when he got none, headed into the Ming room.

Ian followed with some impatience. If Ackerley had meant he wanted to see the bowls, why hadn't he simply said so?

Ian began the tour of his collection in the usual way. He pointed to a bowl from the very early Ming period, the 1360s. "The first one is here." He swept his arm to the right. "Then this way." He'd categorized the bowls by period and date, and within that, by size. Small bowls rested on upper shelves, larger on lower. Glass doors on the shelves kept out dust and clumsy fingers of ignorant visitors.

Ackerley stood in the middle of the room and turned in a circle. "Good heavens. You bought all these?"

"Bought or traded." Ian had gained the reputation of a hard but fair negotiator among collectors.

Ackerley wandered to a far cabinet, beginning completely out of sequence. "Have you been to China?"

"No." Ian's travels had taken him to France and Italy but no farther. Whenever he grew curious about the world beyond that, he read books. His children were too young yet to travel great distances, and Ian never wanted to be very far from them.

John let out a laugh. "I imagined you bartering for bowls in some dusty backstreet in Shanghai."

"No, with dealers in London."

"Ah. Of course."

"Is that how Ming bowls are sold in China?" Ian asked. Seemed a haphazard way to do it, especially with such valuable stock. No, Chinese gentlemen must have shops, like those found in London and Paris, where dealers in rare porcelain sold their wares.

"Actually, I have no idea," Ackerley said. "I never saw a Ming bowl when I traveled the East. I was in China and India after my time in Africa, as always, collecting souls for God."

Ackerley had been a missionary, taking English Bibles, morality, and hygiene to the darkest corners of the world. Ian had to wonder how the natives of these places had responded to the ignorant good nature of John Ackerley.

Ackerley was standing here alive and well, so obviously the native peoples hadn't killed him. He was proud of himself as well, Ian could see. Ian had grown up around pride—it was the one emotion he had little trouble identifying in others.

Ackerley wandered the room, gazing at bowl after bowl, entirely out of order. He asked no questions, pointed out no details, only looked.

"You have arranged them very precisely, haven't you?" Ackerley asked after a time.

Ian pointed again to the first bowl. "Starting there, with early Ming. Middle period, late middle, and late." His arm moved as he took his pointing finger around the collection. "The last one is from 1641. I have heard of a bowl from 1642 that I will look at after Hart's birthday. In London. Not in a backstreet in Shanghai."

He stopped, waiting to see whether Ackerley noticed he'd attempted a joke. Beth would have laughed, and then kissed him. Ian would have to remember to tell her about it later.

Ackerley's expression didn't change. "It is important to you, the dates?"

Why wouldn't they be? "Aye," Ian answered. Did the man think he should pile the bowls in a jumble?

"And only bowls, Beth tells me. Not vases or pots?"

"No." People asked him this all the time. Ian could not put into words why bowls—small, round, perfect—satisfied him when vases did not.

"And only Ming. Not Tang or Qing."

"No." Ian had seen bowls from other periods in the shops. While he supposed they were beautiful, there was something about the Ming pottery that sang to him. The thinness of the porcelain, perhaps. The exquisite workmanship, the muted colors, the way the flowers or dragons or vines wafted across the curve of the bowls. He'd long ago given up reasoning it out.

"Interesting," Ackerley said, rocking on his heels. "Very interesting indeed. Oh, my dear fellow, I didn't mean to keep you standing while I prattle. You mentioned a sitting room?"

The Ming room had a settee and chairs placed so one could sit and enjoy the collection. Ian made a motion toward them.

"I like this room," he said.

"Of course." Ackerley moved to a chair and politely waited for Ian to sit first. "You have done up the displays well, my lord. Your own design?"

The man seemed more interested in the cupboards than the collection. "Hart had everything built for me," Ian said. "I told him what I wanted, and he brought in workmen."

Ian decided not to describe how he'd come in every day to show the carpenters what he wanted until they got it just right. He'd sensed their frustration but hadn't been able to stay away, and good thing. The room would have been all wrong if he'd left them on their own.

"Ah, your brother, the duke," Ackerley said. "He has helped you much over the years, so I understand."

"Aye."

Ian recalled perfectly the day Hart had come to the asylum and explained that their father had died, and Ian could come home again. He remembered the heat of the afternoon, the closeness of Hart's carriage with its curtains drawn as they jolted along the roads, his bewilderment at being outside in the world again.

Ian had been unable to speak, far too many thoughts tangling in his brain to come out in words. Hart had let him be silent, which Ian had been grateful for. His oldest brother had seemed to know that what Ian needed most was peace.

Ackerley waited for Ian to continue, but Ian had nothing to add. Ackerley's statement seemed final enough.

"And Beth—she has been a good friend to you?" Ackerley went on.

Beth. Her name was like a breath of air.

"No," Ian said.

Ackerley's brows rose. "No? Oh dear. From her letters, I gathered your marriage was a happy one."

"It is," Ian said. The best part of his life had begun the day he'd first seen Beth, had looked into her blue eyes, had been warmed by her touch.

Ackerley blinked at his abrupt answer. The man was obviously a slow thinker.

"Beth is not my friend," Ian explained. "She is . . ." Ian went through all the likely phrases, but none seemed adequate. "Everything."

Ackerley looked pleased and also relieved. "I must say I am happy to find her in better circumstances. When my brother married her, she was in quite a dire place indeed. No money, no family, no friends. I am glad to see she has all of that now."

"And wee ones," Ian said. "We have three. Jamie, Belle, and Megan."

He hoped Ackerley would want to talk about the children. Ian liked to boast how Belle was proving to be so good at maths she confounded even Jamie's tutors. How Megan's sweetness was so like her mother's. Megan was more artistic, and loved music. She could play little pieces by Mozart on the piano quite well, rarely missing a note.

Ian wanted to talk about how strong Jamie was and how

fearless. Jamie loudly claimed he wanted to ride horses for a living instead of continuing school, though his mother had much to say about that. But the lad had a knack for the beasts.

"Yes, your children," Ackerley said. "Your oldest is a boy. Is he much like you?"

Naturally, he would be, since Ian was his father. "He is a Mackenzie," Ian said with a touch of pride.

"Does he collect things as well?"

Ian had to think about it. Jamie sometimes brought home things he found in the woods or boys had given him at school, but he seemed indifferent to them.

"No," Ian said.

"Hm. Interesting."

Ian wasn't sure why it should be. He glanced at the narrow ormolu clock in the corner just as it struck the hour and got swiftly to his feet, his kilt swinging. "I have to leave now."

Ackerley stood in alarm. "Leave?"

"It's time," Ian said.

"That is important to you, isn't it? To do everything at the right time?"

The man was indeed slow. Why would Ian not keep a standing appointment because an old friend of Beth's wanted to ask him odd questions?

"Aye," Ian said, and walked out of the room. Ackerley followed, saying nothing, to Ian's relief. The man liked to talk about unimportant things.

Ian met the object of his appointment at the bottom of the back stairs. Jamie held two fishing poles and a net, and had a box of tackle slung over his small shoulder.

"There ye are, Dad," Jamie said. "I thought you'd *forgotten*."

Ian flashed his son a faint smile as he took most of Jamie's burdens from him. It was a standing joke between them—Ian never forgot anything.

"Mind if I come along?" Ackerley asked. "I've done a bit of fishing in my day. Sometimes it was the only way to feed the multitudes."

Ian immediately handed Ackerley his fishing pole and reached into the nearby cabinet for another. "We only have one rule when we're fishin'," Ian said.

"Oh?" Ackerley held the pole upright, looking interested. "What is that?"

"No talking," Ian said, and led the way out the door.

Chapter 5

Ian knew someone followed them. He led the way through the bracken and brush of the woods a mile or so from Kilmorgan, angling to the stream where fish bit the readiest.

He could hear footsteps moving in time with theirs, the person keeping quiet, or trying to. Ackerley was oblivious, and so was Jamie, but Ian knew someone dogged their path.

Ian hurried a few paces to catch up to his son. "Jamie, take Mr. Ackerley to the stream. I'll follow."

Jamie came alert, but he assumed the responsibility without question. "This way, sir. Watch that bit of ground there—it can be boggy."

Ian sidestepped into the woods, making his way noiselessly back the way they'd come. His heart beat swiftly. If one of the robbers or whoever had ruined his barrels, or an entirely new villain came down the path, Ian would have him. He'd truss the man up and drag him to Fellows, or maybe simply break his neck.

The footsteps came closer, measured, nearly silent. Ian hurtled out of his hiding place and grabbed the shadow as it passed.

A shrill scream echoed in his ears. He lifted the squirming thing he'd caught and found himself face-to-face with his daughter Megan.

As Ian stared at her, Megan's fright turned to indignation. "Papa, you scared me!"

Ian didn't know what to do. He'd just terrified his daughter, a being who was the most precious thing in his life. He didn't have the words to apologize, explain, tell her that she'd frightened *him* and he'd made a mistake.

Ian only knew that she was shaking, it was his fault, and he didn't know how to fix it.

He responded the only way he knew how when words spun in his head without any clear pattern. He hugged her.

Megan hugged Ian back then planted a kiss on his cheek. "I'm sorry, Papa. I was afraid if I called out, you'd send me home."

Why? Ian wondered. Was that what other fathers did? "I won't send ye home, lass."

Megan smiled. "Good. Then I want to go fishing with you."

So simple an explanation. Ian let out his breath. He set Megan down and took her hand to lead her along the path to the stream. Megan skipped beside him, her fright forgotten.

Even as they went, however, Ian knew that his first instinct had been correct. Megan hadn't been the only one following. Someone lurked out there, watching. Ian kept Megan close to his side, putting his bulk between her and the world.

Ackerley, when they reached him and Jamie, broke into a wide smile.

"And who is this?" he asked, leaning down to study Megan.

"Megan Mackenzie," Ian said. "My daughter."

Ackerley stuck out his hand. He liked shaking hands. "How do you do, young miss?"

Megan took his hand properly. "Very well, thank ye, sir. And you?"

"I am very well too," Ackerley said. "I am pleased to meet you."

"Pleased to meet *you*, sir," Megan answered in her usual sunny way. Megan loved everyone in the world evenhandedly.

"Megan wants to fish," Ian announced. He took Jamie's extra pole, the smallest one they'd brought, and showed Megan how to hold it.

"Girls can't fish," Jamie said abruptly.

Jamie had been in a state lately in which he declared that girls couldn't do a good number of things—ride, hunt, shoot, fish, walk across the glen, play cards, understand scientific principles.

Ian had no idea where Jamie came up with these views. Ladies, Ian had seen, could do anything they put their hand to. Violet, Daniel's wife, used a spanner to fix an automobile engine as readily as Daniel; Eleanor was a skilled photographer; and on the last visit to Kilmorgan, the wives of the family had decided they wanted to learn to shoot with pistols. Cam, Mac, and Hart had thought this a dangerous proposition, but Ian had set up a target and taught them.

Isabella had been the best, hitting her target dead center each time. Beth had not been bad, though she tended to pull to the right. Ainsley had mostly hit the target and had been eager to practice. Eleanor had been better than Ainsley and Beth, but she confessed her father's old gamekeeper had taught her to shoot long ago.

Mac had pretended to be alarmed that Isabella was such a dead shot, but Ian could see that he was secretly proud of his wife.

Ian ignored Jamie's declaration, and so did Megan. Ian showed his daughter how the line worked, how to turn the reel to play the line in and out, and how to bait the hook.

Ian thought Megan might be squeamish about putting on the worm—Beth had been at first—but Megan very seriously fished one from the bait box and put it on the hook.

Tenderhearted Megan felt very sorry for the worm,

though. Tears filled her eyes. Ian would teach her fly-fishing, he decided. There was not much to feel sorry for in a large wad of thread.

Ackerley was explaining to Jamie that plenty of women he'd known, including his late wife, fished, and were very good at it. Indeed, in the missions, they'd often relied on the women to help bring in fish for supper. Many native women were extremely skilled at it.

Jamie looked doubtful, but he subsided.

It was a peaceful afternoon, but still Ian could not shake the idea that there was a watcher in the woods. He saw nothing, though, no matter how carefully he searched.

At least Ackerley ceased speaking. After regaling Jamie with stories of women he'd known who'd brought home satisfying catches, Ackerley closed his mouth, and they fished in silence.

The woods were quiet, the stream trickling as it flowed past. This stream was a torrent farther up the hill, but here it widened into a pool, calm and rippling. Summer afternoons on its banks were long and balmy.

Something pinged against a tree by Ian's head. The others didn't turn around, not hearing, but Ian had heard.

He looked down at the ground to see a pebble that hadn't been there before. Not that Ian had counted every single one of them, but he'd been aware of the patterns at his feet, and now that pattern had changed.

The others were out of his line of sight at the moment, clusters of brush at the edge of the stream hiding them from deeper woods. Only Ian had been in the relative open.

Ian leaned down and picked up the pebble. He examined it, then put it into his pocket.

Megan squealed. Ian was out of hiding and at her side in an instant, but she wasn't hurt. She was hanging on to her pole, watching the water in delight. She had a bite.

Ian planted his own pole, leaned down to his daughter, and helped her reel in the fish. It wasn't a very big one—Ian would have released it if he'd caught it, but it was Megan's first.

Ian snatched up a net and brought it in, while Megan bounced up and down in excitement. Ackerley said, "Oh, good show," and even Jamie unbent to be glad for her.

"I'm sorry, Mr. Fish," Megan said as it flopped around in the net, gasping in the air. "Maybe we should put it back."

Jamie rolled his eyes. "Ye'd starve to death, ye would, if ye had to rely on fishing. *Girls*."

"Now, young man; it shows she has a kind heart," Ackerley said. "It's your fish, Miss Mackenzie. You decide what to do with it."

Megan watched the fish desperately try to leap from the net, and her eyes filled with tears. "Let him go," she said. "Maybe he has a wife and wee ones at home."

Ian leaned down, lowered the net into the water, and let the fish swim away. Megan, in relief, waved it good-bye.

Jamie rolled his eyes again. Megan sat down, ready to bait her hook and catch another, but Ian was uneasy.

"We'll come again tomorrow," he said. "Time to go now."

Jamie protested, offered to stay with Mr. Ackerley and catch a ton of fish for dinner, but Ian wouldn't change his mind. Jamie gave in, resigned. He'd learned long ago that when his father decided they would do a thing, God and all his angels couldn't talk him out of it.

Ian looked carefully around as they moved back up the path to the house. He heard nothing, saw nothing, and the prickle between his shoulder blades had vanished. The watcher was gone.

They entered the house through the back passages, cleaning up in the scullery before proceeding into the main house. Beth met them in the staircase hall, with a hug for Megan, a brief kiss on the cheek for Ian and for Jamie. As Jamie and Megan began excitedly telling Beth their fishing story, with Ackerley supplying any missing detail, Ian sought Inspector Fellows.

He found his half brother outside the garden door to the gallery, moodily studying the trees that shaded this part of the grounds. Ian took the pebble from his pocket and held it out to Fellows.

"That came at me in the woods," he said. "From the direction of the hill."

Fellows opened his palm. Ian dropped to his suntanned skin the squashed form of a soft lead bullet.

⁓

Ian had pushed aside his worries about the thieves and whisky while he fished with his children. His time with Jamie, Belle, and Megan was sacrosanct.

Once Jamie and Megan were back in the nursery, however, Ian's mind filled again with the destruction of his barrels of whisky.

He headed downstairs, absently shrugging on the coat Curry handed him against the growing chill. The door in the back of the house led to the path that headed for the distillery. As Ian stepped out to it, he heard someone jogging behind him, then Ackerley fell in beside him, rather breathlessly.

"Are you going to the distillery?"

Ian gave a nod in answer, and he had to force himself to do that. He needed to puzzle out this problem, and distractions were not what he wanted. Ackerley was definitely a distraction.

"Mind if I follow?" Ackerley asked. "I'm fascinated. And we might be able to work out whether the thieves also did this."

Ian didn't answer. He didn't want Ackerley with him, but there was no way to be rid of the man short of locking him into his bedchamber. He knew Beth would not be happy with that solution, so Ian only nodded in silence.

Ackerley struggled to keep up with Ian's long strides as they went down a slope and into the valley between steep hills where the distillery lay.

The courtyard was filled with drays and horses, barrels being loaded to be taken to the bottlers or as is to buyers, which included hotels and restaurants in the cities. Mackenzie malt was much in demand.

Ackerley gazed at the distillery in amazement. "It's a house," he said. "Built right into the side of the hill."

The distillery was older than the house at Kilmorgan, built in the early eighteenth century by the grandfather of Malcolm Mackenzie. The rounded stones of the house rose several stories, and its glass windows and tall chimneys blended with the rocky hills around it, making the place difficult to see until one faced it. Planned that way, Ian knew, to hide it from the excise men back before the Mackenzie family had paid enough to make the distilling and selling of their whisky a legal venture.

Ian, who noticed every detail of the distillery every day only said, "Aye," and led the way inside.

Ackerley wanted to see it all. Ian recruited one of the overseers, a dour man, to take Ackerley around, while Ian and the steward went over the problem of the ruined barrels.

"Do we have enough?" Ian asked him. The exact number of orders and who they were for ran through his head.

The steward shrugged. "Can't say for certain. You'll weather the setback, sir, but it's nae going t' be easy. We have t' decide who's getting their whisky and who won't be. Or what orders will have t' be cut. There's younger batches that just went into the barrels, but they can't be rushed."

"No," Ian rumbled in annoyance.

From what the steward had shown him, the thieves had spoiled just enough to make the Mackenzies look bad when they had to announce to the world that a good portion of their batch was ruined, but not enough to put them out of business. What kind of thief did that?

"Aye, well," Ian said. "Fill the orders as best ye can. The price on the special reserve will have to rise."

"Some won't like that," the steward said darkly.

"But there are those who'll pay no matter what," Ian said. "We'll reward them with gifts or an extra reserve barrel for loyalty, and those who walk away will lose." That was what Hart would do, turn customer disappointment into an advantage.

Ackerley entered the distillery room and was near enough to hear Ian's last statement. "Very crafty, my lord. So this is the still?"

He gazed in admiration at the gleaming copper tubes and pipes that ran every which way, the huge vats that held the fermented brew that would be distilled down to its purer form.

"The newest one," Ian answered.

The steward, well trained, took up the speech. "The original still was blown up by the English army in the winter of 1745. Reconstructed in 1748 by Malcolm Mackenzie, who survived the Battle of Culloden and became the Duke of Kilmorgan once the charge of treason on him was lifted. Parts of the first still remain in this one—pieces have been replaced and the whole thing added on to in the last hundred and fifty years. Except for the few years following the Uprising, this still has been producing the best Scots whisky since the late 1600s."

Ian, who'd heard the story too many times to count, watched Ackerley's reaction instead. He'd expected a missionary to be sternly disapproving of anything to do with spirits, but Ackerley looked over the still and the room around it, a huge vault of a chamber that ran straight back into the hillside, with great interest.

Ian, though he did not talk nearly as much as his brothers, had as wide a mischievous streak as any of them. He might be mad, but that didn't make him weak, or even worse, *nice*.

Ian fixed Ackerley with a sharp stare, forcing himself to look into the man's rather ingenuous brown eyes.

"Come with me," Ian said. "And try some."

Chapter 6

Ackerley looked doubtful as Ian poured another measure of whisky into two glasses. They sat in a little parlor off the barrel room, where clients and privileged tourists were allowed to meet with the steward or a Mackenzie—whichever brother happened to be home—and sample the wares.

Ackerley had already downed one glass of the special reserve and declared it excellent. He seemed content to prudently stop after one glassful, so Ian brought out the *special* special reserve.

"The queen drinks this," Ian said, as he poured it, the liquid making a musical sound.

Ackerley lifted his glass, studying how the amber liquid caught the light, the facets of the heavy crystal throwing warm spangles to the table. "The queen herself, eh?"

Ian shrugged. "Hart says she mostly serves it to guests."

"Ones she wishes to impress," Ackerley said. "Well, I must sip what Her Majesty does, mustn't I?"

Ian watched closely as Ackerley let a droplet flow over his tongue. He sat quietly for a moment, then his face changed. "Good heavens, my lord. That is ambrosia. Pure ambrosia."

Ian topped up Ackerley's glass and lifted his own. He took a sip, letting the smooth liquid tingle over his tongue and down his throat.

Ackerley took another mouthful, closing his eyes to savor it. Ian's respect for him rose a notch. Ackerley didn't swig the stuff, or claim to not understand what the fuss was about. He seemed to share Ian's appreciation for a well-made whisky.

Ian waited patiently until Ackerley finished his glass, then he poured more.

Ackerley shook his head. "Oh no, I should not. I'm not used to spirits."

"Ye are staying at the house, going nowhere," Ian said. "Do ye have to face any of your flock later today?"

"My flock? No, of course not. I've retired. My last flock is still in India, ably tended by my replacement."

"Verra well, then." Ian filled his own glass and lifted the decanter, offering.

Ackerley hesitated, then flushed. "Oh, why not? Just another taste."

The whisky lessened Ian's shyness a bit. Being slightly drunk didn't always help him, especially when he was with a crowd, but sometimes, he'd feel less inhibited. Not always a good thing, Beth warned him.

However, Ian wanted to know all about John Ackerley. And the best way to find out was to loosen the man's tongue and encourage him to reveal things about himself.

"Never thought a missionary would approve of whisky," Ian said. "The Scots' ones are teetotalers. They drive Hart spare."

Ackerley looked amused. "Those of us in the C of E are not quite so uncompromising. Excessive drink is a terrible thing, of course. A taste now and again of a fine wine, or indeed, whisky such as this, is far different from living in a glass of gin. Even our Lord Jesus Christ drank wine. Not that he had much choice in those days—I imagine it was much better for him than the water. Though they had ale as well. An ancient drink, is ale."

Ian did not want to talk about the history of ale or wine in Roman times.

"Beth is happy to see you," he prompted.

"Yes, dearest Beth. As I said, I am pleased to find that her circumstances have much improved. Poor little thing." Ackerley took another sip. "You have done well by her."

"Aye." Ian waited, hoping the man would say something like, *Now that I've seen she is all right, I can be on my way.*

Ackerley drained his glass and studied its emptiness regretfully. "I must confess something to you, Lord Ian. My motives for traveling all this way weren't simply to call on an old friend—my brother's widow, that is."

"No?" Ian snatched up the decanter and refilled Ackerley's glass. "What then?"

Ackerley cleared his throat. He took a fortifying sip, his face reddening with it. "I came here on purpose to see *you,* my lord. To ascertain Beth's well-being also, of course, but I've known for some time she was perfectly happy. She's very polite, but I could tell by her letters that she is quite fond of you and content in her marriage. A man of the cloth develops a knack for reading people, you know."

Ian fixed on the man's first sentence. "To see me?"

"Indeed." Ackerley rested his hands on the table as though resisting the temptation to take another sip. "I've traveled the world. Once I made my decision to retire and left the mission, I did not come straight home. I took my leisure to visit places I'd longed to, staying with friends and other clergy of my acquaintance as I moved across the Continent. A missionary does not retire with much funds in his pocket, you understand."

Ian curbed his impatience. Was Ackerley trying to touch Ian for money? Ian would happily give him all he wanted, if he would go away.

"I spent some time in Vienna," Ackerley went on. "A

fascinating place, and a beautiful one. And the work being done there by philosophers and doctors is equally as fascinating."

Ian sat back in the chair, the amount of whisky he'd drunk warming him. He saw no reason to respond to this, so he simply waited.

Ackerley said, "I learned much about the new work done on various madnesses. I spoke to one doctor in particular, who had a patient with difficulty in speaking to people, who couldn't meet their eyes, did not answer direct questions, broke out in non sequiturs, disliked water that was too hot, insisted that everything in his life be ordered in an exact way, and so forth. The doctor was making remarkable strides with him. I learned all I could. The patient made me remember how others have described you. And I thought— why not toddle along to Beth and tell her about this possible cure?"

Ian said nothing. His gaze slid to the stone wall behind Ackerley, his heartbeat quickening.

Ackerley continued, "I confess, you do not appear to be as mad as this other fellow. I suppose it comes in degrees."

Ian opened his mouth. Nothing came out for a few seconds, then words burst into the silence. "They tried to cure me at the asylum. It was torture. I was a child. It made me worse."

Ian tried to tamp down the memories, but they spilled upon him. The trouble with being able to remember everything was not being able to shut the bad things out.

They'd put Ian into ice baths to cool down his tempers, shut him alone into dark rooms when he became violent. The electric shocks were the worst, bursts of white-hot pain through his body, meant to erase his troubled thoughts.

Ian's hand closed around the whisky glass until the facets pressed into his palm. Ian was a large man, his hand strong, but the glass was made of heavy lead crystal and didn't break.

Ackerley watched him with a look of sympathy. "My dear fellow, this is not the same sort of thing at all. I heard what you went through. Those asylums of twenty years ago were positively medieval. Many insisted on using techniques from the early years of the science, which have proved useless. I am surprised they did not claim you had demons inside you and tried to exorcise them. I have studied the problems of the mind for many years, and I must confess I became more fascinated when I learned that Beth had married you. I believe, my lord, that I can help you."

Chapter 7

Help him.

Help me do what? Be normal? Give Beth a husband she doesn't have to apologize for, change her life for, be ashamed of?

Ian sat very still while the memories of the asylum receded and his true life came back to him. He was in his distillery, which made the most famous Scots whisky in the world, facing the brother of his wife's late husband.

"Did Beth tell you about me?" Ian asked. Beth didn't like to talk to others about Ian, didn't like *anyone* talking about him. But perhaps she'd been more forthcoming to Ackerley.

"No." Ackerley sounded frustrated. "She says little about you except what extraordinary things you achieve. She is very proud. But—and I hope this does not offend you—your, shall we say, unique character is common knowledge. It is the subject of journal articles."

Ian hadn't known that. But then, he wasn't much for perusing medical journals. He read about Ming bowls, whisky distilling, mathematics, and astronomy, and read children's stories to his son and daughters. Plus he read, in privacy, the occasional tome about bed play that his brothers always seemed to be finding. These, Ian enjoyed discussing at length with Beth.

He could be in bed with Beth right now, the two of them laughing while they explored the more creative positions of the *Kama Sutra*. They'd concluded after much experimentation that some of the positions simply couldn't be achieved, but it had been quite agreeable to attempt them.

Instead of enjoying himself with his wife at the moment, Ian was entertaining Beth's brother-in-law, who peered at him in earnestness, offering him a cure for his lingering madness.

Was it possible? Thinking of cures brought back the horrible years at the asylum, and darkness flickered at the edges of Ian's vision. The tiny amount of hope that someday he might be free of his oddities made the memories worse. He felt the air leave his lungs, a crushing weight on his chest.

Some days life dealt bad cards, Beth liked to say. Metaphorical decks were impossible to calculate probabilities for, which Ian thought highly unfair.

He rose abruptly. Beth would not be happy if Ian deserted her brother-in-law, but Ian's thoughts took hold of him and danced and spun like the will-o'-the-wisps that haunted the woods around here.

The room began to blur, stones, Ackerley's black and gray clothes and worried brown eyes, the paintings on the walls, the window that looked into the barrel room, spinning until Ian was dizzy.

He saw the door coming toward him, and he angled for it, letting his feet propel him out.

Behind him he heard Ackerley calling after him, asking what was wrong, but Ian was gone, the world a place of colorful, flickering lights.

When Inspector Fellows faced Beth Ackerley downstairs in the gallery, he decided not to mention the bullet her husband had passed him.

He recalled the day, long ago, when he'd first met her. Beth, daughter of a confidence trickster and a gullible gentlewoman, had stood before him in the sitting room of a lavish house in Paris and dared to tell *him*, an inspector of Scotland Yard, that she would not allow him to persecute Ian Mackenzie any longer.

Fellows had dismissed her but soon realized his error in judgment. He hadn't understood the connection she'd made with Ian, or her tenacity in protecting those she loved.

Beth still had that tenacity, which she used to fiercely guard her children and the rest of the Mackenzie brood.

"This man who has come to visit," Fellows said to Beth now. "You are certain he is John Ackerley?"

Beth gave him a bewildered look. "Of course. Why wouldn't he be?"

"You'd be amazed at the number of crimes I've worked on where the long-lost brother was anything but. Confidence tricksters know how to assume guises, how to worm their way into your trust. Be careful."

Beth shook her head. "I met John Ackerley at my wedding, and again a year later, when Thomas passed. John has not altered all that much. Grayer, his face more lined, that is all."

"Hmm." Fellows believed her, but the cynicism deeply ingrained in him didn't let him dismiss the idea. "Perhaps I grasp at straws, but that is because I have so bloody little to go on. What did you see the night of the robbery?"

"Not very much." Beth looked unhappy that this was the case. "I was heading down the stairs to see what the noise was about when a man came charging out of this corridor,

Ian behind him. There wasn't much light—the man was smaller than Ian, with dark hair, and he wore black trousers and a black coat. Ian chased him to the front door, which he opened and ran out of. Not much to go on, I know. I'm certain thousands of men in Great Britain fit the description."

"That can't be helped." Fellows had heard similarly vague descriptions from many a witness, and still managed to find the culprit in the end. He wasn't discouraged. "It is a beginning."

"Do you think you can recover the artwork?" Beth asked. "Some of it is priceless."

Of that, Fellows was not as optimistic. Art thieves were of two breeds—the opportunists who didn't always know what they'd stolen, only thought it looked valuable, and those who targeted a specific piece or collection, usually with a buyer lined up beforehand. Fellows's best course of action was to find the buyer on the other end and put the fear of God into him.

"I'll have a damned good try," Fellows said. "I'll ask Hart when he arrives, but do you know if he has enemies who would wish to ruin him? By robbing him, destroying his distillery? To gloat if nothing else?"

Beth flashed him her smile. "You are asking whether Hart Mackenzie has enemies? He has many of those, dear Lloyd. You know that. You were one of them once."

True. Fellows had hated his half brother with great intensity, and he knew plenty of gentlemen in Britain and across the Continent who held that kind of animosity toward Hart. "I agree, I could shake the nearest tree and a dozen men who wanted Hart's head would fall out. Well, I will shake many trees very hard before I find the right person. But find him I will. Or her."

"You believe a woman could do this?" Beth asked, interested.

"I never underestimate the ability of women for being

criminal masterminds," Fellows said dryly. "Men with fancy degrees talk a lot of rot about the female brain not having the capacity or strength to endure male pursuits, but such men are fools, the lot of them. I've seen women orchestrate the most insidious crimes and get away with them."

"I suppose you have a point." Beth's eyes twinkled. "Imagine what the Mackenzie ladies could do if we put our heads together. If we were evil enough to be criminal masterminds, that is."

Fellows suppressed a shudder. The Mackenzie ladies could take over the world and rule with a collective iron hand if they chose. He did not exclude his own wife, a Mackenzie sister-in-law, from this group.

He would have said more, but John Ackerley himself chose to come bustling into the gallery.

Fellows studied him with clinical detachment. Ackerley was not a small man, though relative to the Mackenzies he'd not be considered tall, perhaps four inches shy of six feet. He had skin with the leathery texture of one who'd spent decades in strong sunlight, unkempt brown hair going to gray, and a closely trimmed beard, with more gray in it than in his hair. His eyes were brown, wide, and worried.

"Sister-in-law, did your husband arrive home? Is he here?"

Fellows came alert, and he watched Beth change from reasonable woman to Ian Mackenzie's avenging angel, who'd turn the wrath of heaven against any who harmed him.

"Why?" she asked in a sharp voice. "What happened? What did you do?"

Ackerley blinked. "I did nothing. We were speaking in his distillery, quite calmly, when he simply rose and walked out. Very fast. By the time I reached the courtyard, he'd vanished. Those I asked said he headed in this direction, but I never saw him, and your servants claim he didn't come inside."

"What were you speaking *about*?" Beth's gaze was hard, her politeness gone.

"Oh, this and that. My travels . . . I only want to make certain he is well, my dear Beth."

The man was lying, Fellows knew. Whatever Ackerley had said to Ian had upset him, and Ian had gone off to be alone and think about it. Fellows knew this was what must have happened, and Beth knew it too.

She gave Ackerley a narrow look. "I will search for him," she announced. "Lloyd, will you help? John, if you retire to your chamber, the housekeeper will bring you tea. You must have some sustenance after your journey."

"I will help you find him, of course," Ackerley said. His face was flushed, his words slurred, which told Fellows exactly what he'd been doing in the distillery. Some revelation, loosened by whisky, had disquieted Ian enough to send him off.

"Best you stay here," Fellows said sternly. "We know the house and grounds far better than you do. We don't want to have to make a search for *two* of you."

Ackerley pursed his lips, as though coming up with further argument, then he subsided.

Fellows, whose pocket felt suddenly heavy with the bullet Ian had slipped him, tried to hide his unease, but he couldn't subdue it. Hart had an enemy out there bold enough to rob him of thousands of guineas' worth of artwork, brave enough to shoot at his brother in the woods. Ian could have burst away in one of his muddles, or he could have gotten an idea of who had done this and marched out to confront him.

Either way, Ian must be found.

Ackerley at least let himself be persuaded to stay behind. Fellows called together a troop of footmen and groundskeepers to help him search. With Beth at his side—who firmly would *not* be dissuaded—Fellows left the house by the garden door and began the search.

Ian didn't come out of the half muddle he'd sunk into until he was on top of the hill, surrounded by the ruins of Kilmorgan Castle.

Once upon a time, Malcolm Mackenzie and his father had been driven from this place by an army. Malcolm had returned, undaunted, not once but many times, indefatigably clinging to the land and making it his.

Ian had that same doggedness, or so he'd like to think. He was part of this place. No matter what the world did to him, Ian could come to the top of this hill and sink into the ground, the weight of centuries rendering his troubles insignificant.

The September afternoon was warm. Ian stretched out among the old stones, facedown, soaking up the heat from the grass and earth. His sporran was an uncomfortable lump under him, and insects buzzed around him, but Ian wasn't bothered. He watched a worm emerge from a hole, inch along the dirt, and dig itself into another.

Ian's frustrations eased, brushed away by the quietude. He began to forget why he'd been upset, but he knew the reasons would come rushing back when he rose and went down the hill. Better to stay here awhile until he could face his troubles again.

The darkness of the past tapped on his senses. Fear and anger, the two emotions that had chased Ian most of his life, wanted to reclaim him.

They had blotted out every other feeling. Contentedness, hope, and most of all, love, had not been able to penetrate the miasma of fear and rage that were his constant companions. Not until Beth.

Thinking of Beth eased him further. She had the sweetest smile. Even when Ian aggravated her to the point of exasperation, the smile waited to warm her eyes.

Beth had eyes blue like a deep Highland loch. Ian had

fallen in love with her eyes first thing, when he'd seen her watching him in the box at the opera, nothing but interest and innocence when she'd looked at him. Ian hadn't realized that what he'd felt was love—he'd put his fascination with her down to yet another of his obsessions—but time had proved that a deeper emotion had been at work.

When Beth had found him, Ian had been existing in a constant pit of despair. He'd learned to survive, but the walls of his mind had closed him in, trapping him. He'd lived a half life, able to walk through the world, but keeping the walls between it and himself.

Beth had given him that lovely smile, stretched out her hand, and helped him claw his way from his darkness into the light.

For that, Ian could never repay her. He could only love her with all his strength, want to be his best for her. Could he ever be?

Ackerley's speech had jolted Ian out of his complacency. Before Beth, Ian had been so long denied any happiness that once he'd found it, he'd dived in, wallowed in it, and not wanted to come out.

He'd begun a comforting routine with Beth, his son and daughters, and his life at home. Breakfast with the children, attending to business while the wee ones had lessons and Beth wrote letters, lunching with Beth, taking Jamie and the girls out for long tramps or Jamie fishing when they were home in the Highlands, to see sights when they were in London.

In the evening, Ian and Beth sat in the nursery as the children dined, and then Beth and Ian took supper together, privately. When they were in London, they might attend a play or opera, or one of the few balls or soirees Beth felt obligated to drag Ian to. Or they'd simply spend the rest of the evening in, which Ian liked most of all. His brothers and families might visit, or one of the McBrides with their wives and children, or Fellows would come with Louisa and sons.

Best of all were the evenings Ian and Beth would be alone, to talk or sit in silence, simply enjoying each other's company.

And then to bed . . . Ian let his imagination drift to Beth's arms around him, her lips warm, her hair tangling him as he slid inside her, where he belonged.

He'd indulged all his senses in his new life. Ian never wanted things to change, saw no reason for them to.

But what if Ackerley was right? What if Ian had sunk into comfort because it helped him ignore his madness? Instead of facing it and conquering it, perhaps he'd simply tucked it away, letting Beth indulge him. He'd been bloody useless against the robbers, hadn't he? Plus Ian had looked at Ackerley, when he'd arrived, and wanted to drop the man into a well. The deep fear that Beth and his new life could be taken away from him lingered, threatening to bring back the darkness.

Ian couldn't push aside the fact that perhaps Ackerley *could* help him. What if the man held the key to releasing Ian from the last box of his madness? Could make him a whole man, instead of one who preferred to sequester himself from the world with his wife and children? Beth loved to go out—Ian knew this—but she deferred to his shyness and stayed home with him most nights.

What if Ian could give her a man who could boldly escort her everywhere, could look others straight in the eye at first meeting and give them a bluff, hearty greeting, as his brothers did?

Was it worth hearing what Ackerley had to say?

At the same time, Ian's mind shrank from what Ackerley's cure might entail. The doctors at the asylum had all but flayed his skin from his bones—that was what their experiments on his mind had felt like. They'd used him to test every quack treatment, every far-fetched idea they'd come up with, often in front of an audience, and no one had stopped them. They'd displayed Ian, showed their colleagues what a quick mind he had, then punished him for it. Hart would have stopped such things, had he known, but Ian's communications with the outside world had been monitored, his letters suppressed. In the end, Ian had lost even the ability to speak.

Ian did not like dilemmas. He preferred things to be laid out in plain and simple facts—one choice right, the other wrong. Ambiguity made him uncertain, and uncertainty unsettled him.

Mathematics and geometry had no ambiguity. A squared plus B squared equaled C squared, every time. The Fibonacci sequence never varied—each number was the sum of the two numbers before it.

". . . twenty-one," Ian began to murmur. "Thirty-four, fifty-five, eighty-nine, one hundred forty-four . . ."

His words echoed hollowly on the stones of the old castle. Most of the sound was captured by the breeze, but the wind was echoing too.

Echoing on what? Ian let his voice grow louder. "Two hundred thirty-three, three hundred seventy-seven, six hundred ten . . ."

The numbers bounced back to him, the stones reflecting them. When Ian raised his head, the echoing receded. Only when he lay flat did he hear it again.

Ian skimmed his hands over the grass where he'd been lying. It moved. Not the individual blades, but a section of tufted grass over stone shifted.

Ian tugged at it. Earth and rocks crumbled as he brought up an entire chunk of sod. It came away far faster than it should have for dirt that had lain undisturbed for a century.

The slab of grass, which had obviously been set in place

deliberately, came out from under Ian, revealing a large, rectangular hole.

Unfortunately, most of Ian's torso was right over the hole. Ian's body folded forward, and he slithered abruptly and silently down into inky darkness.

Chapter 8

"Ian?" Beth's throat was raw from shouting, her breath coming faster as every fear sprang to life. "Ian, where are you?"

Fellows's party of searchers had been all over Kilmorgan—the house, the grounds, the distillery and its environs, the hill of the castle and the ruins on top. Night had fallen as they searched, and lanterns bobbed through the darkness, tiny points of swaying light.

Ian hadn't vanished like this in a long, long time. After the first golden days of their marriage, he'd sometimes gone for his extended walks, disappearing into the Highlands and returning when he was ready. Their first row after Ian and Beth had taken up residence in their cozy house had been about Ian walking off without a word.

Beth understood why he'd gone—he'd still been learning to deal with life and all its uncertainties. She'd finally instilled in him the need to at least leave a note when he decided to go tramping, and he'd come to understand why this was important.

Ian wasn't worried about himself, his logic went, so why should Beth be? To this day, Beth wasn't certain he believed how much she would be devastated if something happened to him. But he'd conceded that telling her when and where he was going made her feel better, and he was happy to do that for her. Sometimes, he'd take her by the hand and pull her off with him.

After the children had come, and especially after Megan was born, Ian had ceased his lonely rambles. He continued to enjoy long walks, but he liked to take one or all of the children with him. His time of needing absolute solitude had ended.

So what had occurred to make him go this time? Or had Ian gone at all? There were men out there willing to rob Kilmorgan, to incur Hart's wrath. No sane person would, which meant whoever it was must be dangerous.

Conclusion, Ian had decided to take a short tramp to ease himself from the strain of meeting John, and had come to some danger.

As the night deepened, Beth's fears did as well. The local police sergeant and constable had recruited men from Kilmorgan and nearby villages and crofts to join the search. But so far, nothing.

"Ian!" Beth shouted desperately. She was halfway up the hill to the castle ruins, shivering in the biting wind. "Please answer!"

Fellows came down the path from above. "Best you go inside now, Beth. Believe me, I will keep searching. You falling in the darkness and hurting yourself won't help him."

Beth jerked from Fellows's steadying hand. "I've been scrambling up and down this hill for years. Why should I fall now?"

"At night?" Fellows gave her a severe look. "While you're upset, with your thoughts fixed on your husband's well-being? When I find Ian, I don't want to have to explain why I let you break your leg climbing around in the dark. Trust me, I do not want to have that conversation with him."

A small part of Beth knew Fellows was right. Letting herself come to harm would accomplish nothing.

At the same time, practical considerations were the last things Beth was concerned about. Her husband was lost, perhaps hurt, maybe by the ruffians who'd come to rob the house. She could not rest, sit still, even think until he was found and she could release this breath she was holding.

Fellows did not give her the leisure to decide. "Simons, escort Lady Ian back to the house," he said to the constable from the next village. The young man was English, from Yorkshire, sent to patrol the wilds of Scotland. To him, a chief inspector of Scotland Yard outranked a Scottish noblewoman, no matter that her brother-in-law was a duke.

"Yes, sir," the constable said. "My lady?"

Beth knew that Fellows could recruit half a dozen men to escort her down the hill, bodily if they had to. She sighed and conceded.

As she reached the bottom of the hill, she saw lights on the drive, heard the clatter of horses' hooves and carriage wheels on gravel. Beth increased her pace, running by the time she made her way across the lawn to the drive, the constable panting behind her.

The carriage bore the ducal crest of Kilmorgan—a stag's head surrounded by laurel leaves. A footman dropped off the back of the coach and hurried to open its door. Beth heard Eleanor's voice even before the bulk of Hart descended.

"I know there is something dreadfully wrong," Eleanor was saying as Hart helped her to the ground. "An entire village does not disappear in the middle of the night, especially when they know *you* are coming, Hart. They line up to greet you. No one, nothing, and your coachman is being maddeningly vague." Eleanor paused to shoot the coachman an admonishing look. The man remained on his perch, pretending not to notice. "Ah, here is Beth to enlighten us. Beth . . . ? What is it, darling? What has happened?"

Beth ceased running, her arm folded across her stomach. "Ian is missing. Truly missing. We can find him nowhere.

Not here, not at our house, not at his fishing places, not any-where . . ."

Eleanor caught Beth as she swayed. Beth's eyes filled with tears, fear closing her throat. She wanted to keep running until she saw the bulk of Ian against the night. She wanted to feel his strong arms around her, hear him reassure her that everything was all right.

Hart said nothing at all. He'd gone utterly still, his gaze fixed on Beth.

Beth had always been able to rise to Hart's stare, to look him in the eye and not let the formidable man intimidate her. Tonight, that resolve deserted her. Ian was special to Hart. Ian was Hart's vulnerable little brother, the one he protected at all costs. When Ian had first met Beth, Hart had tried to protect him against *her.*

And now she'd gone and lost him.

"I'm sorry," Beth said, tears choking her. "I invited my brother-in-law here, he upset Ian—I should have known Ian wasn't ready for someone from my past."

"Great heavens." Eleanor drew Beth against her. "Ian missing is hardly *your* fault. Tell her that, Hart, instead of standing there like a monolith."

"It *is* my fault," Beth said mournfully. "I should have stayed with him, not let them be alone."

"Absolute bloody nonsense." Eleanor's vehemence cut through Beth's descent into despair. "You need a drop of something to steady your nerves. Hart will find Ian, and all will be well. Go on, Hart. You know this place better than anyone."

"Not better than Ian." Hart uncurled the gloved fingers he'd clenched into his palms. "Beth, calm yourself and tell me exactly what happened."

Beth drew another ragged breath, but Hart's curt command was what she needed. She related the tale of the robbery, John Ackerley's arrival, Fellows's worries, and Ian walking off into the blue.

"It must have been too much for him," Beth said. "I know John said *something* to him, but the blasted man won't tell me what."

Eleanor rubbed Beth's shoulder. "That's the spirit. Hart will join the hunt, and you and I will interrogate Mr. Ackerley. I assume you kept him inside so he wouldn't get lost while all the men are running about?"

Beth could only nod. Hart reached out and put a hand on Beth's shoulder. A reassuring hand, one with steely strength that the last ten years hadn't diminished.

"No one takes care of Ian better than you, Beth," Hart said, his voice a quiet rumble. "But Ian's his own man. If he takes it into his head to do something, none of us can stop him, not even you. I'll find him. Ian has repeatedly said he can always find me, but the reverse is also true. I can always find him." Hart's fingers squeezed before he released Beth. "Go with Eleanor. I won't stop until I bring him home."

Beth's tears stung her cheeks, but they were tears of relief. No man was as resolute as Hart—except Ian, of course. Hart would find him, whether Ian was hurt or well.

Beth tried not to think about Ian hurt, or gone forever from her. But Beth had been raised in workhouses, seeing the horrors of the world at too young an age. Bad things happened, and they happened quite often. She would have to face that.

Eleanor's arm tightened around Beth, and Beth sank into her sister-in-law's warmth. Hart, without another word, turned his back and strode off into the darkness.

⁓

Too much bloody darkness. Ian lay tangled on something hard, blinking and trying to see. His head and body hurt, his mouth was dry, his eyes sandy. He had no idea where he was, or where he'd been. This was no room in Kilmorgan Castle or in his house where he lived in peace with Beth.

Panic swept over Ian, whirling him back to the old days,

when he'd lain on a brick floor, shivering and wet, as so-called doctors tried to drive the madness from him with ice-cold water. Or, when he went on one of his screaming rants, they'd lock him in a little room with no windows, no light, no sound. Both to calm him and to assure he didn't hurt anyone, they'd claimed. They'd been afraid of him, not knowing what to do with a panicked and lonely young man.

Waves of fear continued to strike, trying to drive Ian back to his state of rage and terror, when nothing made sense, and no one understood him.

The need to pound his fists against the broken ground and scream until he was hoarse worked up inside him. He'd do it—he'd go mad, locked away in this place of darkness, forgotten, and alone.

". . .Six hundred and ten, nine hundred and eighty-seven . . ." The clarity of the numbers, the equation that existed in eternal perfection started to penetrate the fog. He was Ian Mackenzie, husband of Beth and father to Jamie, Belle, and Megan. Children with no madness in them, and clever, all three of them in different ways. Children to make a man proud.

Ian drew a long breath, and another. Daniel's wife, Violet, had taught him how to slow his breathing, which would still his thoughts. She'd learned it as a performer, as a way to calm herself before facing an audience. Ian lay still and focused on the lift and fall of his chest. The air was dank but not heavy, with a touch of movement. That meant that this place was not sealed off, an airless tomb. There was a way out.

Ian cautiously felt the ground in front of and around him. His hands touched stones, but not necessarily natural ones. Some had the rough, flat feel of bricks, which crumbled when he pressed them. Others were jagged and hard, with the smooth feel of granite.

Rational thoughts came back to him. Ian had been lying on the hilltop, unhappy about the revelations John Ackerley had given him, and he'd fallen. He must have struck his head and been rendered unconscious, waking sometime later in this confused state.

There was nothing wrong with him then. Ian spent a moment in thankfulness, letting the feeling well up and warm him. He had not gone raving mad. He'd simply met with an accident.

He had fallen into a hole from the top of the hill down to . . . where? The old castle had cellars, he knew—he'd explored the ones that could still be reached.

But the cellars opened up into another area of the ruins. Hart had ordered that doors be fixed over them from the top so that the many children who now played at Kilmorgan wouldn't fall into them. Ian had been lying nowhere near those trapdoors.

Perhaps he was in another part of the cellars, long walled off. In that case, who had dug the hole down to them? Who had fixed the squares of dirt and grass over the openings above to hide their existence?

Ian's fears receded as the puzzle took hold of him. Who had done this, and why? And where exactly was he?

How Ian would get out did not worry him as much. He'd find a way, even if he simply had to climb back up the wall. Also, those looking for him—and they would be, if he knew Beth and Fellows—would see the hole in the top of the hill and explore it.

Ian carefully probed the wall and ground around him, before he pushed himself to a sitting position. His head didn't strike a ceiling, and he could feel only emptiness above him, no matter how high he reached. He concluded that he was in a deep hole indeed. It was somewhat warm down here, no cool breeze to chill him. While the afternoon sun had been warm, the wind hadn't been—it never was at Kilmorgan.

A light would be handy. Ian's leather sporran, on his belt, carried all sorts of practical things. He knew exactly which items were it, and put his hand unerringly on a box of matches.

Ian's fingers were steady as he opened the box, withdrew a sulfur match, and struck it against the rock wall.

Light flared, making his eyes screw up. The small flame couldn't much penetrate the heavy darkness, but it was comforting.

By the match's illumination, Ian saw that he'd been right about the brick and also the natural rock. This was a cellar, or a tunnel, carved out of the rock of the hill and shored up against collapse.

Interesting. Perhaps the Mackenzies of old had understood the need to have a back way out of the castle, or a route to bring in supplies if they were besieged. Ian's ancestors had joined the national pastime of smuggling, and tunnels would be a good place to both store the contraband and sneak it away from any excise men who came to call.

The match burnt out. Ian stubbed out the spark on a rock. He crawled a little way along the tunnel, sharp stones cutting him, then he withdrew another match and lit it.

One fear Ian did not have was the fear of underground spaces. While darkness used to send him into absolute terror, exploring caves and tunnels awoke his sense of wonder, the need to learn and understand something absolutely. When Hart and Ian had gotten themselves trapped in the underground rivers and sewers of London years ago, Ian had known the exact layout of every tunnel. This had annoyed Hart, he remembered. Losing Hart down there had haunted him for years.

This time, Ian had lost only himself, which didn't worry him. He would find a way out. He always did.

As Ian waved his match around, the light caught on the gleam of something that glinted back almost as brightly. The last of the panic fled as Ian's curiosity seized him and overrode all other emotions.

He carefully crawled toward the gleam. Not an animal's

eyes—animal eyes in the dark were different, vibrant, aware. This glint was static, unmoving, inanimate.

Ian's match went out. The last of the flame burned his hand, making him let out a curse in Gaelic before he dropped it. He then found the match and ground it against the rock, making sure it was truly out. Fire was nothing he'd be careless with.

The next match bloomed in the darkness. Its light fell on something gold. Not solid gold, Ian realized, his heart beating faster. Gilding. On a frame of a picture painted by Mac Mackenzie and lying in a jumbled pile atop other paintings, with frames either broken or missing entirely.

Before Ian's match went out, it caught on the oval face of a Madonna, a pudgy baby in her lap, painted in the unmistakably vivid colors of the artist called Raphael.

Chapter 9

Fellows called his men together after several hours of searching, taking their reports. Nothing.

He knew that in daylight, he might be able to trace a trail—footprints, broken branches, the snag of a cloth in Mackenzie plaid. Of course, with the men of three villages and the crofts in between swarming all over, any evidence of Ian's passing likely had been destroyed.

Fellows could not lose him. Not only would Beth blame him forever, but Hart was here now, a man who would punish the world if harm came to his beloved younger brother.

Besides, Fellows had grown fond of Ian. Once upon a time, he'd been convinced Ian was a crazed murderer, but he had admitted that his prejudice against the Mackenzie family had colored his judgment.

Hell, it had blotted out his judgment with opaque paint. In his pursuit of Ian, Fellows had only proved himself to be as mad as the rest of the Mackenzies.

He'd come to appreciate Ian's brain, the quietness that hid lightning-quick thoughts. Ian had the ability to see into the heart of a problem, unswayed by the emotions and biases that clouded the eyes of most observers.

That is, Ian had that ability when he didn't go into one of his muddles. Then his clarity was erased, his sharp rationality destroyed.

Ian must have gone off today in one of these storms in his mind, and perhaps had run straight into whoever had shot at him earlier.

Fellows comforted himself by the fact that none of the men had stumbled over Ian's dead body. They would have, he was certain, if Ian had come to that kind of harm.

Unless, of course, the resourceful killer had dumped him into the river.

Damn it all. Fellows faced his men now, asking for reports. No one had found any sign of Ian.

"We need to wait until morning." The words came from Fellows reluctantly. He wanted to search, no matter what, but he knew the chance of finding Ian would be better in the light. "Then we walk a line across the hills, leaving no stone unturned. Understand? Spread the word—we'll need more men to search, able-bodied boys as well. Boys can sometimes find what grown men can't. For now, rest and prepare for tomorrow."

"No." Hart Mackenzie materialized out of the dark. "We aren't stopping until he's found."

Fellows knew he'd have this confrontation. He faced his half brother, the two close in age and temperament. Hart's eyes glinted in the light of the lanterns, the desperation on his face matched only by stubborn determination.

"If they continue thrashing about in the dark, they'll miss him," Fellows said. "Wasting energy that can be used to find him tomorrow."

"Meanwhile, Ian is left exposed to the cold and the night, which could kill him." The harsh gravel of Hart's voice grated. "I'll not leave my brother out here alone."

"I didn't say *I* wouldn't stop looking," Fellows returned. "And you are free to do what you like. I've run many a manhunt in my time, and I know the odds of finding a person in the night with an exhausted search party."

Hart's gaze didn't waver. "And are your manhunts always a success?"

"Yes." Fellows had never given up a hunt before the quarry was found, whether he searched for a criminal hiding from the police or a missing child.

Hart took a step closer to him. "Do you always find them alive?"

Not always. Fellows had to admit that. Sometimes he was simply too late. "A high percentage of the time, yes."

They watched each other, a few feet apart, eye level with one another. Wind stirred Hart's hair, his well-tailored coat, and his kilt, his clothes the finest money could buy. Fellows was in a rumpled suit with a stained greatcoat, his hat squashed down upon his head. Stripped naked, the symbols of who they were gone, there would be little difference between them. Or so Ian would claim. The blood of the Mackenzies would ring true.

A man shouted in the woods. Another shouted back, in Gaelic, which Fellows didn't understand, but Hart came alert.

Without a word, Hart turned from Fellows and strode into the darkness, his steps changing to a run. Fellows went after him, the swift jog he used for chasing villains through London letting him easily catch up.

Hart and Fellows followed the voices along the hillside below Kilmorgan Castle, and deep into the woods beyond. The ground was uneven, and Fellows stumbled more than once. Hart, who'd known the paths from boyhood, kept a rapid pace.

The woods ended at the top of another steep hill, which rolled down to the nearby sea. A man in a kilt was striding up from the rocky shingle, village men with lanterns surrounding him.

Hart uttered a cry that Fellows knew very few ever

heard, one of vast relief and thankfulness. Hart shoved aside those in his way and caught the tall Scotsman in a hard embrace. Lantern light fell on Ian's face, which was streaked with black dirt, Ian's eyes sparkling among the grime.

Ian jumped slightly at Hart's hug, as though surprised his older brother had been worried about him. Fellows, the same relief as Hart's washing through him, watched Ian stare at Hart in perplexity, then bring his hands up to pat his brother's back.

When Hart finally pulled away, Ian said, "Come and see."

He broke from Hart and strode back down the hill. Hart said severely, "Damn you, Ian!" But Ian kept walking, heading back for the shore, disappearing behind a bend in the hill.

Fellows, his curiosity pricking, followed.

Ian moved quickly, Hart growling as he tried to keep up. Fellows fell into step with Hart. "Did you expect anything else?" Fellows asked him. "The bloody man is unfathomable."

Hart only muttered under his breath and quickened his pace.

Ian led them through a thick stand of trees then stopped before a slab of rock that ran straight down from the hill above. A niche in this rock, a mere shadow under the light of the village men's lanterns, proved to be the opening to a cave.

The cave had a low ceiling—they had to bend double to follow Ian inside—but it opened up after a few yards to a tall tunnel, carved out by water and wind. Long ago, human beings had shored up parts of it with bricks and stones like those used to build the original castle. The bricks had crumbled into red-brown dust, but the quarried stones remained.

Ian was moving down this tunnel like a freight train on its way to its final delivery. Hart, uttering colorful phrases in English and Gaelic, hurried after him. Fellows brought up the rear in silence.

"I'll be buggered." The voice of Curry, who'd followed, echoed in the darkness. "Who'd steal a houseful of artwork and dump it in a hole?"

The lantern light fell on a mess. Paintings were strewn about, some ripped from frames and folded in half, lesser paintings piled haphazardly on those that were priceless. The sculptures by Mr. Degas lay in a ruined heap, the horses' legs entwined. Two other sculptures—the head of a young lady and a Chinese bronze—lay nearby, scratched and half buried in stones.

Fellows's breath caught. Not only did the destruction of the valuable and beautiful things kick him in the gut, but the scenario was familiar. Memories of a long-ago day, when he'd been a very young man, just admitted to CID, flitted into his head. Not his first case, but an early one. He hadn't thought about it in a long time, but the crime was the same. A house robbed of famous artwork, but the pieces then broken and found in a drained pond nearby.

One of the villagers suggested, "Maybe they stashed it to return later, after they found somewhere to sell it."

Ian shook his head. "They'd have taken care. Bundled it up to keep it safe. This was abandoned."

"Why the hell—" Hart broke off, flushed with rage. "This is a man who wants to punch me in the face. Maybe my whole family." He swung around to look at Fellows. "Who?"

Ian was watching Fellows, seeing him realize things. "Sedgwick," Ian said. "Remember?"

"*I* remember," Fellows said sharply. "How do you? That was nearly twenty years ago."

"I read of it." Ian rubbed a hand over his face, smearing it more with grime. "Look into it."

Fellows had planned to, but Ian's high-handedness, after they'd all feared him gone to an early grave, was irritating. "Sedgwick is dead. And Radcliffe. All of them."

Ian fixed Fellows with his unwavering golden gaze, as though all the players in an old case being deceased was of no moment. "You will have written things down."

"I know that." Fellows's case notes had been meticulous throughout his career. "But they are in London."

A foolish statement, Fellows knew, as soon as it left his mouth.

"Then go to London," Ian said, and turned away, back to Hart and the paintings.

~~~

Ian's interest in the artwork and why it had been abandoned in the tunnels fled when he saw Beth running toward him from the house. Her skirts rippled and her feet skimmed the ground, as she hurtled herself at Ian. He caught her in his arms and let her drag her down to him, their mouths meeting in a fierce kiss.

Beth was Ian's world. His life. Her warmth came to him now, cutting the chill of the tunnels and the night. Her lips moved beneath his, her body pliant under his hands as she held him.

The hunger in his heart had been satisfied when he'd met her. Pain and fear eased, light and heat taking its place. Beth clung to him, deepening the kiss, holding him close.

"Ian." The harsh sound of Hart's voice cut through the bubble of comfort Beth wrapped around him.

Ian ignored him. Hart was hard about the edges, gruff sounding, and smelled like he'd been traveling for hours. Beth was softness and sweetness, her scents water and soap. Much more pleasant.

"*Ian.*" Hart's hand landed on Ian's shoulder.

Beth stepped back. "You must forgive me, Hart," she said, voice shaking. "Only I've just learned that my husband is alive and well."

"You took us on a merry chase, Ian," Hart growled. "What the devil were you—"

Beth stepped in front of Hart. "Kindly do not lash into him," she said coolly. "Ian has had an ordeal. Let him rest and calm, and then you may ask your questions. Politely."

Ian suppressed a smile. Beth liked to defend Ian against Hart—against the world—with well-bred snarls and kitten claws.

Ian knew exactly how to divert Hart's attention from berating him for being found, unhurt. "Someone dug a hole at the top of the hill, near the keep. Hid it with a plug of sod. Board it up. Keep the children from falling in."

Hart stared at him with his golden eyes for half a moment, then he turned around and started bellowing orders at the men who'd been on the search.

While he did so, Ian, no longer interested in stashes of art and tunnels under the old castle, let Beth take him into the house. She ordered Curry to draw him a bath then shooed Curry away and took up the sponge to Ian's body herself.

That led to some interesting kisses, water all over the bathroom floor, and Ian making hard love to his wife on the damp carpet.

~~~~~

Ian went in search of John Ackerley the next morning, after Hart and Fellows at last ceased interrogating him. Ian had repeated his story several times, though he told the same tale again and again. He was beginning to think *them* mad when he finally turned and stalked out of the gallery where Hart and his staff were sifting through the art to see what they could save.

Neither Fellows nor Hart tried to stop him. Not that Ian would let them.

Ian spied Curry hurrying across staircase hall and beckoned to him. "Ackerley?"

"No, me lord." Curry pressed his hands to his chest. *"Curry."*

Ian gave him an impatient look. "Where is he?"

"You're in a mood, ain't ye? Mr. Ackerley, brother-in-law to your lady wife, is strolling in the gardens. Saw him heading to the far end. Probably off to do some exploring."

Without a word, Ian stepped past Curry and headed for the garden door.

"You're welcome, me lord," Curry's voice drifted after him. "What I put up with . . . Should 'ave stuck to the streets and avoiding the 'angman."

Ian took no notice. Curry loved to drone on about the hell his life had become since he'd begun working with Ian. Since Curry had never once taken the opportunity to leave, Ian had ceased listening.

Ackerley was indeed at the far end of the garden, making for the gate that led to the wild lands beyond. The gardeners Malcolm Mackenzie had hired years ago had only tamed the land *inside* the gate. On the other side of it, the glen dropped into crags and rivers, beautiful and rugged. Fine for a Highlander born to it, not so much for a soft Englishman, never mind he'd survived India and Africa. Scotland had a mind of its own.

Ian put his hand on the low iron gate, an artwork in itself, brought over from Italy by Hart when he inherited the place.

"Aye," Ian said when Ackerley looked at him in surprise. "I will try your cure. What do I have to do?"

Chapter 10

Ackerley's cure seemed to mostly involve talking. Of course it would, Ian thought as Ackerley faced Ian across a table in one of Kilmorgan's lavish sitting rooms.

The ceiling soared high above them, artwork that depicted the Trojan War, from Paris presenting the apple to Aphrodite to Helen's abduction to the fall of the great city, marching across it. Achilles died in agony in one panel, a reminder to all that every man was vulnerable.

Ian had spent hours in this room as a child, lying on the carpet, taking in the pictures, while Hart had explained the story to him. Hart had been a youth then, angry and in sometimes violent conflict with their father, but had always taken time to be kind to Ian.

Ian remembered every word of the stories Hart had told even now. He also remembered thinking that Helen had an oddly shaped face, the spears wielded by the fighters were out of proportion, and Paris looked like a sour-faced footman.

"My lord?" Ackerley cut through Ian's memories.

"Mmm?" Ian dragged his gaze from the ceiling and settled it on Ackerley. *He* didn't look sour faced; more like a happy pieman who'd already sold plenty of pies that morning.

"Are you ready to begin?"

Ian gave him a nod, not bothering to answer. If he weren't ready, why would he be sitting here?

"I will ask you a series of questions, taking you back into the past," Ackerley said, excitement edging his voice. "Deep into the past. The idea, you see, is to find what triggered your . . . er . . . malady. If we can deal with that memory, break its power, it will free you."

Sounded unlikely. Ian leaned back in his chair, folded his arms, and stretched out his long legs. His socks over his firm calves were thick, woolen, and patterned with Mackenzie plaid, his shoes sturdy leather.

Ackerley pulled a notebook out of the worn satchel he'd brought with him, picked up the pen Curry had provided, and dipped it into the inkwell Curry had also brought. Ackerley smoothed a page of the notebook, and let the pen hover over the paper.

"Now then, let us begin with your school days—what school did you attend? What did you like to study there? Were your brothers with you, and how did you feel about them watching over you? Tell me everything you can remember."

Ackerley asked nothing about the asylum, Ian noticed. Fair enough. Ian didn't want to talk about his years there in any case.

"I never went to school," Ian said.

Ackerley stopped. "Never? But you are so learned—a brilliant mathematician, Beth says."

"I taught myself. They tried to put me inside a school, but I ran out again."

Ian remembered it perfectly—the boys at Harrow, where all the Mackenzies attended, staring at Ian as he'd tried to take his place among them. They'd heard of his madness, he'd supposed.

At the time Ian had not understood how different he

was—he only knew the weight of all those stares had caused rage to well up inside him, and terror. In the classroom, under the Latin tutor's nose, Ian had launched himself into two other boys, leaving them bloody and with broken limbs before Mac had rushed in to pull Ian away and carry him out. Ian had fought his way from Mac and had run, run, run . . .

"My lord?" Ackerley's polite voice again shattered the memories.

Ian snapped his gaze to him. "I read books."

"Ah. What sort of books?"

Was he a slow-wit? "All sorts. Books on language, art, science, mathematics—Chaussier, Darwin, Lamont, Lavoisier, Lucas, Maxwell—"

Ackerley held up his hand to halt the flow of words. "Perhaps you could give me a list later."

Ian gave him a nod. "I'll have Curry write one."

"Curry." Ackerley's eyes took on a bright light. "He has been with you for many years."

"Aye."

"A pickpocket, I believe he was."

Many people were interested in Curry's history. "Cameron caught him trying to pick his pocket. Curry begged for mercy, and Cam liked him." *Charmed me, the blackguard*, Cameron had said. When Curry proved himself efficient and un-spookable—Cam's word—he'd sent the man to attend Ian in the asylum.

"Curry wasn't afraid of me," Ian said. "He made sure I was looked after, helped me hide things from my keepers—books, pictures, cheroots. Did everything for me."

"Still does, I gather."

"He looks after Beth now too."

"It never worried you that he was a criminal?" Ackerley asked as he made notes.

Ian drew himself closer to the table and pressed his palms to it. "No. He never stole from me."

"How did you know you could trust him?"

Ian watched Ackerley write in a slow, careful hand. Ian could read the words upside down. *Curry becomes a father figure? Delivering the care a parent could not?*

Ian had never thought of Curry as a father. A friend, yes, a conjurer sometimes, the way he was able to almost magically make things happen. But never a father. That was different.

Ackerley stopped writing and held his pen in both hands. "I would like to know about your father."

"He was an unpleasant man, and he's dead." The words came out in a staccato monotone. "He beat us. Hated us, Hart says, because we took our mother's love from him. Hart says he was mad and didn't know it."

"What is *your* opinion, Ian?"

Ian didn't have to ponder. "That we should leave him in the past. He was a madman; he's gone now, and Hart is duke."

"I am curious to know." Ackerley dipped his pen in the ink once more. "What is your first memory of him?"

"Beating me." Ian's lips were tight. "My mother had swept me into her arms. My father took me away from her and backhanded me. He shouted at her—*They'll become soft and weak, like women, if ye touch 'em in that disgusting manner. Leave off, ye daft bitch.*"

Ian's voice had taken on the cant of his father. The words rose in his head, every one imprinted on his damnable, unrelenting brain.

"Do you know how old you were then?" Ackerley seemed to be speaking from far away, behind thick glass.

"Three. It was m' birthday."

The pen stilled, and Ackerley looked up. "Three? Are you certain?"

Of course Ian was certain. He forgot nothing. "Aye."

"Do you remember what you did? Your response?"

"Wept," Ian said without shame. "I was a child. He

cuffed me for that, and the nanny was sent for to take me back to the nursery. Mac tried to console me. Hart went downstairs and shouted and swore at our father, and our father broke his arm."

That memory was admittedly dim—Ian remembered only the significant points of the day. Hart's screams, which cut off, then the pure hatred in Hart's eyes while the doctor was setting his arm. Hart had been about thirteen at the time. The overt battle between Hart and his father had commenced that day. The house had not known peace thereafter.

"I don't want to talk about m' father," Ian said abruptly.

"Hmm." Ackerley scribbled. "Very well. I don't wish to distress you."

The man had not thought it through if he hadn't realized speaking about Ian's father would be distressful. Ian drummed his fingers on the table. If Beth were here, she'd soothe him with a warm touch, a light joke that she'd have to explain to him later.

But no, Ian didn't want Beth there. Not if they would dredge up horrors of the past. Ian wanted Ackerley to cure him. After that, he'd find Beth, tell her he wasn't mad anymore, and *then* let her soothe him, in many interesting, and possibly sticky, ways.

"Now." Ackerley caught Ian's eye, turned a bright shade of red, and flicked his gaze to his notebook. People did that when they were uncomfortable, Beth had told Ian. What did Ackerley have to be uncomfortable about?

"I do not wish to embarrass you, Lord Ian," Ackerley said, his tanned face going redder. "But it is important to this treatment to discuss, er, the ladies."

Fine with Ian. He liked women, and discussing them gave him no qualm. "What about them?"

Ackerley cleared his throat. "Your first. Can you tell me about that? Not in great detail, of course," he added quickly. "But who was the lady, and why did you decide . . . ?"

"A maidservant at the asylum. She was kind to me, and very pretty. I was seventeen; she was nineteen. She taught me well. I decided . . . because I wanted to."

Ackerley kept his gaze on his paper. "You fell in love with her? Was it difficult to learn it would not be a permanent thing?"

"No," Ian answered. "And, no."

"She seduced you?" Ackerley looked up, his expression going indignant. "She must have, older than you, more experienced, you vulnerable as a patient. That is simply not on."

"I seduced *her*," Ian said. "I gave her many presents. I wanted her, and I had her. Cam had told me what to do, as did the books he lent me. I was very pleased with myself. I did not know then that it was called seduction."

"I see." Ackerley was back to embarrassment. "I am sorry to speak so indelicately, but it is important to the process. I was under the impression that this encounter caused you to seek women who were . . . shall we say . . . not those you would marry. Once out of the asylum and back in your brother's home, you did not court a respectable woman of your class."

Ian shrugged. "I was a madman. They did not want me. The ladies I paid would look the other way at my oddities."

"I'm certain that was upsetting," Ackerley said, sadness in his eyes. "To know you could only have softer company if you paid . . ."

"The house Hart's mistress owned was very comfortable," Ian said. "The women were kind to me. I didn't love them; they didn't love me. It was an agreeable arrangement."

Ian had no interest in talking about women of the past. He'd relieved his physical needs, and that was an end to it. Hart and Cam had enjoyed the ladies' company—they would talk with the ladies and laugh, play cards, and drink, while Ian read a newspaper and waited until they were ready to leave.

"There was a terrible tragedy at that house, I believe," Ackerley began.

"Aye." Ian's quick mind ran through the events from beginning to end. "I feared my brother had murdered a woman. I was mistaken." That too was in the past and didn't worry Ian anymore. "Hart and I and Fellows have long since reconciled. What has this to do with curing my madness?"

Ackerley laid down his pen. "The idea, you see, is to sift through your memories and find the key. Once we discover that, we can begin there and repair your mind, as it were."

Again, Ian wasn't certain he agreed, but he spread his hands, ready to go on. If this was what it took to cure him, he'd put up with it.

"Now," Ackerley said. "I . . . ah . . . have heard that some of the things you did at the . . . er . . . houses such as the one of your brother's mistress were not quite, shall we say . . . straightforward."

"Perversions," Ian said. "I believe that is what they are called."

Ackerley's face was as red as fall apples. Ian was beginning to enjoy seeing how many different colors the man could turn. "Yes. Quite."

"My brother Hart had the proclivities, not me. I believe he still does have them."

Ackerley stared, astonishment replacing his discomfiture. "Still? But he's married to a respectable lady . . . the daughter of an earl."

"Aye," Ian said calmly.

"You mean he continues to visit houses? I am shocked, I will say, my lord. I had understood from Beth that the duke was now a family man."

"He is," Ian said. "Hart stays with Eleanor. He would never betray her."

"Then I cannot imagine what you are suggesting."

Ackerley very much wanted to know. As generally oblivious as Ian usually was to other people's emotional

states—people not Beth or his children, that is—Ian sensed
his intense curiosity. Ackerley hid it behind indignation and
disbelief, but he was titillated and desired to know more.

Ian couldn't resist. "Hart likes tethers—leather or silken
rope. He has cords that lace all around the woman's body,
allowing her limbs to be pulled into various positions. He
collects different floggers from France and the Orient, and
devices a person can be strapped to. Since he married Eleanor he has also become interested in photography. For
private pictures, of course."

"Good heavens." Ackerley's mouth had sagged open. He
leaned forward, hanging on Ian's every word.

"Do not write it down," Ian said, pointing at the notebook. Ackerley's pen hovered over it, a drop of ink ready to
fall and blot the page. "I believe much of what Hart pur-
chases is not legal."

Ackerley jumped, and the ink fell, splotching the clean
paper. "No, no, of course not. Wouldn't dream . . ."

"But those are *Hart's* proclivities," Ian said. "They have
nothing to do with my madness."

Ackerley took out a handkerchief to mop up the ink.
"They might. If you witnessed such a thing too young, it
could have had a fevered effect on your brain."

"Hart took care that I did not see until I was older, and
after I had already been bedding women."

"But perhaps when you were *very* young, you saw . . .
Maybe you do not remember."

Unlikely. Ian remembered everything. "I did not."

"Or perhaps . . ." Ackerley finished wiping up and laid the
pen on the stained handkerchief. His voice gentled. "Your
father with your mother?"

"No," Ian said without worry. He'd barely been allowed
near his parents and certainly not on the floor that housed
their bedchamber. Ian's father had been many things, but
he'd overall been a bit of a prude when it came to his wife.
After her death, the old duke had taken his needs to a string

of mistresses, but what he'd done with Ian's mother had been strictly private.

"Are you certain?" Ackerley asked.

The man was obsessed by the act. Ackerley leaned forward again, as though he wished Ian to pour out a confession that he'd seen his father and mother do the things Hart was now famous for.

"Certain," Ian said. "I would not have forgotten."

Ackerley's eyes lit. "Ah, but there are such things as memories that are buried—harrowing things hidden deep within the mind. I know a technique that will draw them out. Might I . . . Might we try it?"

He looked as eager as the youngest dog in Ian's pack when it wanted to play. Ian doubted Ackerley could pull out any more memories than Ian already had—his head was stuffed full of them, and they never went away.

But Ian was as curious about Ackerley as Ackerley was about him. And, Ian was willing to try whatever might give him relief from his madness.

He gave the bright-eyed Ackerley a nod. "Aye. What do I have to do?"

Chapter 11

Ian watched with curiosity as Ackerley lifted the satchel and drew out a coin. Ian peered at it and was disappointed when he saw it was an ordinary coin, a French franc.

Ackerley polished it with a cloth, as though the silver bit were the most precious gold. "I'd like you to recline on that sofa, if you don't mind. Much more comfortable for you."

Ian glanced at the carved-backed gilded couch from the eighteenth century. "Won't fit me. That was Will Mackenzie's."

"Will?" Ackerley asked, interested. "Who is *he*? A cousin?"

"My great-great-great-uncle. He lived in the court of Versailles and used to send back furniture."

"Good heavens." Ackerley gave the sofa a look of new respect. "It must be quite valuable."

Ian nodded. "From the stories, Uncle Will had many things and lost track of most of them. He was killed in battle by English soldiers, but lived in France most of the time he was dead."

"Lived . . . most of the time he was *dead*? What on earth do you mean?"

Ian rose. He'd found diaries in the attics, reams of them,

when Hart had first brought him home from the asylum. Ian had hidden up there, terrified, but unable to sit still, he'd gone through all the boxes and trunks, unearthing family secrets long buried.

Lady Mary Lennox, who'd married Malcolm Mackenzie, had kept journals. She'd written of her life from her own childhood to meeting Malcolm and her breathless courtship with him, ending up running off with him—and his entire family—to Kilmorgan.

Her journals had been endlessly fascinating to Ian, and he remembered every word of them.

"Will Mackenzie was reported dead at Culloden," Ian said. He wandered in a circle in the middle of the big room. "But he escaped to France, listed dead ever since. So were his brothers Alec and Malcolm. Malcolm was allowed to come back to life, and he built this house . . . This will be better."

Ian took himself down to the carpet, stretching full length. From here, he could see the entire glory of the Trojan War from beginning to end, played out before his eyes. Menelaus, rage on his face, sword raised as he ordered the war on Troy, had always reminded Ian of his father. Small wonder Helen had run from him.

"Better for what?" Ackerley was on his feet, staring down at Ian in puzzlement.

"Comfort. And following the story."

Ackerley's frown increased. The man was rather slow. Ian pointed to the ceiling.

"The story. When I was small, I thought I was Hermes." Ian's finger moved to the corner where a god lounged, covered only with a loincloth, and watched the action. The god in the painting had red-brown hair and the build of a Scotsman, skin tinged pink from the weather.

Ackerley looked up and gaped at the art dashing across the top of the room. "Hermes. Now, that is interesting. The messenger of the gods. Why did you think you were like him?"

Ian shrugged, shoulders moving on the carpet. "He looks like me."

And he watches, Ian thought, but didn't want to say out loud. *He watches, unnoticed, but knows everything.*

Ackerley studied the painting for a while, then looked back down at Ian. "Well, I suppose this will do. Must fetch a chair to rest my old bones."

He lifted one of the carved wooden chairs with surprising strength and set it down next to Ian. "Now, then, Lord Ian, watch the coin."

Ackerley held it toward Ian's face and started turning it back and forth. "Watch the movement of the coin. Focus only on it."

Ian tucked his hands behind his head and crossed his feet. It *was* rather comfortable on the floor. Perhaps he'd bring Beth down here, late at night, when they weren't likely to be disturbed.

Ackerley was talking, saying something about Ian following his voice and doing what he commanded. Ian studied the ceiling, watching the heroes Hector, Ajax, Achilles, bulging with muscles, swords raised, grim determination on their faces. The fall of Troy was blamed on a woman, but these men and their pride had destroyed a lavish city and all within it. Bloody fools.

Suppose Ackerley had come rushing at Ian with sword raised when Ian had absconded with Beth. He'd spirited her off to a side-street pension in Paris, and had married her in the morning.

No army had come after them, razing the city to avenge Beth. Beth was worth fighting for, though, far more than any person or place in the mural above him.

Ian pictured her in the painting too, smiling down at him, then she descending to stand at his side. She was wrapped in the flowing clothes of the Trojan women, one fold of her drapery slipping down to bare the swell of her breast.

"What are you doing, Ian?" Beth asked, her beautiful

smile in place. "You aren't teasing my brother-in-law something awful, are you?"

"Aye," Ian said. "I am."

"What was that?" Ackerley cut in. "Whom are you speaking to, Lord Ian? Whom do you see?"

Beth's laughter wound around him. "You are a rogue, Ian Mackenzie. You pretend to be cryptic and locked away, and all the time you are laughing at us." She nudged him with a bare foot. If Ian had been able to move, he would have caressed it.

Beth looked up at the portrait of Hermes. "He looks far too smug. Like you."

She floated upward, back to the painting. Hermes *was* Ian, his expressionless face and golden eyes softening as Beth went to him. She kissed the god's cheek, winked, and settled on his lap.

Unfair. "Come back," Ian said. "It's nice here."

"Whom do you see?" Ackerley repeated.

"Beth," Ian said. "I always see Beth."

"And your mother?"

Ian's brows drew together. The man was a simpleton. "No. My mother is dead."

"That made you very sad, didn't it?" Ackerley said. "How did you feel when they told you your mother had died?"

Fool, slow-top, bloody ass. Ian had been in the room when . . .

He was there now. Ian froze in growing horror as his father's study formed around him, every piece of furniture placed exactly as he remembered it. The painting of Kilmorgan and portraits of Mackenzie ancestors marched up the walls, and the windows, open, had no curtains, because his father disliked dusty brocade drapes and had ordered them pulled down.

Ian saw himself, a small boy, come alert as he heard voices in the hall. He crawled quickly under the huge desk, where he folded himself into a terrified ball.

His father burst into the room, shouting—he always shouted—and Ian paid no attention to the words. Only the duke's voice, filling the space, vibrated Ian's bones.

His mother came after her husband, weeping, pleading. "I never did. You are mistaken."

"I'm a liar, now, am I?" the duke demanded, his Scots voice flowing in Ian's memory. "I didn't see ye fluttering your eyes, twitching your skirts, making sure your bosom rose high? He's my friend. *Was*. He'll be denied the house now."

"I've never betrayed you." Ian's mother had been a frail creature, but he heard now the desperate steel in her voice, the sincerity. "Never."

The duke rounded on her, shouting into her face. "I *saw*. I saw the looks passing between the pair of ye, the way ye dote on him, making sure the servants tend to his every need."

"He is our guest." Tears streamed down the duchess's thin, ethereal face. "I do such things for all our guests."

"No!" The duke had his hands on her arms. "Do not mock me, wife. *Wife*—ye make the word a travesty. I know what I see. I see a woman lusting after a man in me own house. How many of my good-for-nothing sons are truly mine? Is this why Mac fills his copybooks with drawings of flowers? He's no Mackenzie. I'll break his fingers, all of them. Hart defies me to my face, and *Ian* . . . a dolt and backward fool, can't even understand a simple word ye say to him . . ."

"They're *your* sons." His mother's voice broke with her sobs. "All of them. I love them so."

The duke shook her. "What did I tell ye about making them soft? The only one who's mine is Cam—the others, by-blows of your lovers."

Ian's mother couldn't speak anymore, and her eyes squeezed tight against her tears. She was so much smaller than her husband, her dark hair soft, her arms too thin, but they'd felt just right when she'd put them around Ian.

"Why are ye doing this to me?" The duke's words rang

against the ceiling. Ian watched himself draw into a tighter ball, but he was not crying. His eyes had been dry and burning.

His father had released the duchess for a moment, but only to slam the door and turn the key in the lock.

"Now, woman, you're going to tell me th' truth!"

"You used to love me," Ian's mother sobbed. "Why, why did you stop?"

"Stop?" The duke gave her an incredulous look. "I never stopped. What is the matter with ye? Ye're a weak fool, ye always were, but I gave you *everything*. Ye repay me by making soft eyes at that bloody Carmichael. I'll kill him!"

"No." The duchess's eyes widened, shining with fear. "No, leave him be, for God's sake."

The duke stopped. Ian, watching now with adult understanding, saw that until this moment his father had not truly believed his wife had fallen in love with another. He'd been blustering as usual, wanting to bring the duchess to heel, to make her tell him he was the most important thing in her life—more so than her sons, herself, her own happiness.

In the moment the duke had threatened the hapless Lord Carmichael, and Ian's mother begged him to leave Carmichael alone, he'd realized. She'd not pleaded because she feared what would happen to the duke if he committed murder, but because Carmichael's life was precious to her.

That moment changed everything. The duke's berserker rage burst out of him, a bellow that shook the walls, smothering the duchess's cries and Ian's small moan of distress.

"Lying, filthy *bitch*!"

He seized her. The duchess screamed in terror, but the duke's violence seemed to unleash something inside her.

"Yes!" she choked out. "I love him. I'm leaving with him. Divorce me if you please, ruin me, but leave him alone!"

"Bloody, stinking, dirty whore . . ."

"Let me *go*!"

The duke's eyes brightened with fury. He shook her,

shook her, hard, harder, while Ian's mother pleaded, and her husband called her terrible names.

And then came the sound Ian had never forgotten. The duke's strength had overwhelmed the smaller, weaker body of the duchess. Her head had rocked back on her neck as he shook her.

One audible snap, and the duchess's head rolled to the side, her cries cutting off, her eyes becoming wide and staring.

The duke had kept on shaking her until he realized that he held a limp bundle of limbs. Then he dropped her. "Elspeth." He fell to his knees beside her, his eyes wide in shock. *"Elspeth."*

He put his hand on her chest and jostled her, rolling her body back and forth. The movement came faster as he couldn't make her respond.

"Elspeth!"

A cry of anguish jerked from deep within him, and the boy Ian couldn't contain his faint sound of despair.

That tiny gasp sealed Ian's fate. His father rose like a terrible god, gaze going unerringly to the shadow under the desk. The duke reached in and pulled out Ian, who struggled futilely against the grip that had just killed his mother.

"Ye tell no one." His father's eyes had been wide, mad, filled with a horror so deep it had pierced into Ian and nestled there. *"No one!* Answer me, boy. Promise!"

Ian could only hang in his grasp, terrified, grief-stricken, knowing in the next moment, he would die.

The duke strode to the door on the opposite side of the room, opened it, and threw Ian face-first into the corridor. He slammed the door, and locked it.

Ian's perspective switched to that barren hall, as he hauled himself to his feet and ran. *Run, run, run.* Down through the house, out into the day, *keep running.* Ian sped far over the Kilmorgan lands, unaware of which direction he'd headed, until his legs gave out, and he had to stop. His breath came in shuddering gasps, his head spinning with lack of air.

Finally, Ian fell to the mud and grass, at last his throat opened, and the roar of anguish came out.

"Nooooo!"

Ian heard it even now, echoing around him, the word turning to a wordless keening. He felt carpet at his back instead of earth, heard his deep voice tearing through the room.

He opened his eyes, which had flooded with tears. Through the blur, Ian saw John Ackerley gazing down at him in concern, the coin frozen in his hand.

"What did you see?" Ackerley asked breathlessly. "What is it? Have we found the trigger?"

"He killed her, ye gobshite!" Ian thrust himself up on his elbows, his face wet, his throat raw. "Killed her in front of me."

"Who?" Ackerley asked, fearful. "Your brother . . . ?"

"No, ye pox-rotted simpleton. M' dad. He killed m' mum as I sat and watched. And I did nothing. *Nothing!*" Ian scrambled to his feet, his berserker rage, the curse of the Mackenzies, flooding him. "Do ye think *that* drove me mad? It didn't. I was mad before that. I have always been. I couldn't stop him, because I was too small and too *insane* to know what t' do."

Ackerley could only stare, opening and closing his mouth. He clutched the coin, which glinted in his hand as though satisfied.

The door banged open with a jarring noise, but the rustle of skirts that accompanied it was like gentle rain on Ian's soul.

Beth was in front of Ian in an instant, facing Ackerley. The scent of her hair put paid to Ian's remembered stench of fear.

"What the devil are you doing?" Beth snapped at Ackerley. "What have you been saying to him?"

"I . . ." Ackerley's face had gone red, his eyes moistening. "I never meant . . . I was trying to help."

Ian closed his arms around Beth. "He's making me remember," he said, his voice hoarse and broken. "But *you* make me forget. My Beth, help me forget."

Chapter 12

Beth's heart wrenched as she felt her husband's arms around her, his strong embrace one of need.

John Ackerley stood before them both, looking thoroughly ashamed of himself, and sorry too. He was a kind man underneath, Beth knew, as Thomas had been, though a bit naïve. Well, Thomas had been naïve as well, hadn't he?

"What on earth have you done, John?" Beth asked. Naivety was no excuse for bedeviling her husband.

"I . . ." John glanced at the coin in his hand as though it were to blame. He held it up, sheepish. "Trying a bit of mesmerism. It works wonders."

"I have also heard of its dangers," Beth said tightly. "Why would you try such a thing on Ian? I do not recall you mentioning you were an expert on the technique."

"Well, no," John said in a small voice. "I've only done it once before. But with good results—the young man remembered things he'd buried long ago."

Beth held out her hand. "Give me that."

John gave the coin another bewildered look. "This?"

"Yes." Beth reached out and took it from him. "No more of this nonsense."

She closed her fist around the coin at the same moment Hart decided to storm in.

"What the devil is happening?" Hart was every inch the duke, forbidding, hard-faced, staring down Ackerley, who looked as though he wanted to crawl under the table.

Ian leaned over Beth, burying his face in her neck. She felt dampness on her skin, Ian's tears.

"Never mind, Hart," Beth said. "It is finished."

Hart ignored her. "Tell me, man," he snapped at Ackerley.

Ackerley buckled under Hart's stare. "I was . . . I was . . . It is a very sound, scientific technique, being tested in Vienna. Quite well accepted." Ackerley gave both Hart and Beth a defiant look.

"Scientific shite." Hart's snarl held his deep fear for and protectiveness of Ian, which always came out in Mackenzie anger.

Ian raised his head. Beth felt Ian's body strengthening, the muddle he'd been sinking into easing away. "Leave him be, Hart."

"I heard you yelling all the way downstairs, Ian." Hart returned his stare to Ackerley. "It's best *you* take yourself elsewhere for a time." His rumble grew louder. *"Now."*

"Oh, for heaven's sake," Beth began, when Ian gently pressed her aside.

Ian's eyes were red-rimmed and wet, his face mottled, his breath ragged. He clenched his large fists, the hands rough from wind and weather. "Hart, I said *leave him be.*"

"Not until you tell me exactly what is going on. Who is this charlatan?"

The brothers faced each other, so alike, yet with ten years' difference between the two. Their hair was a few shades of red apart, but their eyes held the same golden intensity, neither giving way to the other.

"Ian," Hart said, impatient.

"He's curin' me," Ian said. "Leave him alone."

Beth drew a sharp breath. "Curing?" She looked at

Ackerley, who opened his mouth to explain. Beth held up one finger, and Ackerley popped his mouth closed again.

Hart had gone dark red. "What the hell kind of shite has he filled your head with, Ian? If he said that, he *is* a charlatan, a quack. Beth, I know he's your acquaintance, but this needs to cease."

Ian took yet another step to Hart, forcing Hart's attention solely to him. Ian was looking into Hart's eyes, a natural act for most people, but one Ian had struggled to master. Hart fell silent, quelled by the gaze of the little brother who'd taken so long to learn even this simple feat.

"He's family," Ian said. The rawness had left his voice, and control returned. "He is Beth's family, which makes him *my* family."

Hart could look at nothing but Ian.

Beth realized Hart no longer noticed Ackerley or even Beth, or the curious servants peering into the room—one of which was Curry. Beth heard Curry saying, "Let me in there, ye daft cove. I need to look after 'im."

Hart was caught in the moment of Ian standing straight and strong, no longer the terrified, confused youth or the quieter man who'd withdrawn inside a shell his brothers couldn't breach.

Ian regarded Hart with an anger as sharp as Hart's own, speaking in a commanding tone that came as naturally as breathing.

Hart's eyes glistened, and something like a shudder went through him. "I don't want him to hurt you, Ian."

"He's an old man," Ian said, jerking a thumb at Ackerley. "He can't hurt me. I won't let him. The past can't hurt me. It's gone."

Hart went quiet again for another long stretch. Beth could almost see the thoughts in Hart's head, his arguments, his pain.

Finally, Hart gave Ian a nod and cupped his shoulder

with a big hand. "You're right, Ian. The past, it's gone. For-ever. *Now* is what's important."

Ian gave Hart the look he got when he was impatient at another person's slowness. "I know. *Trust me.*"

Hart let out his breath. "All right then. I ask your pardon, Beth. And Ackerley."

He said the last awkwardly, as though the apology came out with the greatest reluctance. He didn't trust Ackerley an inch, it was clear. Of course, Beth, at the moment, didn't trust him much either.

The awkwardness shattered when another voice, clear and feminine, came down the hall.

"Good heavens, what is all the ruckus? Is there a circus performance?" Eleanor pushed through the servants, who had stepped backward in hasty deference and also relief. The duch-ess was here, and all would be well.

Eleanor took in the situation with quick, shrewd eyes as her tongue rattled on. "Hart, why is all our artwork in a jum-bled pile in the hall, ready to be trodden on? It must be sorted through, cleaned, restored. Ian, so clever of you to have found it. Hart, darling, since the frame is ruined, *can* we send that Raphael to a museum? I know art critics like to come here and coo over the thing, but it gives me the shivers every time I look at it. Let them coo over it in a museum far from here. Now, Mr. Ackerley, we will have a lovely tea out on the terrace—such a nice afternoon. Beth, come along and help me arrange it. You know I get into sixes and sevens about everything."

Her stream of chatter continuing, the duchess swept out, servants hastening to obey her scattered commands. Hart, his face like thunder, moved at a quick pace in her wake.

Beth turned to the bewildered Ackerley. "What Eleanor really means is that we should all leave you alone and cease interfering. Just be careful." She gave Ackerley a stern look. "We love him."

"I only want *you* to love me, Beth," Ian rumbled behind her. A hand landed on her shoulder, warm, strong, caressing. "Hart can lose himself." Ian leaned down and pressed a kiss to Beth's cheek.

The kiss sent fire through her blood, which would warm her until she could be alone with him again. Beth kissed Ian's cheek in return, then rustled away to leave Ian to do what he felt he must.

As she closed the door, she heard Ian rumble, his timbre restored to normal, "All right, then, what do we do next?"

Beth had little time to speak to John alone until after tea. Eleanor could send the household scurrying in all directions when she set her mind to it. She kept Beth plenty busy, which Beth understood was Eleanor's way of making sure Ian was left in peace.

Beth worried, however. The past ten years had taught her that Ian had resilience, and plenty of it. And yet, small things could trouble him, like tiny sparks from a firework, seeking to burn away that resiliency.

Ian seemed calm enough during tea—that is to say he inhaled an entire plate of cakes and downed several dainty cups of steaming oolong as though it were cool water. Beth pretended not to notice Curry dribbling a tiny amount of whisky into Ian's cup.

Afterward, Ian went to the children, but Beth lingered and cornered Ackerley in an empty hall.

"I know you mean well," Beth began. "At least, I trust you do."

Ackerley regarded her with eyes so like Thomas's. "Of course I mean well, dearest sister-in-law. Why wouldn't I?"

Beth held on to her patience. "It is just . . . Too many people have been interested in Ian. The doctors at the asylum used him as a showpiece. When we travel, everyone from learned physicians to outright confidence men want a look at him. Ian is excellent at ignoring these people, but now you are telling him you can *cure* him? That might be rather cruel, do you not think?"

Ackerley's bewilderment was true. "Gracious, I would never do anything to hurt you. Or your husband. Thomas was a saint, as you know, and I'd never attempt to harm anyone he loved. I truly believe I can help."

"Ian believes it." Beth knew inside herself that John was not evil. He might act from ignorance but not malice. "Which is rather more worrying."

Ackerley put his hand to his heart. "I give you my word that if I think my methods are injuring Lord Ian in any way, I will cease."

"He might not let you cease," Beth pointed out. "Ian can be quite persuasive."

"Yes, I see that." Ackerley's expression softened. "He persuaded you to marry him when you had no intention of marrying again after your broken engagement, or so you claimed in your letters. You love Lord Ian very much, don't you?"

"I do." Beth felt a swell of affection. "Ian is . . . unlike any other man in the world. This is not to detract from Thomas at all—please understand. What I had with Thomas was special. Ian is different, but Thomas wasn't lesser."

"No, he wasn't." Ackerley's sorrow showed in his eyes. "I still miss him, dash it all."

Beth put her hand on his arm. "I know. Let us make a pact—after the chaos of Hart's birthday ends, we will sit down and talk all about Thomas. Remember him properly, his good deeds, and when he made us laugh at him."

"Excellent." Ackerley gave her a nod. "You are a fine woman, dear Beth."

"Thank you." Beth patted him, then stepped away. "Just be careful with Ian. And make sure he is careful with you. If you need to break through that stubborn Mackenzie façade, you come to me. Promise?"

"I do, indeed," Ackerley said.

Beth let him go then, and Ackerley turned away, looking vastly relieved the interview was over.

~~~~~

Beth was going to scold him. Ian knew that as they met in the nursery that evening to put the children to bed.

Jamie, along with Hart's son and heir, Alec, had received permission to share a bedroom two doors down, older boys together—no girls. Ian said good night to Jamie and sent him and Alec off with Eleanor, then he and Beth turned to tucking in their daughters, and Hart's very young son, Malcolm.

"Papa," Belle said to Ian as Beth settled Megan. "Aunt Eleanor says you've asked Uncle John to cure you of your madness. But you're not mad, Papa." Her expressive face furrowed. "'Centric, certainly. Not mad. I've been reading about madness in my books. You don't appear to have any of the symptoms the physicians write about. You don't talk to people who aren't there, or wear clothes wrong, or forget who you are and how to find your way home."

Ian became aware that Beth, at Megan's bed, had stilled to listen.

"'Tis not that sort of madness, love," Ian said to Belle.

"There isn't another sort," Belle answered with conviction. "I'm going to be a doctor, you know. I've been studying."

Ian had no idea how to reply. Beth always did, but Beth now seemed incapable of speech.

Ian had spent all afternoon with Ackerley, while Ackerley asked Ian more and more questions about his earliest memories. Ackerley had wanted to know about Ian's need to run when faced with unpleasant situations, and delved into Ian's hatred of his father, which had begun long before the awful day of his mother's death. Ian had found himself pouring out the details of his life. It had been almost a relief to share the memories, even as they hurt.

Daughter Belle reached out and touched Ian's hand. "You see? You are not mad, Papa. You may cease worrying about it."

Ian studied her for a long time, Belle with her quick thoughts and love of books. She was smart and resourceful, and a quick learner, like Ian was. His pride in her ran deep.

He wasn't certain how to answer Belle, so Ian pressed a kiss to her forehead. Belle, satisfied she'd solved all the problems, smiled and closed her eyes.

Ian went to Megan's bed, stooping to kiss her as well. Megan said sleepily, "Love you, Papa," and snuggled down with her velvet stuffed giraffe.

Beth took Ian's hand and led him from the room, not letting go until they entered their own chamber downstairs.

Yes, Beth was going to scold. Ian watched her firm her shoulders, draw a breath, and harden her expression. Only one thing to do.

He reached to Beth's bodice and started undoing her buttons. A row of them, black and shining, marched to her waistband, the placket parting to show Ian the silk and lace she wore underneath.

Beth's undergarments were sleek and smooth—she did not like the excessive frills, ribbons, laces, and bows that other women did. Ian preferred Beth's style, which allowed him to run his hand over silk and feel the warm woman beneath.

Styles of dress had changed in the ten years Ian and Beth had been married, and so had undergarments. Beth didn't favor the full corset that covered the hips—hers stopped at her waist, its low décolletage cupping softness.

Beth's body was a song to him. Music rippled through Ian when he touched her, growing fuller and more melodious the more his hands found. Her waistband opened under his fingers, and as her skirts and petticoats fell away, he slid his touch to the swell of her hips, the fullness of her buttocks.

Ian kissed Beth's neck while he caressed her then drew his hands up her back to open the corset cover and pull loose the laces of her stays.

Beth hummed in her throat as she flowed to him. He heard her take another breath, steeling herself to continue her lecture, and Ian bit her now-bare shoulder.

"Ian." The whisper floated around him. Ian closed his mouth on her skin and suckled.

Heat ran through him as he remembered the joy of teaching her about love bites, the remarkable day she'd approached him and asked him whether he would mind if they became lovers.

Ian still had not recovered from the stunning blow of that question. The beautiful woman who'd fallen into his life and left him dizzy had asked *him* to be her lover.

Ian, not being a fool, had immediately acquiesced.

"Ian, we must talk." The words held no conviction, Beth's resolve failing her as Ian tasted her warmth.

Ian finished the love bite and licked the reddening patch on her shoulder. He also kissed the darker red of the bite he'd left last night.

The corset came away, the laces fluttering as it fell to the carpet. Beneath was another thin garment, combinations that hugged Beth's body from shoulders to knees.

She never believed Ian when he told her how beautiful she was in her combinations. The fabric outlined her breasts, waist, hips, legs, enhancing the plump softness of Beth's body. Now that she'd borne three children, Beth thought herself too sagging, but Ian saw nothing wrong. She was *his* Beth, her body as enticing and beautiful as when he'd unwrapped her for the first time.

Ian kissed his way down her body, landing on his knees, which were cushioned by his kilt. He skimmed his hand over the abdomen that had cradled his children, the miracles that were Jamie, Belle, and Megan.

She'd given him life many times over.

"There's no honey in the house," Ian said, pressing a kiss to her stomach through the fabric.

"No? Oh." Beth moved on restless feet. "That is a pity."

"Only yours." Ian reached up to peel the combinations down her body, taking her stockings as he went. The garments fell away, opening her to him like a gift.

Nothing was better than Beth's own honey, welcoming his mouth. Ian drank her in dark enjoyment, while Beth's bare toes curled on the carpet. Her fingers closed on his hair, the sounds coming from her throat making his already tight hardness tighter still.

Ian collapsed onto his back and lay full length on the floor. Beth remained above him, staring down at him. Ian enjoyed the view of her full breasts, curve of hip, curls of dark hair now damp where he'd licked her.

He looked his fill for a few moments, then Ian reached up, locked strong hands on her waist, and pulled his wife down to him. Beth came willingly, her smile widening. Ian fumbled his plaid aside and brought her to him, Beth's body pliant and warm.

Soon Ian's beautiful Beth was surrounding him as he eased her to straddle him, and he slid deep inside her. Her eyes half closed as she rocked on him, her soft breasts swaying as Ian began to thrust.

No matter how mad Ian might be, *this* was never maddening. Sweet Beth made love to him without shyness, without shame. Her truest feelings showed on her face, sounded in her voice.

"Love you, my Beth," Ian said as he came into her, faster, harder. Beth's head went back as she gave herself to pure joy. "Love you, love you, love you."

Ever since the day he'd learned to say it, Ian had formed those words in his mouth, savored them, *understood* them. Beth had given him this.

Beth's cries rang out as she found her deepest pleasure. "I love you, Ian Mackenzie—I do love you so *much.*"

Yes, my Beth. This is love—and madness has no place here.

Beth collapsed on top of Ian, spent and breathless, at the same time his white-hot release flooded him, and he sent his seed hard into her. "Beth, m'Beth, *love you.*"

Ian fell back, gathering the woman he loved more than his own life into his arms, and everything went impossibly still.

Chapter 13

Fellows returned from London by the overnight train, bringing with him his efficient former sergeant, Pierce, now an inspector in his own right.

Pierce had met the Mackenzie family before, but he'd never been to Kilmorgan. As the coach moved over the bridge and the enormous house spread before them, Pierce let out a whistle.

"Blimey, that's a pile. Why don't you quit policing and move in here, sir?" He looked around in wonderment. "His Grace the duke's always eager to share with you, so you tell me. I say take him up on it."

"You'll understand in a day or two," Fellows answered. "I like my job, Pierce."

Pierce's eyes glinted with humor. "Tell you what, sir. You keep on doing your job to please yourself, but hand over all your salary to me, seeing as you are so high-minded that you turn down riches and work for pleasure."

Fellows sent him a quelling look, and Pierce answered with a delighted laugh. "You're a snob, sir," Pierce said. "You just don't want to be posh."

No, Fellows didn't. For all his rage in his younger years

that his mother wore herself out on the keeping of him
while the Mackenzies lacked for nothing, Fellows now realized he didn't resent them for the material goods they
owned, or even for their money.

As a child, Fellows hadn't understood what made him so
angry, but as an adult, he knew that he'd simply wanted to
be acknowledged. Even if the old duke hadn't given him a
penny, Fellows had wanted the man to look at him and concede that Fellows was his son.

The duke never had. He'd died without admitting he'd
fathered Lloyd, hadn't recognized Lloyd when he'd seen
him on the street. The bitterness of that rejection had run
deep.

It still did, but Lloyd no longer blamed the Mackenzie
brothers for it. They'd suffered at the hands of the old duke
far more than Lloyd had. Fellows had come to find common
ground with them, and even liking.

Cameron, for instance, had become a good friend. Cameron was largehearted and generous, and he and Fellows
attended the races together, enjoying the finest whisky afterward. Cam was also at home in the pubs in Fellows's neigh-
borhood, easily lifting a pint in Fellows's local and talking
readily with his friends. Fellows didn't understand Mac as
much, but he appreciated the painting Mac had done of
Louisa and their children, as a gift to Fellows. Mac too had
a wide streak of generosity in him.

Hart and Ian were tougher nuts to crack. Ian possessed
the same openheartedness as his brothers, though not as
obviously. The amount of money Ian Mackenzie donated to
the care and study of the infirm and the mad was incredible. At one time, a research hospital had wanted to name a
wing after him, and Ian had refused. He hadn't done it for
the building, he'd said, but for the people inside it.

And then there was Hart, a man who'd had to hold himself distant for so long that he had no idea how to open to
others. Eleanor had pried him loose, that was certain, and

Hart was most loving to her and his children. Even so, for a man who was so eloquent in his speeches to Parliament, Hart had difficulty talking casually to others.

He'd softened a huge amount in the last ten years, Fellows had to admit, and the two of them had become much more comfortable with each other. Fellows now had no difficulty running lightly up the stairs to Hart's study when he reached the house, without asking the majordomo to announce him.

Hart called, "Come," when Fellows tapped on the door, and rose to cross the room and warmly shake Fellows's hand when he entered. Fellows returned the grip then turned to present Inspector Pierce.

Hart nodded at the man and shook his hand in turn. "Pleased to see you again, Pierce."

"I've come to tell you a story," Fellows said, accepting the whisky Hart poured after they'd exchanged greetings and settled in. Though it was early, Fellows wasn't fool enough to turn down the famous Mackenzie malt no matter what the hour.

"Once upon a time . . ." Fellows sat back in his chair, took a sip of whisky, and savored its smooth heat. "There was a man who collected art, though he was not particular how he came by it. He hired the best of thieves to bring him works of art he craved, and paid them thousands of pounds for it. I was a sergeant at the time this man 'collected,' and worked with an inspector tasked to finding the thieves he used and bringing them in. We couldn't touch the man; that had been made clear."

"Who was it?" Hart asked.

He'd seated himself again, not at his desk, but on a wide chair, his kilt falling modestly over his knees. Hart had declared he'd never wear anything but a kilt in his family's plaid until Scotland was free of England's yoke.

"Lord Ethan Sedgwick," Fellows said. "Now recently deceased."

"Mm." Hart didn't look one bit surprised. "Sedgwick was always an arrogant bastard. Did you catch his pet thieves?"

"That we did," Fellows said. "My inspector at the time, Radcliffe, left the details to me. I got a man inside Sedgwick's house as a footman, and he obtained plenty of information. Sedgwick was one who didn't believe servants could see or hear, so he wasn't careful about closing doors when discussing business. After a few months of surveillance, we knew what artwork he wanted to obtain, where it was, and when the thieves were going to steal it. It was only a matter of getting policemen into place and nabbing the thieves when they came out with the goods."

Hart shot him a narrow look. "Sounds ideal."

Fellows paused to take a deep drink. The humiliation of the failure still bit.

"Wait 'til you hear the rest," Pierce said to Hart. "Before my time, but I remember the air was pretty thick about it even when I was a young constable."

"We caught the thieves," Fellows said after letting a quantity of whisky float down his throat. "They had the painting they'd gone to nab all right, but in exchange for making sure they didn't get the noose, the thieves talked. Told us all about Sedgwick and the things they'd stolen for him over the years and where he kept them. While I knew I could not arrest Sedgwick—or at least, I'd been told not to—I saw no reason I shouldn't find the stolen artwork and return it to its rightful owners. So, I went to the place where Sedgwick kept his private collection—a sort of summerhouse on his grounds. Not well guarded, the idiot. I went inside and found a veritable museum. He'd stolen every old master he could put his hands on—Rembrandt, Rubens, Raphael, van Dyck, Holbein, Velázquez . . . more I didn't know. A stockpile that would astonish you."

"I am suitably astonished," Hart said mildly. "Are you telling me these same thieves have done me over?"

"No." Fellows shook his head. "Let me explain. I returned to London and reported to Inspector Radcliffe. I told him I'd secured the latest painting Sedgwick had caused to be stolen, though I'd leave to him the decision whether to arrest Sedgwick for receiving stolen goods and hiring the thieves for the rest of it.

"Radcliffe was furious with me. Sedgwick and his father, a marquis, had a lot of pull in the Home Office and could make life difficult for those of us in Scotland Yard. Radcliffe told me that simply by investigating Sedgwick I'd forfeited my career, and his, and that of anyone who'd assisted me. I was to stand down, turn my back, pretend I'd never seen the paintings, get the thieves a conviction for what I'd actually caught them stealing, and that would be that."

Hart's eyes were alight with interest now. "But you, being you, could not do that."

"Of course not. I returned to Sedgwick's estate, intending to box up the art as evidence. The law was the law, even for the too-rich son of an English marquis."

Hart grunted a laugh. "What happened? I see that you're still alive."

"The chief inspector—Radcliffe's superior—surprisingly backed me. He was tired of aristocrats getting away with high crime and wanted to make an example of Sedgwick. He went with me to supervise shipping the artwork back to London. But when we got to Sedgwick's home, the paintings were gone. Every single one. The frames of many were left, the paintings cut out. Sedgwick, smiling like a naughty schoolboy—he was fifty at the time—told us he'd been burgled."

"Obnoxious bastard," Hart rumbled. "Always was. His father with him."

"Sedgwick's father decided that the chief inspector who supported me was to blame for persecuting his son and had the man dismissed. Thirty years the DCI had given to policing, and he was turned out without a shilling. Radcliffe, who had tried to prevent the mess, was spared, as was I, but I received a severe reprimand, and I nearly lost my newly acquired rank of detective sergeant. The Home Office decided I'd acted from naivety, not malice, and let me remain, though I wouldn't be allowed to work on any more sensitive cases."

Hart pressed his fingertips together as Fellows spoke, a sparkle in his golden eyes. "I am going to wager that didn't stop you either."

Fellows took another sip of whisky. "I investigated the so-called burglary on the sly. I knew Sedgwick had hidden the paintings, waiting for the day we stopped paying attention. He'd restore them to his collection room, and no one would be the wiser. Except . . . I found them."

Hart gave him a frown. "I know you're not suggesting that Sedgwick hired a set of thieves to turn over Kilmorgan. Sedgwick is dead, and his father. Sedgwick had no heirs, and the marquisate reverted to the Crown. Or is it some beloved retainer of his waiting this long to gain Sedgwick's revenge on you—using me to do it?"

Hart didn't believe any of this, Fellows knew. He was outlining possibilities, as he liked to do. Hart was always thorough.

"Sedgwick had nothing to do with your theft," Fellows continued. "The similarity lies in the state in which I found the art stolen for him. There was a deep pit on Sedgwick's estate, an old pond that had been drained at some point in the past. The art was buried there—and not very well. Rolled up and dumped, covered with a tarp to keep out the weather. Pictures still in frames stacked up, much of it ruined.

"Sedgwick was outraged when I found it, of course. He didn't care that many of the paintings had been destroyed by his act—if he couldn't have the art, he said, then no one could. I believe he was a bit disturbed in the mind."

"A bit," Hart said, his tone drier still.

"Even when I presented the evidence to the highest authority, little was done. At the time, Sedgwick's father had too much influence. The artwork that wasn't destroyed was quietly restored to the original owners, and nothing was ever said. Sedgwick went on collecting art, though never again through theft. His father had a talk with him about that, from what I understand."

"The old marquis was a hard man," Hart said. "If it makes you feel better, I imagine his chat with Sedgwick was more effective than imprisonment or transportation." He paused. "You found the art in the same condition you found mine, thrown away to rot. Whoever did that knew the story of what had happened with Sedgwick. Or, it's an amazing coincidence—and I don't believe in those."

"Nor do I," Fellows said. "Back then I still could not drop the matter. I kept digging until I found out who had warned Sedgwick that I was retuning for the art, who had helped him with the fake burglary, who had suggested the removal of the chief inspector, leaving the way open for a promotion. I had suspected, but became certain when I was invited to Inspector Radcliffe's home, and his wife served me tea under the very Raphael that eventually made its way to *your* house. I had seen it among Sedgwick's collection in his summerhouse, but it hadn't been among the paintings he'd thrown away."

Hart's brows climbed high. "Inspector Radcliffe took a payoff?"

"He did indeed." Fellows remembered the anger, the betrayal he'd felt. His own inspector, whose cleverness he'd admired, had been corrupt and a party to fraud. "Their plan was for Sedgwick to have himself robbed and claim insurance on the paintings he'd acquired legitimately. The stolen paintings would vanish—no proof he ever had them. Radcliffe was rewarded with one to make sure no one found out." Fellows took a final sip of whisky, letting the past fall away. "He received me in the room where he'd hung the Raphael, thinking me too stupid to know what it was. I went back to Scotland Yard and anonymously sent a report of Radcliffe's involvement to the very top of the chain, to a trustworthy man who couldn't be toppled. Anonymously, because I'd learned my lesson about announcing my findings. I sat back and waited for the music to play. Which it did, eventually. Radcliffe was arrested but the charges dismissed. He retained his job as a policeman but was sent to some backwater to rusticate the rest of his days."

"Is he still living?" Hart asked. "Is this *his* revenge on you? Why wait twenty years for it?"

Fellows shook his head. "Radcliffe is dead. Everyone connected with the case has passed on, including my DCI and the man I informed of Radcliffe's connection."

Hart shot him an impatient look. "Then why tell me the story?"

"Ian suggested I dredge it up," Fellows said. "And since Ian has an uncanny way of being right, I went back to London and went through my old case files. I kept notes at the time, and reread them all. I suggest that someone else knows the story and decided to make use of it. Perhaps they want to imply that you had the artwork stolen yourself for the insurance. The paintings were stashed where they'd eventually be found in order to embarrass you or ruin you." Fellows shrugged. "Something."

Hart went silent a moment, his hands stilling on the arms of his chair. "I have too many enemies," he said after a time. "Any number of them could have decided to come after me. I am trying to think which of them would likely know of this story."

"Very few do," Fellows said. "Radcliffe's role was hushed up, because the Yard didn't need the scandal. Sedgwick's father also made sure most of the details stayed hidden."

"Did Radcliffe have sons?" Hart asked. "Sedgwick

didn't, we know. Did Sedgwick have daughters? Women can be as vengeful as men. More so, in my opinion."

"Radcliffe's children predeceased him, and Sedgwick had no issue at all," Fellows said. "There was rumor Sedgwick was as impotent as a dead fish."

Pierce snorted a laugh. "Never shirk at a bad word about your betters, do you, sir?"

Fellows gave him a chilly look. "Sedgwick might have been born to a higher station in life, but I wouldn't consider him better for it."

Pierce only grinned, undaunted. "It's a pleasure to work for you, sir."

"Fellows is refreshingly unbiased when it comes to the aristocracy," Hart said, meeting his half brother's gaze. "He has always been so."

Fellows lifted his whisky glass to Hart, and they shared a look. The two had been through much, but it was a fine thing to have buried their enmity in the past. Fellows had found a like mind in Hart, and he was proud to call him brother.

Beth scrambled out of bed the next morning and hurried to insert herself in front of her husband, who was about to leave the room.

The scoundrel had loved her well into the night, effectively making sure she had no opportunity to speak with him. Every time she'd opened her mouth, she'd found it engaged with something interesting. Ian had kissed her gently as she'd fallen asleep, spooned against him, and she'd known nothing more until she felt Ian's warmth leave the bed.

He'd pulled on a kilt, likely planning to slip into the dressing room to shrug on whatever clothes he found and be gone before Beth could catch him. It did not help Beth's resolve that Ian, wearing nothing but a kilt around his hips, the sun catching the red of his hair, was a heart-stopping sight. Ten years had not diminished him—his habits of walking, riding, fishing, and tramping over the Highlands kept him fit and hard-muscled.

Thinking of those strong hands fitting themselves to her breasts, waist, hips, lifting her to him in the night didn't help either. Beth wanted to kiss her way down his bare chest to his abdomen, follow the thin arrow of hair to the waistband of his kilt.

She forced her gaze from his delectable body and cleared her throat. "Ian, we need to talk."

Ian gazed at the open hall beyond her, as though willing Curry to charge along and interrupt the scene. "I'm late."

"Your own fault," Beth said. "If you'd not kept us awake most of the night . . ." Ian's eyes flicked back to her and filled with warmth, the corners of his lips curving.

Beth waved her hands at him. "Stop that. You know I want to scold you for letting John talk you into believing he can *cure* you. What on earth makes you think so? He is no physician or scientist—he's a missionary who has too much curiosity than is good for him. Thomas was the same. Besides, Belle is right—there is nothing wrong with you."

Beth let the words tumble out quickly, because she knew Ian could simply lift her aside and go if he wanted.

Ian lost his half smile. "You have always known that I am not . . . right." He pressed his forefinger to his temple. "Not like my brothers."

"Thank heavens for that," Beth said fervently. "You recall I met Mac and Cameron before I married you. And then I met Hart, which clinched the matter. I definitely chose the right Mackenzie."

Red crept into Ian's cheeks. "They do things I can't."

"What of it? None of the rest of you can paint as Mac does—I don't believe Cam knows which end of a brush is which, yet I do not see him yearning to be just like Mac."

"Not what I meant."

Ian's golden eyes took on a slight look of distress, but there was something else in them today, some distraction she didn't understand.

Beth pointed a stiff finger at his chest. "I know exactly what you mean, Ian Mackenzie. You are an arrogant Mackenzie male. You are brilliant and your family loves you, but that's not enough for you. You want to waltz into a card room and be the life of the party. You want to have people fluttering over you, hoping to befriend you because you charm them." Beth took a step closer to him. "Well, let me tell you, if I'd wanted a smarmy, unctuous husband, I'd have married Lyndon Mather and been done. I threw him over for you, if you recall. He was horrible, which you so bluntly pointed out to me, but that was not the only reason I jilted him. I'd met *you*, and knew I'd found the better man. I knew I'd never be pleased with anyone else. I do not want you or John upsetting that better man and taking him away from me—can you understand? *Ian . . ."*

Ian's gaze had drifted from her again, his brows lowering as he studied a point on the wall behind her.

Beth knew she'd lost him. She'd made her speech too long, and somewhere in the middle, Ian had drifted away to one of the hundreds of thoughts that spun constantly in his head.

"Ian—"

"You jilted him." Ian kept his gaze on the wall. "Threw him over."

"I've just said. Gladly. You will also remember that he recovered and married another heiress, and they are both living with his mother somewhere in Kent."

Ian wasn't listening to a word. He'd gone off somewhere in that brain of his, thinking, thinking, thinking.

Ian put his hands on Beth's shoulders, moved her aside, and walked out of the room past her, ignoring her reaching fingers. *"Curry!"*

Beth rushed after him, but Ian had started for the main

staircase, his loose kilt swirling around his bare legs. "Ian?"

She reached the staircase as Curry came out of a back passage. "Ye bellowed, me lord?" the small man asked. "Can ye not yank on a bell, like the rest of your family?"

"Find me clothes," Ian growled at him as he started up the stairs.

"Oh yes?" Curry asked, watching him. "And where am I to put them on you? In the attics, is it?"

"Aye!" Ian called down as he quickened his stride. The kilt moved to show Beth his strong thighs and a glimpse of firm backside, and then he was gone.

Chapter 14

Some part of Ian's mind told him the household was upset at him again, but that part was a dim, flickering voice. The foremost part of his mind told him that the answer to the mystery lay in Fellows's old case and in the attics.

Curry carried up an armful of garments as Ian started through the stacks of journals he sought. Curry muttered and grumbled as he always did, but that was Curry. Ian shrugged on his shirt and pulled on socks and shoes against the cold then pointedly ignored Curry and his questions until the man snarled and went away.

No one came to disturb Ian after that, so Beth must have been making certain they left him alone. He loved her for that—he loved her for so many things.

He knew she would not rush in panic to Hart or Fellows to pry Ian from his endeavors. She'd learned that when Ian fixated on a task, that task was of great importance. Though others might not be able to discern its importance at first, Ian's instincts were usually correct.

He loved Beth for that understanding as well.

An hour later, Ian did hear a step, and lifted his head, irritated, to see John Ackerley emerging into the attic.

"Lord Ian," Ackerley said, giving him a nod.

Ian returned his attention to the words in his hands. He would have ignored Ackerley entirely, but he remembered Beth's painstaking instructions to be courteous to guests.

"I'll be down later," Ian said to him. "We'll continue then."

Ackerley cleared his throat. "Beth has made it clear she disapproves. And I must apologize. I grew excited at the prospect of helping you. When I became acquainted with the society of philosophers in Austria who are trying so many new methods, I was haughty enough to believe I could replicate their experiments. I am guilty of the greatest of the seven deadly sins, I'm afraid. My wife, bless her, was quite good at sticking a pin into my pride and deflating it. I was ever out to save the world."

Ian heard Ackerley's words, registered every single one of them, and stored them for later.

"Can you read old handwriting?" Ian held out a leather-bound journal to him, the cover worn and flexible with time.

"Pardon? Oh . . . I suppose so. How old?"

"Seventeen hundreds. Her script is fairly clear."

"Yes, I find that our grandfathers wrote in better hands than we do now." Ackerley took the journal with a look of curiosity. "Why?"

Ian told him what name to look for as Ackerley settled himself on an armchair that came from the time of the last Stuart queen. The pages of the journals were fragile, but Lady Mary's writing rang clearly from the past.

"It's important, is it?" Ackerley asked.

"Aye," Ian said, returning his gaze to the page he'd been reading. "It will tell me who stole Hart's paintings."

"Ah." Ackerley's voice lost its morose note and became brisk and interested again. "Well, of course. I am happy to help, my lord."

For the next hours, silence reigned in the attic as the two men read. The peace was occasionally broken by Ackerley leaning excitedly to Ian and saying in a hushed voice, "Is this anything?"

Ian would read what he pointed out and either note it or shake his head.

The journals had always fascinated Ian. Lady Mary Lennox, who became Lady Malcolm Mackenzie, and later, the Duchess of Kilmorgan, wrote in a straightforward and breezy style, without the forced witticisms or ponderous explanations of others of her generation.

Alec paid us a visit with his daughter in tow. How changed Alec is, but only for the better. Of Will, of course, he could say nothing. Dear Will. I am certain stories of his secretive life are many times more interesting than our domestic tales.

In later years, Mary wrote, *Our Angus is home, with Willie Ian, my favorite grandson. What a charmer he is! At ten years old he has made the household fall in love with him, and he gets away with anything he pleases. Mal, the wretch, sees himself in the lad and indulges him something terrible.*

Mary continued with an account of her travels with her son and grandson from Kilmorgan to London, praising the comfortable modern coach and the quickness of the journey along the new roads. In 1790, a journey of a number of days seemed swift to her, while now, a hundred years later, the same journey happened in less than a day and a night on the train.

I took Willie Ian for a walk in Hyde Park, and to my great astonishment, spied a familiar face. Well, I should not say "familiar" as such, because I have not seen him for many a year, and he is quite in his dotage, not the rather good-looking man he'd been in his younger days. I speak of none other than the Earl of Halsey—the man must be approaching eighty.

He was in a two-wheeled conveyance, driven by what looked like a manservant who was a bit nervous at the reins. And no wonder. The lad could not move the carriage in any direction or slow down or speed up without Halsey snarling invective at him.

I, being a polite woman, bowed and bid Lord Halsey good day.

"Stop!" Halsey bellowed at his man, who pulled the carriage up so short the horse began to rear. The driver calmed him with expertise, but Halsey scowled at him for that as well. "Good Lord, it's the Duchess of Muck," he said to me, and then laughed at his pretense of cleverness. "How are things in your Scottish pigsty?"

"Dear Halsey," said I. "You remain as courteous as ever. My husband would send his regards if he had any for you, which he does not. Of course, I do not think he gives one thought for you from one day to the next. Much water has passed under the bridge since the Jacobite days, and yes, we do have bridges at Kilmorgan."

"None but a duke would do for you, eh?" Halsey proceeded to say. "I'm sure you have paid the price, living in the wilderness with your mad whisky-brewing husband. English earls ride in carriages inlaid with precious stones while Scottish dukes go barefoot."

I knew quite well that if Halsey drove around in carriages encrusted with diamonds or some such nonsense, it was because he'd wed a very rich woman indeed. "When I married Malcolm I had no idea he would ever become duke; therefore your postulation does not signify," I replied. "And Malcolm does wear shoes—when he remembers to."

Halsey spat a laugh, but not at my little joke. "He wronged me, and I have not forgotten. I shall never forget. He owes me a debt I shall not forgive even when I am in the grave."

"Then I pity you, sir," I said. "The past is gone. To hold

such old hurts close is foolish. You have had a fine life, and I have a fine husband."

"A Scottish pig in his own muck," Halsey said, returning to his earlier theme.

"It is a bit mucky when it rains, I grant you. But I will take Kilmorgan over all the mansions in London, thank you very much. I learned very quickly that family is what's important, not riches or gold-leafed drawing rooms. Good day to you, sir. My family awaits me at home."

Halsey, true to his nature—which has not changed one whit—could not leave well enough alone. "He should never have been duke. He should have been hanged or shot, like the rest of them."

At that, my rage got the better of me. All I could think of was poor Duncan, poor Angus, men a hundred times better than Halsey ever was, and the dead and dying at Culloden.

"That they are gone and you have lived to a somewhat overripe age is a crime," I snapped. "You are a bad-tempered, high-handed, rather disgusting, arrogant ass, and always have been. I thank the Lord every day for my lucky escape. Again, I say, good day to you."

I doubt anyone, especially not a woman, had ever dared speak to Halsey thus, because he only gaped at me. I saw he'd lost most of his teeth, the old coot. His driver, who had his back to Halsey, wanted to laugh and laugh—I imagine the tales in the servants' hall this evening will be lively.

Halsey spluttered as I walked away, back to where Willie Ian waited with his nanny. "One day I will ruin the Mackenzies," *he called after me.* "I swear that with my last breath. I will task my heirs to ruin them and on through the generations. The Mackenzies shall never be out of reach of my wrath."

I ignored him utterly. Cards and castles, what a vindictive old git! His mind must be starting to go. One should pity him, I suppose—he is only a horrible, sad man drowning in his own bitterness.

"Who was that awful old man, Grandmama?" Willie Ian asked as I joined him. *"He looks like a wet goat."*

With his shaggy hair and glittering eyes under slammed-together brows, Halsey did rather resemble a goat. I laughed and tousled the lad's hair. *"Believe it or not, I was betrothed to the man, once upon a time,"* I confessed. *"Until I came to my senses and ran away with your grandfather."*

Willie Ian, who, in his kilt and boots, his red hair and golden eyes, was the perfect likeness of his father at that age, and I imagine Malcolm as well, looked after the two-wheeled conveyance with interest. *"Why didn't Granda' shoot the Sassenach?"*

"We were far too busy to pay him any mind." I took Willie Ian's hand. *"To be honest, I have not thought about Halsey in many years. Our circles rarely cross, thank heavens. Now, let us return home and have many good things to eat. I will kiss your father, whom I love very much, and then I'll go back to Kilmorgan and kiss and kiss your grandfather."*

Willie Ian gave me a dubious look. *"You and Granda' like to kiss."*

"Indeed, we do. 'Tis a wonderful thing, is kissing. We'll be doing it until we fall into our graves, then we will continue it in heaven, where there will be plenty of whisky and bannocks."

Willie Ian gave me another glance, which the young reserve for the foolishness of the old. *"When I grow up, I shall be verra kind to the ladies. Not like that old goat."* He gave the slowly retreating cart a look of approbation. *"Verra kind indeed. They'll love me."*

I hugged him close, which he put up with, with good grace. *"I'm sure they will, my gallant little lad."*

With that, we turned our steps back to Grosvenor Square and so home—at least our London home. Home for me will ever be the wild lands of Kilmorgan, with Mal.

～

Ackerley read over the passages after Ian had shoved the journal at him and pointed at the pages. Ackerley gave Ian a bewildered look when he'd finished.

"What are you implying? This was written a hundred years ago. Do you mean that Lord Halsey's heirs have a long enough memory to want to carry out their great-great-grandfather's vengeance?"

"Aye," Ian said. "'Tis a possibility."

This was Beth's fault. When she'd reminded Ian of Lyndon Mather's vindictiveness when she'd jilted him, Ian had remembered Lady Mary's stories of Lord Halsey.

"Mind you, some of these old families have long memories," Ackerley admitted. "In some places on the Continent families can carry on feuds for generations."

Ian took the journal back from him, carefully marked the passage with a scrap of paper, and closed the book. He stood up. "We will make inquiries."

Ackerley's brows rose as he climbed to his feet. "We?"

"The current Lord Halsey inherited the title two years ago. He is a direct descendant of the earl Lady Mary threw over. He has opposed every one of Hart's proposals in the Lords, and his father worked against Hart back when Hart wanted to be prime minister and free Scotland. Halsey is English to the bone, from an old family, and hates anything Scottish. We are still Jacobites to him."

Ackerley held up his hand to stem Ian's flow of words. "You said *we* would make inquiries. Do you include me in that pronoun?"

Ian gave him a nod, impatient. "Aye. Halsey will admit you, an English missionary looking for funds, but not me, brother of Hart Mackenzie. You will find out all you can and report to me. Do not tell him of your connection to Beth."

Ackerley thought it over, his lips parted. Then he popped

his mouth closed, looking interested and determined at the same time. "You can count on me. But . . . it is far-fetched, isn't it, old chap? What if you're wrong?"

"Then we look elsewhere. We keep looking, until we find the right person."

Ackerley gave him an approving nod. "A sound method."

Ian knew that. Finished with his exploration, he walked past Ackerley and down the stairs to the main floors, calling for Curry on the way.

The sooner Ackerley visited Halsey and determined whether Ian was correct or off the mark, the sooner Ian could return to peaceful fishing with his children and long nights touching the satin warmth of Beth's skin.

Beth, thrown into preparations for the arrival of the rest of the family, noted with relief that John and Ian seemed to be getting along quite well today. John had followed Ian up into the attics at Beth's suggestion—to report to Beth if anything were wrong—and Ian hadn't sent him running down again.

The fact that Ian hadn't minded John staying with him assured Beth that Ian was simply in pursuit of one of his ideas. Ian didn't always mind others with him when he was focused on a task, as long as they let him be.

A few hours later, Ian and John came down, John with an eager expression, Ian with brows drawn. Ian ordered Curry to fetch the coach, and strode out with John to meet it, John speaking rapidly to Ian as they went. Ian kissed Beth without a word, then the two got into the coach when it appeared, and the conveyance sped off.

Ian hadn't said good-bye, or explained where he was going, or what he was up to. But that too was typical when he had his mind on something important. Beth knew that Ian would reveal all later.

"I shouldn't worry," Eleanor said to Beth as Beth stood

in the front drive, watching the carriage go. "Our coachman is a tough old soldier—he won't let Ian murder Mr. Ackerley and push him into a ditch. Though Mr. Ackerley *can* talk, can he not? I shouldn't wonder that he converted many a native to a Christian life in his missionary days. I imagine they agreed to anything to make him be quiet."

Beth shook her head. "He is a good man, Eleanor."

Eleanor tucked her arm through Beth's and the two went back into the house. "Oh, I can see that. Goodness oozes from John Ackerley. One can simply have too much of it. Give me a little badness, and I am happy. That is why I fell in love with Hart, you know. He was as bad as bad could be. He looked at me, and I wanted to touch his fire, no matter how much it might burn. I knew I was a wicked woman then. No virtuous gentleman for *me*. I wanted Hart and everything that went with him."

Her eyes shone as she spoke. Eleanor had loved Hart for years, and Beth had seen his love for her long to come out. Beth was happy that they'd finally found each other again.

Eleanor continued her stream of talk. "Virtuous gentlemen are often hypocrites, in my experience, do you not think? They profess they'd never dream of offending a lady with harsh language or anything so base as holding her hand or kissing her cheek. The next moment, they rush off to their mistresses and do as they please, or they marry the lady and immediately become parsimonious and persnickety. When Hart kissed me the first time and didn't give a damn whether he offended my sensibilities, I knew the truth about myself. I wanted all the wickedness he could dish out to me. He was a high-handed, arrogant wretch, that is true, but life hadn't yet played its cruel tricks on him, poor man. Hart is a bit tamer now, but not too tame, if you know what I mean. I certainly wouldn't want *that*."

"No," Beth agreed, keeping her face straight. "We wouldn't want to tame them entirely."

"But never tell them," Eleanor said. "They believe they've reformed. As though a Mackenzie ever could. Oh." She broke off as one of the untamable Mackenzies strode down the long gallery toward them. "Good afternoon, Lloyd. You look grim. What news?"

Fellows, ever correct, stopped and gave both ladies a polite nod. "I can find no one in the house—not Hart, not Ian."

"Ian ran off with Mr. Ackerley," Eleanor said. "And Hart is visiting the farms. You may deliver your grim news to us, Chief Inspector. We are resilient."

Fellows studied them both a moment, his brows drawn over eyes that were a match for Hart's. "We've gone over all the artwork Ian found in the castle," Fellows said. "Most of it is there, but five paintings and several bronzes are unaccounted for. Also, Hart's majordomo, Wilfred, says that men from the firm that insures Hart's artwork have been sniffing around, investigating a rumor that Hart instigated the theft himself. I've sent them away, but I know they'll be back."

"Oh dear," Beth said. Hart would be furious—she rather pitied the hapless insurance clerks. "Have you had any progress in finding the culprits?"

"Not as yet." Fellows's mouth hardened. "And I might not have the chance to. I have more or less been told by my superintendent at the Yard that I'm under suspicion for helping Hart perpetrate a fraud, and I have been ordered off the case."

Chapter 15

The current Lord Halsey lived on his estate in Lincoln-shire, and Ian purchased tickets for himself and Ackerley on the next train going that direction. Curry came running as the train pulled out of the station at Kilmorgan Halt, and jumped on at the last minute.

Curry swung into the compartment where Ian and John were settling, and scolded Ian for leaving him behind and buying the train tickets himself. A gentleman didn't pur-chase things, Curry declared, but had his man do it for him. This was an ongoing argument. Ian was glad to see Curry, however, and Curry, after he had said his fill, went and or-dered tea for them.

Ackerley was entranced by the first-class carriage. He marveled at the marquetry and gleaming brass, the velvet cushions, the draperies, the wide windows that framed the vast Scottish scenery rushing by.

"I've taken many a train in my life," he said as Curry returned with tea and brandy, carried on a silver tray, with porcelain cups for the tea and crystal goblets for the brandy. "I've trundled up and down the entire world in a train, it seems. In India, the roof is as good a seat as any, you know, in all weather. Cars rumble down the tracks, teeming with people clinging on for dear life to the sides and top. It is quite a sight. But, needs must." Ackerley shrugged and downed his tea.

"I would like to see that," Ian said. He gazed out at the familiar Highlands, the mountains he knew every foot of, the glens of lush green and thick trees, lochs that stretched wide and blue under the sky. "And the rest of the world."

At one time, Ian hadn't liked to travel. He'd gone to Paris and as far as Rome with his brothers and Daniel, but he'd preferred the circle of what he knew. He'd become well acquainted with Paris and was comfortable there, but the thought of venturing farther had daunted him.

Now, as he listened to Ackerley paint pictures of hot skies and dry grasslands, green jungles and days of rain, his interest quickened. His brother-in-law, Elliot McBride, had told Ian stories of the Punjab and its beauties, intriguing him. Ian had read about these places in books, and remembered every word of every description. At one time, that would have been enough for him. Now, he wanted more.

"When my children are more grown," Ian said, "Beth and I will visit the world. The children can come with us."

Curry, clearing the tea things, stopped and gave a dramatic groan. "Never say it. I can see me trying to keep you out of trouble in foreign parts, you wandering about the 'eart of the Suk, trying to look at everything, drawing down eight different vendettas on yourself without even knowing it."

Ian flicked a glance at him. "Stay home, then."

"Oh, not bleeding likely. I made a vow a long time ago, didn't I? To look after you. Her ladyship needs all the help she can get, and don't think because children are grown that they won't need looking after as well."

Curry clattered the porcelain onto the tray, scowled at Ian, and banged out again.

Ackerley chuckled. "I believe he'd be offended if you left him behind. He certainly ran hard to catch this train."

"Curry is a good friend," Ian said, and went back to looking out the window.

Of course Ian would bring Curry with him when he and Beth, Jamie, Belle, and Megan set off to circle the globe. He couldn't imagine life without him. Curry fussed, cursed, and complained, but he'd always protected Ian from the most terrible things. He was part of the fabric of Ian's life.

In due course, after changing trains in Edinburgh and then hiring a carriage in Lincolnshire, they reached the Halsey estate. The drive to the house rambled for a mile under beech trees, likely planted for the purpose a century ago. The house surrounded a huge courtyard, the front gates opening to let them into the tall enclosure flanked by four wings. The front door of the residence lay opposite the gates, and a run of stairs swept from courtyard to door. The coachman stopped them directly in front of the steps, and a footman hurried down to the carriage to inquire their business.

Ackerley scrambled down, asked to speak to the master of the house, and then glanced back into the coach in alarm when Ian didn't follow.

"Are you not coming in with me?" Ackerley asked. "I know you don't wish to speak to him, but your presence outside whatever room in which he receives me would be most comforting."

Ian shook his head. "I'm a Mackenzie. You need to go in."

"Yes, yes, I take your point." Ackerley looked agitated, but he followed the footman up the flight of steps. He squared his shoulders and lifted his chin before he went into the house, as though steeling himself to face a warrior tribe on a South Sea island.

Ackerley was admitted without impediment, as Ian had suspected he would be. A so-respectable gentleman, a member of the clergy, would be able to gain access to an enemy that Ian could not.

Ian knew his theory about the current Lord Halsey could be entirely wrong, but the thought didn't bother him. He would examine each possibility until one proved to be the correct solution. If he had to tear up and down England, recruiting Ackerley to go where a large, mad Scotsman could not, then he would.

Whenever Ian was forced to sit and wait, one of two things happened. Either Ian would become absorbed in a problem inside his head and not realize the time had passed, or impatience would seize him and not let him keep still.

Today, impatience won. Ian tried to focus his mind on all he'd done with Beth last night, the best thing he could think about, but the details slipped away into a misty stream. Remembering Beth was not nearly as pleasurable as actually being with her.

Ian managed to wait fifteen minutes before restlessness got the better of him. He glared at the watch his children had given him for his last birthday—engraved *To Papa with Much Love, 1891*—and willed the hands to move.

After five more minutes, Ian shoved the watch back into his waistcoat pocket, slammed the carriage door open, leapt down, and ran up the steps to the house. He heard Curry, who was conversing with the coachman, cry after him, but Ian did not stop.

The door was shut. Ian banged on it with his fists until the haughty footman yanked it open.

"Sir?"

Ian strode inside, forcing the footman out of his way. "Where did you take him?"

"The missionary gentleman, sir? He's with his lordship."

Ian leaned to the footman. He didn't want to touch him—he disliked touch with anyone outside the family—but he'd shake the answer out of the lad if he had to.

The footman swallowed, looking Ian fearfully up and down. "Are you . . . with him?"

Ian had arrived with Ackerley—why wouldn't he be with him? "Where are they?"

The footman pointed upward. "Library, sir."

Ian considered for one second asking the footman to lead him there, then discarded the thought. How difficult could it be to find a library?

He raced up the creaky grand staircase, which swayed under his weight. The upper floor, unfortunately, became a maze once Ian left the gallery at the top of the stairs. The house was very old and had been modernized by throwing in a wall here, blocking a door there, until the earls of Halsey lived in a jumble. Ian ran down corridors, ended up back at the stairs, and still couldn't find the blasted library.

Finally, he stood in the middle of the gallery and roared, "*Halsey!* Where are ye?"

A door slammed open in the distance. "Lord Ian?" Ackerley's voice floated to him. "What is it? Is everything all right?"

Ian followed the sound of his voice. Ackerley waited uncertainly in a corridor outside an open door, and Ian pushed past him and into the library.

The room rose in dark walnut panels and was lined with shelves upon shelves of books. They momentarily distracted Ian—he loved books, and had the sudden desire to start at one end of the room and read his way to the other. Perhaps after he had Halsey arrested, Ian could return to this library and peruse it as he liked.

Halsey, a middle-aged man, rose from behind a giant of a desk and peered at Ian. "Who the devil are *you*, sir? An ill-mannered Scotsman, obviously."

Halsey stood the same height as Ackerley, but where Ackerley was on the stout side, Halsey was spindly. Halsey's brown hair was a fine down on his head, and though he'd made an effort to grow side whiskers, the result was hair that straggled down his cheeks. His body was a bit androgynous, no real shape to fill out his expensive clothes. Only his eyes, hard and blue, told Ian he came from a long line of arrogant men who believed themselves superior to all around them.

Ian opened his mouth to shout at him, but strangely, no sound emerged. This happened sometimes when Ian worked himself into a state of rage—he either bellowed or was rendered mute.

Ackerley turned to Halsey. "This is Lord Ian Mackenzie, my lord. He's come to help me petition for—"

"Mackenzie?" Halsey fixed his gaze on Ian with a sparkle of delight. "Not one of the notorious Mackenzies of Kilmorgan?"

"Indeed," Ackerley went on. "He has come to—"

"No, let him speak. Why has the ancient enemy of my family descended upon me? I am most intrigued."

Ian forced himself to unclench his fists. Beth had made him realize that when he couldn't speak, it was because every one of his muscles had tensed, including those in his throat. His body would tighten until he made himself a wall against the world.

Ian took a long breath, and then another. If he could ease out of the stiffness, his voice would open up, and his mouth work.

"Ye ruined my distillery, ye bugger."

Halsey's brows climbed high in his sallow face. "Such language. But so-called Scottish aristocrats are only barbarians someone once bestowed a title upon at knifepoint. Or was it claymore-point? Why on earth should I care about your distillery, Mackenzie? Sell your muddy whiskies wherever you like—I won't drink them."

At that moment, though Ian had no evidence whatsoever, he knew that Halsey was responsible for the destruction at Kilmorgan. He *knew*. The conviction took root in Ian's heart, filling every cell in him with certainty.

The certainty relaxed him the rest of the way. Ian had no

more need to threaten Halsey or search for the right words to accuse him. It was only a matter of time before Ian proved it, and then the Mackenzies would win and Halsey would lose.

Ian took a step toward Halsey. Halsey edged away, putting himself behind his desk.

Ackerley lifted his hands. "Now, my lords, we can settled this amicably, I'm certain."

Ian, ignoring Ackerley, moved to the desk and leaned his fists on it. "What did ye do with the paintings ye didn't dump in the tunnels?"

Halsey blinked at him across the solid piece of furniture. "Pardon?"

"I saw what was in the tunnel under Kilmorgan. I know what was taken from Hart's gallery. Not all of them were there. Where are the others?" Ian knew exactly which paintings were missing, from the robust angels in the Rubens to the odd pair illuminated by a lightning strike in the Giorgione.

Halsey's laugh was thin. "I have no idea what you are talking about, Mackenzie. First it's your whisky, now it's artwork. It's rumored you are quite mad, and now I believe it." He turned to Ackerley with a look of false sorrow. "I pity you, sir. Do you have the keeping of him? Perhaps I *will* make a donation to your charitable works, if you are trying to help poor idiots like him."

Ian only pinned Halsey with a stare worthy of Hart. "I know what ye've done," he said quietly. "And I know why."

The flicker in Halsey's eyes told Ian he was right. "You are a pathetic form of humanity," Halsey said, his arrogance undimmed. "Your entire family is and always has been. Mr. Ackerley, will you, a sensible Englishman, please take him away?"

Ackerley gave Halsey a thoughtful look. "Do you know, Lord Halsey, that I have traveled quite a bit of the world? I have met men from the basest savages to rulers of kingdoms

holding extraordinary riches. I have seen incredible goodness and vast evil—both of which exist under the same sun.
Thus, I have learned to judge a man, not from what he has or
in what circumstance he was born, but from his character.
Believe it or not, the native living in the crudest hut can be as
gracious and full of goodness as any highborn Englishman.
More so, perhaps, depending on the man." Ackerley drew a
breath. "In this room, at this moment, I know who is the better, sir, and I am proud to call him friend. Good day to you,
my lord, and thank you for receiving me. Perhaps we *should*
go, Lord Ian. A pint in a local brewery would be just the
thing for driving away the taste of this bad business."

Ian wanted to laugh. Ackerley's tone was as haughty as
Halsey's, and he spoke with no deference, and no fear that
he was wrong.

Halsey was nearly green with anger, his eyes glittering.
Ian doubted anyone in his life had ever disagreed with him
or challenged him in any way.

Did the fool think he could get away with poking at the
Mackenzies? And for such a ridiculous reason?

Ian lifted himself from the desk. He had nothing more to
say to Halsey, so he kept silent, turned his back on the man,
and strolled from the room.

Ian remembered the way out, now that he'd found the
route once, and he descended through the house without hesitation. Ackerley followed swiftly, neither man
speaking.

Curry was nearly dancing with worry outside the front
door, kept from charging inside by the harassed footman.
"You'll send me to an early grave, ye will," Curry said.
"What th' devil did ye mean by it?"

"No harm done," Ackerley said, when Ian said nothing. "I
think we should go, and quickly."

Once the carriage rolled out through the gates, leaving
the high-walled courtyard that cut off the world, Ian felt a
weight lifting from him. His quest was over. He'd done

what he'd set out to do, and now he could go home and leave the burden behind.

He cast his eye over Ackerley on the opposite seat. Ackerley was mopping his face with a handkerchief, red and sweating, though the September air was cool.

"Did ye convert many?" Ian asked him after a time. "In your missions?"

"Beg pardon?" Ackerley said, folding his damp handkerchief. "Of course not, not everyone. But we were quite successful. Though I ceased believing after a time that a man was damned for following his own beliefs. God has a place for everyone."

"Mm." Ian's spirits rose as they left the avenue of trees for brighter sunshine. "Ye mentioned a pint."

Ackerley laughed. "I did indeed, Lord Ian. Shall we ask our coachman to take us to the nearest pub? One friendly to strangers, that is."

An ordinary wife would have been furious at her husband for abruptly departing the house, absconding with a visitor, going who-knew-where, and returning the next day in a hungover state.

But Beth, Ian reflected when he and Ackerley, followed by Curry, dragged themselves from the coach and into the house at Kilmorgan the next morning, was not an ordinary wife at all.

She stood poised on the bottom step of the staircase, obviously having rushed from wherever she'd been when alerted to their arrival.

Curry spoke first. "I did me best, my lady. They missed the train out of Edinburgh last night because they lingered at every pub between Halsey's estate and Lincoln. By the time we finally reached Edinburgh, the last train north had gone. A pair of reprobates, they are."

Ackerley, his eyes red, his movements slow because of

the headache he'd complained of all morning, gave Beth a feeble smile. "My fault, I'm afraid. I suggested we enjoy the local brew, and Lord Ian took me at my word."

Ian, with his iron constitution, had only a slight headache, but he wanted a nap. One with Beth.

Ignoring the others, he started up the stairs. The children would be having lessons at this hour, and he'd learned not to disturb them. For now, he turned his steps to his porcelain collection. Beth would know to look for him there once she'd seen Ackerley settled.

The bowls were in place, each one nestled against its velvet cloth, shining softly in the sunlight.

Ian got lost in the perfection of the first bowl he'd ever purchased, years ago, when he'd finally emerged from Kilmorgan after his time in the asylum. He'd found it in a shop in Paris that Isabella had taken him to, and had become mesmerized by its beauty, the stark blue on white, the patterns of the chrysanthemums and dragons.

Ian reached into the shelf and lifted the bowl out.

He knew Beth stood behind him, even though he'd been concentrating on the bowls. Beth remained quiet, waiting for him to notice her. She wouldn't risk startling him with a loud noise or a sharp word, lest he drop a precious bowl.

Indeed, she was no ordinary wife.

Ian set the bowl into its place and turned to her.

Beth did not look angry. Ian had learned to read the signs of that. Her mouth was turned up at the corners, and her blue eyes shone with interest.

"Well?" she asked. "Did you see Lord Halsey? What was he like?"

Chapter 16

Ian did not answer at once, but this didn't worry Beth. Ian was like that.

He'd remain silent while he considered the question and its many possible answers. He'd also be deciding whether the question needed a response at all, and then, out of all the answers he could give, which was the most important.

"He had a portrait of the old Lord Halsey in his library," Ian said after a time. "The one Lady Mary was betrothed to. He was strong. This Lord Halsey is not. Too much inbreeding has weakened the strain."

"Not something Mackenzies need to worry about." Beth felt a smile come. Mackenzies down the ages had married whomever they pleased, no matter what the lady's pedigree.

"Aye, ye breed a horse too close to its line, and it can be weak and sickly," Ian said. "The same goes for people."

"That's all very well." Beth knew Ian could take up a topic and pursue it while the original question went unanswered. "Do you think he did it, Ian? Did Lord Halsey steal the paintings?"

"Aye."

The one word, and then silence.

"*Aye*, you think so?" Beth asked. "Or *aye*, he actually did it?"

"I'm certain he did." Ian stopped again, then seemed to realize Beth wanted more. "Halsey has kept some of the art for himself. I saw it in his eyes when I accused him of it. He thought we wouldn't notice the absence in the jumble the thieves left in the tunnels. But I saw that they were gone when we found the stash."

"Good heavens, Ian, why didn't you say so at the time?" Beth exclaimed. "Fellows and Hart realized only yesterday that the paintings were gone."

Ian shrugged. "Everyone saw what I saw."

"I agree," Beth said in exasperation. "They should have been brilliant and concluded immediately that not all the paintings were there. Now Hart is being accused of fraud, and unless you can prove that Lord Halsey has the artwork then . . . Ian?" Beth stuttered to a halt as Ian removed a square velvet box from the pocket of his coat. "What is that?"

Ian touched the box's soft lid. "We had to sleep in Edinburgh."

"I know," Beth said. "I received John's telegram."

Ian held out the box, waiting for her to take it.

Beth knew that, for Ian, simply stating he'd stayed the night in Edinburgh passed for a clear explanation. She could read him enough by now to follow what had happened—Ian had decided he needed to bring her a gift to placate her for not telling her where he'd gone the day before, and for staying away all night.

Beth could assure him that an apology gift was not needed, but Ian's presents were always . . . interesting. She took the box and carefully opened it.

And stood, dumbfounded. "Ian, this is . . ."

Breathtaking. A strand of diamonds lay on white velvet, not a simple string, but a complex mesh like a spider's web, glittering with multicolored stones. The necklace dipped to a point in the middle, from which dangled a large round diamond, sparkling in the soft light.

"Oh . . . *Ian*." Beth looked up at him, her heart squeezing. "Why?"

Ian's brows drew down, the gold in his eyes glinting. "Because I thought you would like it. If you don't, I'll have Curry take it back to the jewelers."

He reached for the box, perfectly serious. Not offended, Beth knew—Ian would reason that if Beth did not like this gift, he'd simply exchange it for another until he found one she did like.

Beth gripped the box and took a few swift steps backward. "No, no, no, it is not going anywhere. This is lovely, Ian. Exquisite. *Perfect*."

Ian relaxed. "Then you do like it."

"Of course I do." Beth hugged the box to her chest, then gave him a puzzled look. "But it must have been far too late when you arrived in Edinburgh for shops to be open, and far too early in the morning before you left it."

"Our jeweler's shop was shut, yes. I knocked on the door this morning until he opened it."

"I see." Beth envisioned Ian pounding on the door with his fists, unrelenting, while the jeweler stumbled down the stairs in his nightcap. "Poor man. But Ian," Beth said, tears in her voice. *"Thank you."*

Ian came to her and took the box from her hands, laid it gently aside, and closed his arms around her. His eyes darkened. "I should have taken you wi' me."

"Indeed, you ought to have." Beth slid her hands around his waist, finding the soft wool of his kilt over his firm backside. "I would have liked to see this scion of the house of Halsey and helped you accuse him."

"Then I wouldn't have had t' sleep alone." Ian leaned to kiss her neck. "I don't like sleeping alone. Not anymore."

Beth smiled, her impishness rising. "You could have put a cot in your bedroom for John."

Ian lifted his head. "He's a large, hairy, snoring man. He snored all the way from Edinburgh t' Aberdeen then from Aberdeen t' Kilmorgan Halt. Why would I want him near my bedroom?"

"I'm teasing you, Ian. You seem to have become good friends."

Ian shrugged. "He'll do." He tilted Beth's face to his. "He talks too much."

"But what are you going to—?"

Ian nipped her lower lip. "Shh."

Beth rose on tiptoe and met him in a heartfelt kiss. Ian parted her lips to kiss her in return, his tongue sweeping in to heat her. He gathered her close, his strong hands bringing her hard against him.

"I remember when ye first undressed for me," he said, his voice going soft. "In Mac's studio, in Paris, when ye brought me a present."

Beth remembered perfectly. She'd given him a gift—a gold pin to wear on his lapel—to apologize when she thought she'd stirred up trouble for him and his family. Ian had accepted the pin without understanding exactly why she'd given it to him, then told her he wanted her to undress for him, to show him her body. Beth, after a few heart-pounding moments, had.

"You asked me to explain love to you that day," Beth said. Her arms were around his tall body, and she felt the thickness of his arousal against her abdomen. "I was confounded, and did not know what to say."

"Ye said well enough." Ian's low rumble made her shiver. "And now, ye no longer have to explain."

"Good." Beth swallowed. "I remember being very bad at it."

"Ye've made me know it instead." His voice became a dark whisper. "Love you, m' Beth." Beth's eyes moistened. "I love you, Ian Mackenzie."

Ian's arms were solid around her, and at the same time, Beth felt herself falling. But the carpet on the floor of the Ming room was soft and giving, and Beth landed safely, cradled by Ian.

He undressed her, as he had last night, as he had that afternoon in Paris, and so many days and nights in between. Beth's clothes came away a piece at a time, to lie strewn about the floor. Beth undressed Ian in turn, his coat, waistcoat, shirt. Finally Beth unpinned his kilt, the folds of it falling away to bare her husband to her.

Ian took time to look at Beth, laid out before him on the plaid he'd slid beneath her. His golden eyes took in everything, heating as he slid his gaze down her body.

He rose abruptly to his feet, sunlight through the windows playing on his nakedness, shadows sculpting muscles. Before Beth could ask where he was going, he returned with the box containing the necklace. Stretching himself next to her, Ian opened the box, drew out the necklace, and spread it across her breasts.

"There," he whispered. "They're more beautiful when they're on you."

Beth glanced down at the diamonds, emeralds, sapphires, and rubies that reposed on the swell of her breasts. Clusters of diamonds glittered on her nipples. "Um . . ." Beth began, "I do not think the necklace is meant to go quite in that spot."

Ian slanted her one of his rare smiles, this one full of wickedness that went with the sin in his eyes. "It does now, m' Beth."

Beth's heart beat faster. The stones and slim chains were cool on her skin, but Ian against her was as hot as fire.

Ian cupped his hand under her breast, not disturbing the necklace as he kissed her, the kiss deep. She touched the line of his jaw, loving the burn of his whiskers against her fingertips.

The jewels did not move as Ian lowered himself on top of her, kissing her, touching, his hands strong and gentle at the same time.

Ian slid inside her, the intense pleasure of him opening her and stealing her breath.

"I love ye, my Beth," he whispered. "M' wife. M' everything . . ."

The house was in chaos that afternoon. The remainder of the family was due to arrive soon, and Beth had to return to assisting Eleanor. Ian decided that the next time he visited their jewelers he'd have them make matching pieces to the necklace to adorn Beth in other places.

Ian regretted having to relinquish Beth. He'd prefer to lie with her on the floor in the Ming room, languidly touching her, trying to decide where the necklace looked best on her. He'd kiss her when he wanted to, or come together with her for more lovemaking.

Beth's kiss good-bye before she hurried off to Eleanor held promise, but Ian would rather have her now than the impatience of waiting for later. Everyday life, in all its details, ground on too long, in his opinion.

Ian unfortunately had plenty of details to attend to. He conferred with Fellows about what had happened with Halsey, then returned to the distillery to give orders about how to clean up the mess there. Once Ian had finished with that, he looked for Beth, but she was still rushing about with Eleanor, the maids, and the housekeeper. Ian knew she'd be some time, so he hunted up Ackerley and told him he wanted to continue the cure.

Today, this involved Ian talking about himself and his brothers and how he'd felt about them as a child. Though Hart, Cam, and Mac had often confused Ian, he'd always liked and admired them. Cam had taught him to ride and to drink; Mac had taught him about women and art; Hart about numbers and money. Ian had absorbed it all.

"I don't know how I *felt*," Ian said irritably after a time. "I didn't know how to feel anything. I didn't *feel* until I met Beth."

"Ah yes." Ackerley looked up from writing his notes. "Dear Beth. She is a sweet woman. How did she . . . well, teach you to feel, as it were?"

Ian had no trouble meeting Ackerley's gaze now. "I don't know. I wanted . . ." He groped for the words that swooped and swirled past him like elusive fish. "I wanted to be with her. See what she saw; hear what she heard. She taught me to understand. What is here." He touched his forehead. "And here." He placed his hand over his heart. "And the day I thought I'd lost her . . ." His emotions had buried him, and he'd realized that every loss he'd ever endured before Beth would be as nothing if she went. He loved her with his whole being.

"I see," Ackerley said softly. "I see."

"No, ye don't," Ian growled. "Ye talk about m' father and m' mother and brothers, and what I did as a lad, but *it doesn't matter*. It's all gone. Beth is now. M' family is *now*. I don't care about a long time ago."

Ackerley studied him with renewed interest. "Indeed? I shall have to think about that."

Ian sprang up, restless. "When ye've thought, and ye can cure me, ye find me and tell me. I have many things t' do."

With that, he left the room, sensing Ackerley's fascinated gaze on him all the way out the door.

~

At dinner, there was more interminable discussion, this time about Lord Halsey and his culpability.

"Unfortunately, Ian," Fellows said, as the meal began, "I can't rush down and arrest Halsey without any proof of your suspicions."

Ian saw no reason why not, but he knew Fellows liked to follow the rules—unless expeditious not to. "Doesn't matter," Ian said. "Watch him. He'll do something wrong sooner or later."

"Let him hang himself, you mean," Fellows suggested.

"Aye." Ian, finished with the discussion, applied himself to his food.

Hart, obviously, was *not* finished. "Your solution is to do nothing until Halsey makes a mistake?" He scowled at Fellows and Ian. "What if he never does—or does in twenty years? I've been accused of fraud—not openly yet, but that will come."

"Insurance men are so tiresome, aren't they?" Eleanor put in from the foot of the table. "Why should Hart want to throw his own paintings into a hole?"

"For the money, of course," Beth answered, her gentle voice a caress to Ian's soul. "As though Hart would ever let his finances become so unsound."

"The vulgar insurance man implies so." Eleanor made a face. "He doesn't come out and say it, thinking it is too gauche to mention money at all. At the same time he drops little hints, such as *Very odd thing for a thief to do, isn't it? Leave most of what he stole behind? Almost as though he knew he could come back for it whenever he liked.* Pompous prig."

Ian swallowed a mouthful of buttery fish. "Hart can talk his way out of it." Hart was good at that.

"True," Eleanor said before Hart could reply. "Perhaps we should invite Lord Halsey to stay here," she went on, her fork poised. "For the birthday celebration. We could surround him and get him to confess. Or, I could take him up to the roof . . ."

"*El*," Hart said.

Eleanor blinked her very blue eyes at him. "To show him the view, of course. It's a fine one, you must admit." She gave Hart a sweet smile, and returned to her meal.

Hart watched her, his golden eyes holding a mixture of

wariness, affection, and heat. As much as Hart growled, Ian knew he loved Eleanor's impetuous boldness, her fearlessness. They made a good match—the fearsome duke and the warmhearted woman.

After dinner, Ian returned to the nursery with Beth. The children were unrulier than usual—tomorrow, the rest of the cousins would arrive, and the excitement of this had them animated.

Ian worried a little about that—his own son, Jamie, was the ringleader, and could incite his younger cousins to do anything he could think of. Ian would have to keep a careful eye on them.

When the girls and small Malcolm finally settled in the nursery, and Beth chivvied Alec and Jamie into their own room, Ian went wearily to bed. He'd never imagined how exhausting children could be. His father had tried to quell the high-spirited Mackenzies with iron control and vicious beatings. Beth had been showing Ian for the last ten years that there was a better way—patience and love.

Ian had tucked the necklace into the bedside table, and decided he wasn't too tired to show Beth how much he appreciated her teaching him about the gentle side of life. He snuggled down with her much later, knowing that the next day, he'd have to again take up the problem of Halsey. He, like Hart, did not want to wait twenty years for the man to put a foot wrong. Ian wanted an end to this. In the meantime, he let himself drift off with Beth, knowing he'd come up with some idea if he let himself.

In the small hours of the morning, in velvet darkness, Ian snapped open his eyes.

He did not know what had awakened him—a tiny noise, a breath of air—but a tingle swept through his blood, a warning that something was terribly wrong.

Beth slept on in the warm nest they'd made. But in the same way Ian had known when the thieves had invaded the gallery, he sensed that someone was in the house.

In the nursery.

He slid from the bed, wrapping a kilt around his hips, not bothering with shoes or shirt. Ian silently left the bedroom, taking the key from the lock inside and locking the door behind him. He'd not risk one of Halsey's thugs skulking around him and getting to Beth while Ian explored elsewhere.

The hall was quiet, every door closed. Ian moved noiselessly down the corridor, which was lit by moonlight through a large window at the end. The very last door led to the nursery. Its knob turned easily under Ian's hand.

Ian slid inside, becoming a shadow in deeper shadows, and made his way to Megan's bed. He let out a sigh of relief when he found her sleeping quietly, on her belly, her cheek pressed to her pillow.

Ian smoothed the cover over her and moved to Belle's bed, already hearing her soft breathing. Ian let his hand drift over her dark red hair. He checked Malcolm, who was also sleeping, then he left the room, his heart beating thickly with relief. His daughters and wee nephew were safe.

Ian went next to the lads' room, the hall's carpet prickling his bare feet. This door opened as easily, though its hinges gave a faint creak.

Ian's breath stopped. It was this sound, the small noise in the darkness, that had awakened him.

Ian swiftly entered the room, his lungs tight. He saw Alec, Hart's son, sprawled across his bed, his eyes tightly closed, covers barely rumpled.

The bed in which Jamie slept was empty. The blankets and sheets had been dragged down the side of the bed, and the pillow was on the floor, the mark of a large and heavy boot imprinted on the linen.

But apart from Alec, no one else was in the room. Jamie, and the man he'd struggled with, were gone.

Chapter 17

Ian's roar of anguish jerked Beth from a sound sleep. She sat straight up, her heart pounding. She hadn't heard Ian sound like that in many years.

She hastened out of bed, drawing her wrapper around her. Beth found the bedroom door locked, the key gone. Ian hadn't done that in a long while either. Locking her in was his way of protecting her, Beth understood, but she'd learned how to circumvent the problem. She fished in her bedside table drawer for the spare key and let herself out and into the corridor.

The noise came from the boys' room at the end the hall. Beth, every limb cold, raced toward it. The nursery door was closed, and Beth heard her daughters' voices, worried, calling for her and Ian.

Ian stood in the middle of the lads' bedroom, his head bowed, eyes closed, fists balled. He'd ceased making the terrible noise, but he rocked back and forth, his body tight. He had gone into his mind, searching for a place to retreat.

Alec, strangely, was still fast asleep, his chest rising with his even breath. He should have been awakened by his uncle shouting next to him, but he didn't stir.

Jamie's bed was empty.

Icy fear rose up to beat at her. "Ian!" Beth ran to him and seized one solidly fisted hand. "Ian, where is Jamie?"

Ian jumped at her touch. His body shuddered, then he peeled opened his eyes and looked down at her with fathomless anguish.

"Gone," Ian said. "He's gone, he's gone, gone, gone, gonegonegonegone . . ."

Beth's world broke into glittering shards of colors and light. "Gone? What do you mean . . ."

But she knew exactly what Ian meant. She took in the torn-up bedding and the boot print, and knew in her heart that Jamie had been stolen from them.

"No." The word dragged out of her, a cross between a whisper and a moan.

The sound made Ian's continuing *gonegonegone* cease. He seized her hands in a tight grip, his eyes filled with a terrifying anger.

This was the Ian whom Beth needed, the one with the unstoppable determination of his Highland ancestors.

"Find him," Beth said. She heard Curry's voice rise down the hall, from the direction of the main stairs, followed by Hart's and Lloyd's, then Eleanor's. Beth ignored them, her attention all for her husband. "Find my lad, Ian. Please."

When Ian spoke, his voice was low, steady. "Keep them away."

They shared a look. Beth understood. Ian feared, as did she, that if Hart and Fellows rounded up a large, noisy search party, their son's captor might be startled into cutting his losses. This was for Jamie's life.

"Yes," Beth promised in a whisper. "Go."

Ian's hands closed on hers in a brief, hard grip, then he slipped from the room and into the hall, melting into the darkness. Beth, following him, saw him pause at the hidden door in the paneling that led to the back stairs, then he was gone.

Alec still hadn't woken. Beth heard Megan and Belle calling for her, frightened. She wanted to run to them, but there was something wrong with Alec. Beth hurried to his bedside and shook him, her fear increasing.

Alec was sleeping, but unnaturally so. Someone had sent the lad into a drugged sleep, Beth realized, to ensure he wouldn't cry out while Jamie, her beloved son, was kidnapped.

Ian could move around Kilmorgan Castle quickly and in deep silence. He knew the house better than anyone, even servants who'd spent their entire lives there.

He used the back stairs and corridors to emerge into Cameron's wing of the house, empty and waiting for him and his family to fill it up. In Cameron's dressing room, Ian found a shirt and greatcoat, socks, and boots. He was closest to Cameron in size and had no trouble sliding into his clothes.

He ran down the back stairs again, ducking out of sight as several Mackenzie retainers rushed up the staircase. Hart and Fellows would be questioning Beth by now, then they'd organize a search. It would take them some time to round up enough men to begin, and by then, with God's help, Ian would have already found Jamie and dispatched the men who'd dared take him.

Then he would fill his Webley with shining bullets and travel to Lord Halsey's house and shoot him dead. Hart and Fellows would try to prevent him, of course, but Ian wouldn't let them.

Ian made himself halt in the middle of the stairs and think, to go over the scenario logically, reaching past his gut-wrenching fears.

Jamie's bed hadn't been cold—the heat of his body had dissipated but not altogether. Ian judged twenty minutes at most had elapsed since Jamie had been dragged out. He'd heard the noise of the lads' bedroom door. The time it had taken Ian to come fully awake after hearing that, realize something was wrong, and investigate had given the abductors their head start.

Ian continued to the ground floor in the servants' passages, found a side door, and stepped outside. He was clothed against the cold and now pulled on gloves he'd snatched up from Cam's dressing room. They were riding gloves, tough in the palms, tight but warm.

He emerged onto a side path, which was hidden from the rest of the garden by a high hedge. Ian had not gone twenty feet down the path when he was nearly run down by a barrel of a man who hastened toward the house.

Ian seized the man and dragged him back into the shadows. His captive drew a breath to shout, but Ian slammed his hand across his mouth and shook him to silence.

John Ackerley stared wide-eyed over Ian's gloved fingers. Ian noted that the man was fully dressed and bundled against up against the night in greatcoat with scarf.

"What th' devil are ye doing?" Ian demanded.

"I was about to ask the same of you," Ackerley answered when Ian lowered his hand from the man's mouth. "I had opened my window to let in a breeze, and I heard voices below. I thought the thieves had returned. I hoped to follow them and find them for you, but alas, I lost them in the dark."

Ackerley spoke glibly, and Ian stared at him in suspicion. How likely was it that Ackerley had decided to investigate, alone, in the middle of the night?

"Why didn't ye wake me?" he asked. "Did ye think ye could take robbers by yourself?"

"Of course not. I meant to discover where they'd gone and then fetch you and Mr. Fellows. Why are you looking at me like that? Good gracious, man, you don't believe *I'm* in league with the villains, do you?"

Ian at the moment didn't know what he believed. He didn't care. He needed to find Jamie—nothing else in the world mattered. That need pulled at his soul, blotted out every other consideration.

"If ye are in league with them, you'll lead me to them now," Ian said. "If you're not, you'll help me find them. They have my son."

Ackerley's gasp conveyed genuine surprise. "What? Young Jamie?"

"Aye." Ian peered into the darkness, assessing which way to go. "Young Jamie." It hurt even to say his name.

Ackerley's affability became outrage. "Have they, by gum? Well, now they've gone too far, blast them. Of course I'll help you search. We'll put the fear of God into them when we find them, won't we?"

"Aye." Ian's heart warmed a trifle at Ackerley's resolution. Without another word, Ian started off into the woods.

"Wait." Brush and twigs crackled as Ackerley struggled to catch up. "Shouldn't we alert the others? Or at least go back for lights?"

"There's light." Ian glanced at the sliver of moon and the stars on this clear night. "The others will be coming. We must get there first."

"Ah, covertly, you mean. I understand. I'm your man."

"Good." Ian pinned him with a Mackenzie glare. "Now, be *quiet*."

Ian turned away from Ackerley, scanning the wide swath of darkness. Where to begin? The villains would have traveled here in a conveyance, but they would have left it some way off, so the noise of it wouldn't alert the household.

Though Ian could see fine by starlight, it also helped that he knew every inch of lands around Kilmorgan. The thugs wouldn't. They'd blunder about in the darkness, leaving a trail. Or, they'd hide until daylight and they could find their way back to their vehicle. Because they'd left the house in near-silence, and had made certain Alec didn't wake, they likely believed they'd have time to escape before the family woke and discovered Jamie missing.

If they'd gone to ground to wait for daylight, where would they have done so? The tunnels under Kilmorgan where they'd left the paintings were a strong possibility. The thieves already knew the place. Then again, Ian had discovered the tunnels, and Fellows and his men had been all over them for the last several days. Fellows, being the thorough policeman he was, likely had posted a few guards, in case the thieves returned, looking for their treasure.

Not the tunnels then. The river and its thick screen of trees? Too risky for those who didn't know the terrain. A fall into the river, especially at night, would be a disaster. The water was icy and could carry a man far downstream, to his death over rocky falls.

The vast gardens of Kilmorgan held many hiding places, but all were too close to the house, and were in view of the upper windows.

Ian considered the folly—the false ruins Ian's grandfather had constructed on an outcropping overlooking a steep valley—then immediately dismissed it. The folly was at the end of a long, steep, overgrown path, dangerous enough during the day. Anyone who didn't know it risked a fall to his death, plus there was only one way up. The thieves wouldn't chance being trapped there.

The distillery . . .

The distillery was locked at night. The caretaker lived in a cottage about half a mile from it. In the old days, the caretaker had lived inside the distillery itself in the rooms upstairs—at one time the entire Mackenzie family had resided there, after the old castle had been burned and before the new house had gone up.

The distillery was dark at night and empty, the whisky sleeping on its own.

Without a word, Ian abruptly turned and went the shortest way down the hill and along the path that led to the distillery. He expected Ackerley to make much noise as he followed, but the man's footfalls were as quiet as Ian's, and he easily kept pace.

The distillery's walls glittered in the moonlight, the black stone ancient and strong. The house had been built as a secondary residence for the family in the late seventeenth century, then became the distillery when the Mackenzies went into the whisky business.

The windows were dark, no lights anywhere. Ian's keys to the place were back home in his desk drawer, but he knew where the caretaker hid the spare.

No need for keys, though, he saw. The front door was not only unlocked but ajar.

Ian slipped carefully inside, his breath hanging in the chill air. Darkness stretched around him, shapes of things familiar by day distorted by shadows and moonlight.

Ian stood in the middle of the large foyer, looking up at the grand hall that rose two floors above him. The silence was immense.

The abductors were no longer there. The air that flowed over Ian's face was cold but fresh, as though a window had been opened and left that way. In the quietness, Ian felt no presence, no watchers, sensed nothing.

Even so, he decided to make a quick search. Ian groped for lanterns stored in a cupboard near the front door, lit two with matches also kept there, and handed a lantern to Ackerley. Ackerley broke away to search rooms on his own, his lantern held high, saying both of them searching would cut the time. Ian's regard for the man rose.

Ian found an open window in the ground-floor office. The window had been forced, the catch broken. The thugs must have come in this way and left by the front door, which had not been forced, not bothering to close either window or door behind them. They'd also grabbed lanterns from the shelf in the office, along with a spare coat Ian kept here and a bottle of whisky.

Ian left the room to see Ackerley hurrying through the front hall toward him, excitedly waving something. "I found this on the floor, near the still itself." Ackerley thrust a strip of cloth at Ian. "The sort of thing nightshirts are made of."

Ian took the cloth, rubbing his thumb over the softness of the fabric. "It's Jamie's." He remembered kissing his lad good night only hours ago, smoothing his shoulder, which had been covered with this very material.

"Lucky it tore off," Ackerley said. "It shows we're on the right trail."

"Mm." Ian folded the fabric into a careful rectangle and tucked it into his pocket. He knew damn well the cloth hadn't come to be there by luck.

Nothing more to be found here. Ian strode out of the distillery, flashing his lantern across the path outside the gate.

The kidnappers wouldn't have gone south—that way lay the caretaker's house, and beyond it the lane to the village. Too many farms and people down that road. To the north, the way was rougher, the sea close. However, they might risk heading for a boat, especially now that they'd grabbed lanterns from the distillery.

Ian started off on the north-leading path, Ackerley laboring to follow. Ian strode faster and faster, then he broke into a run, fear pushing him on. If he did not reach the men before they took ship, they might never be found. Ian would certainly go to Lord Halsey and beat on the man until he told Ian where to find his son, but by that time, Jamie could be hurt, or dead.

Ian refused to think what would happen to him, and to Beth, if Jamie died.

Ian moved rapidly along the path, his lantern swinging, his feet skimming over rocks and bramble without pause. He scarcely noticed his breath as the way turned to a steep climb—he noticed nothing, everything within him fixed on finding Jamie.

Nothing else mattered. If Ian remained a madman for the rest of his life, unable to follow conversations, uncomfortable in crowds, uncertain how to respond when everyone else seemed to know effortlessly what to do, it didn't matter. He'd take the taunts, thinly veiled contempt, and ignorant questions of the rest of the world—as long as Jamie was all right.

"Wait!" Ackerley panted far behind him. "Wait—Ian! I found another."

Ian leapt back down the rocks to Ackerley, who was wheezing but holding up another strip of cloth. "On the bush. Back there."

Ian seized it, a soft piece of his son's nightshirt. Relief made his limbs watery. "Jamie is alive and well." *Thank you, God.*

Ackerley looked hesitant. "It might have simply caught on a bush as they carried him, I hate to say. You must be prepared, I'm afraid, for the worst."

"No." Ian wrapped the strip around his fingers, using it to vicariously hug his son to him. "Jamie tore this off himself and left it. He knows I'll be following."

Ackerley's face was ghostly pale in the lantern light. "How would he know you'd choose to come *this* way? There are so many possibilities out here."

"He knows," Ian said. He turned to lope up the path again. "Hurry."

Hope gave Ian strength. He ran on, leaping from rock to rock, wind whipping his kilt around him. Ackerley manfully kept up, uncomplaining.

Then, minutes later, Ian emerged on a cliff top that gave him a wide, sweeping view of the sea. Moonlight danced on the water, illuminating a ghostly path to nowhere. Mists were forming on the shore below.

Ian's hopes plummeted. He saw no sign of any ship on the water, no lights, no wake—no indication that anyone had passed this way tonight.

Chapter 18

Ackerley reached the top of the path behind Ian. "Have they gone already?" he asked in breathless worry. "Have we missed them?"

Ian sank down on his heels and wrapped his arms around his kilted knees. *Too late, too late, he's gone, gone, gone, gone, gone . . .*

Ackerley's hand landed on Ian's shoulder. "Steady, lad."

Ian realized the words were coming out of his mouth, surrounding him in sound, filling his ears. *"Gone, gone, gonegonegone . . . !"*

Ian squeezed his eyes shut. *Beth, my Beth, help me.*

But Beth wasn't there. She was at the house, doing what was necessary, keeping Hart and Fellows busy organizing a wider search, stopping them from panicking the thugs too soon. This was what being parents meant, Ian had come to understand—he and Beth doing what they must for their children, together and separately, each contributing their unique strengths to the task.

Beth's strength was her goodness, and her ability to think clearly and lend others courage and hope.

Ian's strength was solving puzzles, reaching conclusions

no one else could, reducing life to mathematical equations. All he had to do was clear his mind, and then sort everything he saw, heard, and touched into neat categories.

This isn't mathematics; this is m' son! his entire being wailed. *My child, my dearest wee lad. M' Jamie . . .*

And I can only help him if I think.

"Zero, one, two . . ." Ian's voice wavered at first, then gained strength. "Five, twelve, twenty-nine . . ."

"Pardon?" Ackerley leaned closer. "What are you saying?"

Fibonacci's sequence was not the only type of number series the mathematician Mr. Lucas studied. The Pell numbers fell into a neat, unending progression that could be spun out to infinity. All Ian had to do was double a number in the series and add it to its previous number—$P_n = 2P_{n-1} + P_{n-2}$.

"Seventy, one hundred sixty-nine . . ."

The mists in Ian's mind began to clear. His heartbeat slowed, the mantra of the numbers restoring his equanimity.

Ian opened his eyes. Ackerley held a lantern high, bathing them in a circle of light.

"Four hundred eight, nine hundred eighty-five . . . If they'd taken ship, we'd see it," Ian said, his words in the same even tone as the numbers. "They could not have gone so far so fast, even with an engine. We'd hear a steam engine—sound carries in the night and across the water. They are down on a shore or in a smuggler's cave, waiting for daylight."

"Then we must go back," Ackerley said. "Inform Mr. Fellows. Have him round up constables—the duke can send word to alert the navy. We'll bottle them up and have at them." He waved the lantern, excitement making his eyes shine.

"*You* must go back," Ian said firmly. "Tell them. I must fetch my son."

Ackerley gaped. "Good heavens, man, you can't go after them on your own. Even if you do find them and corner them, what will you do? You don't know how many men there are—they might be armed."

"Five men." Ian looked down into the cove. "Five distinct tracks on the paths, and Jamie's. They *are* very likely armed."

"Then you shouldn't go alone."

Ian studied Ackerley, looking directly into the man's eyes. "You can't help me with this. You need t' show Hart and Fellows where I've gone. And tell Beth . . ." Ian trailed off, thinking of Beth's blue eyes, her red lips parting whenever she rose on tiptoe to kiss him. "Tell her I will bring our son home. As I promised."

Ackerley appeared ready to argue, then he gave Ian a nod. "Very well. I understand." He stuck out his hand. "God go with you."

Ian gazed at Ackerley's outstretched palm in its worn leather glove for some time, then he slowly put out his own hand and clasped it.

Ackerley grabbed Ian's wrist, gave him a hard handshake, and released him. "I'll be as quick as I can."

Ian stared down at his fingers as Ackerley started to pick his way back along the path. Ian still had to instruct himself to accept an offered clasp, that this was natural, a way people reassured each other. Even now, he did not truly understand when a handshake was necessary, but it no longer worried him unduly. Those who loved him understood.

By the time Ian pulled his gaze from his hand, he was alone in the night.

He extinguished the lantern and set it down, leaving it behind as he made his way to the path that began at the very top of the bluff and then down the cliff face to the sea below.

Ian found them in a cave about half a mile from where the path ended on the rocky shore. He moved like a ghost, using the rising mist to conceal him. He saw the kidnappers' lights darting through darkness, and at the boulders at the bottom of the path, he came across yet another strip of Jamie's nightshirt.

Ian would have chosen a better cave for concealment. Not far from where the kidnappers had chosen to shelter was a narrow fissure that exited into a tunnel that opened to a stretch of shingle on the other side of the outcropping. These men, however, didn't know this shoreline like Ian did.

Ian also knew that if he rushed in with nothing but the knife he'd picked up in Cameron's rooms, a *sgian dubh*, he'd be surrounded, beaten down, possibly shot. None of that would help Jamie.

What Ian needed to do was flush them out, drive the kidnappers into a place of his choosing. Then he could separate them from one another and Jamie, and rescue his son.

Ian rarely debated with himself once he chose a course of action. He made a decision and carried it out.

He faded into the shadows and moved to the most hidden cave in this cluster, one that in the old smuggling days on this coast had been stocked with ample supplies. Not that smuggling had ceased altogether, which was why this cave still had a stash.

Ian gathered what he needed into a canvas bag, which he slung to his back. He picked up a few other useful items then climbed out past the concealing scrub, all the way back up the path to the top of the low cliffs.

He walked along the cliff to the spot he knew was just above the cave the abductors had chosen. Here Ian dropped to his belly and crawled a few yards forward on the sharp rocks. Tufts of grass and heather grew here, the plants as resilient as the Highlanders who'd inhabited these glens forever.

A crack in the cliff rocks formed a natural chimney for the cave below, which was likely why the villains had chosen it. The night was cold—they'd want a fire to keep warm. Indeed, Ian saw a small campfire through the fissure, the flames straining against the draft.

Ian pulled out the wad of oil-drenched rags he'd taken from the stores, opened the small jar of kerosene he'd found, and soaked the rags with the liquid. He struck a match against a black rock, and lit one tip of the cloth. Jamie, if he were conscious, would know what to do. If he weren't conscious, Ian would storm down and grab him after the men boiled out.

Ian quickly shoved the burning rags through the hole, to land right on top of the campfire.

The small fire faded for a second as the wet bundle choked it, then the rags exploded in a glare of blue and yellow light. Black smoke streamed to fill the cave as the oil under the kerosene caught and smoldered.

Men coughed, swore, shouted. They fled the cave, choking, drawing weapons, searching frantically for the source of attack.

A small white streak darted among them and then past. *Jamie.*

Ian's body went slack, his heart pounding until his head throbbed. His relief was so complete, he almost forgot the next part of his mission.

One of the men saw Jamie. "Get after 'im!" the thug yelled, with a cadence that spoke of London backstreets. They were far from their element. "Grab 'im!"

Jamie ran, his bare legs flashing, straight to the path that led to the cliff tops. Jamie's hands were bound before him, but he didn't let that slow him down.

Five burly men chased him. Likely they'd catch Jamie

before he reached safety. Ian, however, wanted them up that path, which led straight to where he needed them to go.

Ian lifted another item he'd brought, the Winchester rifle that had been locked, unloaded, into a crate, along with a box of shells. Ian cocked the now-loaded rifle, sighted well away from Jamie, and shot down into the cove behind the men.

More bellowing, swearing, chaos. Ian recocked and shot, recocked and shot, the repeating action of the Winchester letting him fire several rounds without stopping. The final shot had the last of the five men scrambling desperately for the cliffs.

The path emerged about twenty yards from where Ian lay. Jamie reached the top just ahead of the thugs, and started running, not toward home, but across a field, heading for the woods on the other side of open land.

"Good lad," Ian said under his breath. He got his feet under him but remained in a crouch, not wanting his silhouette to show against the night sky.

Jamie had darted under the trees when his abductors, with their longer stride, caught up to him. One scooped up Jamie—who swore like the best of them—and continued into the woods.

Ian slung the rifle and pack to his back, rose, and ran silently after them.

Ian caught up to the man bringing up the rear just outside the line of trees. This man was a little portlier than the others, a little more out of breath.

Ian had his arm around the thug's throat, hand across his mouth before he could cry out. A fist across the man's temple made him sag, but he struggled, still conscious, so Ian banged him back into the nearest tree. Ian was gone before the unfortunate man landed in a heap on the damp ground.

The next thug did manage a shout before Ian could

silence him. Ian dragged him aside into deep shadow, hearing the others call worriedly after him.

Ian's blow with the hilt of the *sgian dubh* quieted this man right away—or else, the thug decided that folding up and lying still was a good idea. Ian left him and ducked under the trees as one of the man's colleagues came running back to see what was the matter.

This man approached cautiously, but from the way he blundered about, his lantern obviously night-blinded him. Ian was beside him before the man registered his presence, his soft grunt of surprise lost as Ian's fist put him on the ground.

The floor of the woods was muddy, marsh waters oozing through. Ian knew the dry paths and quickly skirted more treacherous footing. He heard the remaining two men snarling as they slipped or stepped knee-deep into mud. Jamie didn't make a sound.

If they'd hurt Jamie—if they'd so much as frightened him . . .

Ian's breath suddenly left him, his feet ceasing to move. He needed to continue, to find his son, but against his will, black panic from the past rose inside him, blotting out all coherent thought.

Ian hated that his mind could do this to him. He'd be perfectly fine, living his day-to-day life, then something would trigger terrible visions—sights as well as sounds and smells, memories he'd hoped he'd never encounter again. Ian's blasted mind forgot nothing.

He remembered how he'd run through these very woods as a lad, terrified of the will-o'-the-wisps that glowed deep between the trees. Ian would run from his father, knowing the man would snatch him up and throw him to the ground if he were caught.

Ian's only refuge had been to find a place as far from home as his legs would take him, which often meant these woods.

His father refused to follow him there—whether from fear or because the old duke simply didn't want his boots dirty, Ian had never learned.

Ian would run until his strength gave out, and he ended up facedown, panting and sobbing, in the mud. After a long time, Hart would find him. Hart would help him up, and they'd sit together on a boulder at the edge of the trees, simply watching the world. Hart never admonished Ian, never derided him for his fear, his need to escape. The two brothers would sit in silence, Hart understanding. Until Beth, Hart was the only one who had.

One night, when Ian had been about seven years old, as he and Hart had waited for Ian to calm enough to walk home, the sky had suddenly burst with color. Waving bands of green had rippled into the heavens, flowing among the stars.

Ian jerked himself to the present. The sky above the trees was glowing with the same bright green, bands of it flaring high into the atmosphere.

He heard the astonishment of the two men who still had Jamie.

"'Struth!" one said loudly. "What the bleeding 'ell?"

"This place ain't right," the other said. "It ain't worth the pay. Kill the lad, and let's be gone."

The raging cry of a Highland warrior ripped from Ian's throat as he barreled through the woods at full speed, rifle in one hand, *sgian dubh* in the other.

The two men had pistols. Green light gleamed on the barrels as they were aimed at Ian, and Ian heard Jamie's shout.

"Dad!"

A pistol went off. Ian wasn't there to receive the bullet— he'd already spun aside in the darkness.

"Dad!"

Jamie's yell came from Ian's left. The shot had come

from the right. Ian lifted his rifle and fired at the man on the right. The thug screamed and collapsed.

Ian levered the rifle and advanced rapidly until he stood six feet from the man who held Jamie.

Jamie hung from the crook of the man's arm, hands bound. The last man standing pointed his pistol at Ian, and Ian aimed the rifle directly at his head.

"Put m' son down," Ian said, making every word slow and clear.

Jamie hung still, not fighting. Not from fear for himself, Ian knew. Jamie worried that a sudden move would make the man shoot, and Ian might die.

"Put m' son *down*," Ian repeated.

The pistol wavered. Above them, the lights continued to soar, the man's eyes shining in their glow.

A sudden burst of red among the green made the thug jump. In that instant, he fired, and so did Ian.

Hot pain brushed Ian's side as he threw himself out of the way. Ian swung in a full circle, kilt moving, until he faced the man again, rifle raised.

Except the thug was no longer there. He was on the ground, Jamie under him. Ian laid the rifle on the ground and approached, his knife held ready.

Jamie crawled out from under his unmoving captor, struggling with his bonds. "Dad, did he get you?" He was shivering, his words shaky. "Dad—ye all right? Speak t' me!"

Ian swept up Jamie, holding him in strong arms while he swiftly cut away the thin rope around Jamie's wrists.

"He missed," Ian said. "Grazed me. I'm not s' old I can't duck a bullet."

Jamie laughed out loud, then he flung his arms around Ian, his body trembling.

Jamie would never, ever break down and cry before his sisters, or his young cousins, or even his mother, but here in the privacy of the woods, he clung to Ian and wept.

Ian held him close, his own eyes wet, rejoicing that his son was warm and alive and safe in his arms. Nothing else mattered, only this now.

Jamie's cries died into sniffles, and he scrubbed a hand across his dirty face. Ian went on holding him, father and son taking comfort in each other, as the aurora spun in its green and red dance in the heavens.

Chapter 19

Under the last flares of the aurora borealis, Beth saw Ian silhouetted on a hill against the sky, a rifle across his back, and a boy in his arms. Beth shook off the well-meaning holds of John and Eleanor and raced up the path, making straight for her husband and son.

Ian stopped and waited for her. Beth, her heart pounding, reached them, sobbing in relief when she saw that Jamie was whole and unhurt.

No words would come as she took Jamie into her arms, holding him tight. He was heavy, her boy, growing so swiftly. At the moment, he was only her firstborn son, the babe the midwife had laid into her arms so long ago. That faraway morning, Ian had put his hand on Jamie's back while the lad lay on Beth's chest, completing the circle.

They completed it again, Ian, Beth, and Jamie. The girls, guarded by Eleanor, came running to them next, crying and overjoyed.

Ian lifted Megan, and Belle flung her arms around her mother and father at the same time. They were a family, whole and together.

The household surged forward to bring them home,

everyone talking at once. Fellows and his men headed for the woods where Ian directed, Fellows giving orders to arrest all they could find. He sent others to the cove, to wait for the ship that had been coming to take away the villains.

Jamie, once he'd recovered his composure, struggled to get down. Beth released him with reluctance, but Jamie was fine, she had to admit. Excited and exhausted, but whole.

Surrounded by family, friends, and protectors, they made for the house, which was fully lit. Beth noticed Ian walking somewhat stiffly, but he said nothing, only carried Megan in silence.

Jamie refused to return to bed. Beth allowed him to sit up in the drawing room to tell his story and fortify himself with hot, milky tea. The girls and wee Malcolm declared they wouldn't go to bed if Jamie didn't. They, and Alec, who was at last awake and furious he'd missed the adventure, sat bundled in blankets and plaids, surrounded by parents, friends, retainers.

"They wanted Alec," Jamie was saying as Curry handed him his cup. Curry had lingered to serve the tea Eleanor poured out, and whisky for the adults, and he made no pretense of not listening avidly.

"I heard the men whispering to each other when they came in," Jamie went on. "They were after the heir to Kilmorgan. So I sat up and told them I was Alec Mackenzie, the duke's son. They didn't waste any time sticking a cloth full of chloroform over Alec's face, and mine. I smelled it and held my breath as long as I could. I drifted off a little, but was awake soon enough."

As Jamie spoke, his voice grew stronger, more confident. "They first wanted to hide out in the distillery until morning. Then they decided it was too risky—ye might come and find them. So they stole a few things and left again. They couldn't see well in the dark, even with the lanterns, but they made me tell them the way to the cove where they could wait for a ship. I guided them to the cave they hid in—I decided it was a good place for Dad to corner them. I was right." Jamie paused to take a sip of tea, his face flushed with heat and triumph. "You should have seen Dad drive them out of there. They ran like their backsides were on fire." He hooted with laughter, proud and happy.

Eleanor leaned down and kissed his cheek, her eyes full of relief. "You are a brave, wonderful lad, my nephew. What made you declare you were Alec and go in his place?"

Jamie gave a shrug so like Ian's that Beth's heart ached. "Alec's littler than me, in't he? They might have hurt him. I'm bigger and older—I could take it."

"I'm not *that* little," seven-year-old Alec said with indignation.

The fact that Alec was Lord Hart Alec Graham Mackenzie, heir to the Duke of Kilmorgan, and Jamie was the son of the youngest son, thus at the bottom of the line of succession, did not keep Jamie from sending Alec a severe look.

"You're little enough," Jamie said. "Those men would have carried ye off like a sack of potatoes. I was protecting ye, lad. That's what cousins are for."

Alec's look, while still petulant, held admiration. "Well, thank ye," Alec said. "'Twas well done."

"It certainly was," John Ackerley put in. "A toast to Jamie Mackenzie, a brave, brave lad."

Jamie only shrugged again as they raised their glasses and cups, his cheekbones red. "Dad was very brave too. He fought them all, single-handed, and put down every one of the bas—er, thugs."

Ian, who had said very little from where he sat next to Jamie, now spoke. "The lights."

Jamie frowned at him, then gave a conceding nod. "Aye, th' aurora distracted them a just a little, I suppose. We were lucky the lights showed themselves tonight."

Ackerley gave him a wise look. "The Lord works in mysterious ways, young man."

"Aye," Jamie answered gravely. "So do Mackenzies."

After an hour or so of celebrating, Jamie began to droop. Beth declared that the children must rest to face the day tomorrow, and that Ian needed his sleep too. Both the younger and older generations made their way to their beds, no longer reluctant.

Ian insisted he tuck the children in, and Beth didn't have the heart to stop him. This time, however, the boys slept in the nursery, the room now guarded not only by the nanny but by two sturdy policemen, who declared no kidnappers would get past them.

Not until Ian and Beth were safely shut into their own bedroom did Beth let herself collapse.

Ian caught her, her tall, strong husband cradling her in his arms. The firmness of his body against hers, his warmth, his solidity, let her finally break down. Ian, the man so many people dismissed as mad, had gone alone into the night, bested five men, and brought Beth's son home to her, alive and unscathed.

"Thank you, love," she whispered, her face buried in his shoulder. Tears wet his shirt. "Thank you."

Ian wordlessly pulled her close. He kissed the line of her hair, warm lips on her skin.

Beth pulled back, taking in Ian's loose shirt, his plaid sagging around his hips. He was delectable.

When she slid her arms around him again, Ian winced, and grunted.

"You *are* hurt," Beth said with conviction. She pushed aside his protesting hands and dragged up his shirt. A thin but deep gash laced the hard muscles of his side, dried blood caking the wound. "Good heavens, what happened?"

"He had a pistol," Ian said, his tone as matter-of-fact as Jamie's had been. "Didn't go in."

"Oh, Ian." Beth rested her head against Ian's chest, feeling his even heartbeat. The injury brought home to her how easily she could have lost him tonight. "Ian," she whispered.

"I'm all right," Ian said, sounding puzzled at her concern.

Beth made herself let go of him. She ordered Ian to sit down, then she fetched a basin of water and a cloth and bathed the wound.

Ian let her, though he didn't hold back his swearing when she dug too deep. As Beth wrapped the final bandage around him, Ian stopped growling, cupped his hand around her hip, and pulled her down to his kilt-clad lap.

The cloth Beth had used to clean the last of the blood fell to the carpet with a wet slap. Ian's bare, tanned torso moved against the pale bandages as he slid his hands up her waist, pulling her close.

His kiss was fierce, savage, all his fears, rage, and joy coming to Beth. His hands found her curves and warmed them.

When he eased the kiss to its close, Beth touched his face, her heart full. "I might have had to say good-bye to you forever tonight, you and Jamie."

Ian skimmed his thumb across her cheek. He studied her with eyes of amber-gold, the eyes that had arrested Beth when she'd seen him for the first time. She'd known, when his gaze had swept over her, that Ian Mackenzie was an extraordinary man indeed.

"I'll always come home to you," Ian said. "My Beth. Ye *are* my home."

"And you know how to melt my heart." Beth brushed a kiss to the corner of his mouth. "You're a scoundrel."

Ian's answer was to draw her up to him for a deeper kiss. He'd said all he would say on the matter, she knew.

Ian kissed Beth until she was breathless, then he shoved aside his kilt and her skirts, moving her to straddle him. Beth cupped his face in her hands, loving to watch his eyes as he slid inside her. Ian made no noise at all as they joined together, but his gaze sharpened, holding hers. He always looked at her now when they made love.

Beth held on to Ian as he thrust up into her, taking her in desperate longing and raw joy.

When dawn came, Ian charged out the front door just as Fellows started to climb into the carriage that waited to take him to the railway station. Fellows paused, startled, but Ian shoved him on into the coach with a hand on his back.

"What the devil?" Fellows growled as Ian swung himself up behind him.

"Go!" Ian called to the coachman. He thumped down on the seat opposite Fellows, who settled in, giving his greatcoat an irritated wrench. "I'm coming with ye," Ian said.

"I see that. Do you even know where I'm going?"

"You're off to see Halsey, and I'm coming with ye."

By now Fellows had learned he could not argue with Ian at his most stubborn. "Does Beth know you're accompanying me?" he asked in a mild tone.

"Aye." Ian had trouble with lies, so he always spoke the bald truth when asked. Ian *had* told Beth he was going with Fellows, even though she'd been half asleep, pleasantly warm and mussed, and could only murmur, "What? Ian . . . ?"

The journey to Edinburgh and then Lincolnshire took all morning, without much conversation between the two men. Unlike Ackerley, Fellows saw no need to converse unless necessary. He didn't talk to fill time or awkward spaces, a trait Ian appreciated in his half brother.

They arrived at Halsey's lavish estate in the early afternoon, the September sunshine warm, though the air was crisp.

Halsey was hosting a hunting party, his footman coolly informed them, but if they cared to follow . . .

As the footman led them out the back of the house and down a sweep of stairs to the lawn, Ian heard horns sounding far out into the woods. Somewhere in the fields, Englishmen in red coats, which they called *pink* for some reason, would be charging about en masse after a single fox.

Halsey, apparently, was not riding with the hunters but lingered inside a pavilion, where he drank bloodred wine with two elderly guests past their riding days.

Ian recognized the two gentlemen—one was an English duke Hart actually respected, the other a knight of the realm, a soldier who'd earned his honors in Crimea.

Ian noted them only in passing. He went straight to Halsey, fisted his large hands in Halsey's shirt, and hauled the man from his chair, hoisting him high. Halsey dangled in Ian's grip, his mouth open.

Words Ian wanted to say flooded his mind—too many words. They jumbled and tangled, getting in the way.

Ian shook Halsey, his hands closing tighter. As he looked into the man's watery blue eyes, pools of arrogance, the confusion of words fell away, and Ian knew exactly what to say.

"Ye took m' son."

Halsey's eyes widened over Ian's fists. "*Your* son? No, not y—"

Ian's voice rose. "Ye took m' *son*!"

"No, not *yours*?" Fellows asked mildly. "Is that what you meant to say, your lordship?"

Halsey stiffened, but he didn't dare take his eyes from Ian. The other two gentlemen in the tent had risen, but only looked on, not speaking, not interfering.

"You intended to kidnap Hart's son," Fellows continued. "Those are the orders you gave your hired men. They *do* work for you—the ones we caught are singing your guilt."

"The devil . . ." Halsey spluttered.

"You conspired to abduct a duke's son." Fellows spoke calmly, but in a voice of granite that brooked no argument. "You *did* abduct the son of Lord Ian Mackenzie, who does not, as you can see, appear to be in a forgiving mood. You should fall on your knees and thank God that Jamie was returned home safely."

Ian slid one hand to Halsey's throat. This was the man responsible for dragging Jamie away, for having him carried off, bound, drugged, threatened. Ian could not forget the spike of fear that had lanced him when one of the thugs had said, *Kill the lad, and let's be gone.*

Halsey's pulse, his life, beat under Ian's fingers. All he had to do was squeeze . . .

"Ian," he heard Fellows say.

The stark terror in Halsey's eyes was gratifying. Halsey truly believed Ian would choke him to death, any moment now.

"Ian," Fellows repeated. "You can't strangle a peer of the realm in front of witnesses. I'd have to arrest you."

Ian put enough pressure on Halsey's windpipe to make the man's eyes bulge. He held him thus for a long moment, then finally he lowered Halsey to his feet but kept his hand around his throat.

"Help me," Halsey wheezed, gazing desperately at Fellows. "You're the police!"

"That I am," Fellows said. "But I've come to arrest you, so I'm not certain what help I will be."

Halsey looked in appeal to his guests, but the two gentlemen stood quietly, listening, saying nothing.

"You can't," Halsey said to Fellows.

"I can. You will be tried in the House of Lords, of course, but I'm not certain how your peers will view you. Child abduction is a heinous offense."

Halsey's fear increased. "It's not my fault. Not my fault! I had to. He commanded me!"

Fellows came to stand next to Ian. The two were of a height, one a Highland Scotsman on the edge of berserker rage, the other calmer, in a London suit, but with a look of steel.

"This is interesting," Fellows said to Halsey. "Who commanded you?"

"My father. And *his* father. On down the line. Ruin the Mackenzies. It's the first oath the Earl of Halsey swears when he takes the title."

"Really?" Fellows gave him a cool look worthy of Hart. "Why has my family not heard of this oath before?"

"Because *I* take my vows seriously! The Mackenzies did my family a wrong. We never forget. I promised to put it right."

The English duke broke in, his tone mild. "Not really the thing these days, Halsey. I believe I will send for my carriage." He strolled away, taking his time, as though the events in the pavilion were of no interest to him.

The soldier merely said, "Bad show, Halsey," and followed the duke out.

"Ian," Fellows spoke quietly. "Let him go."

Two constables appeared at the pavilion's entrance, and beyond the tent's wide flap, horses were crowding into the green field, the guests returning from the hunt. Dogs milled about, clustering, panting, and the noise of horses, dogs, and people filled the quiet afternoon.

Ian yanked Halsey from his feet and dragged him from the tent. In the sight of Halsey's guests, Ian released him, turning his back as the constables moved in to detain him on Fellows's order.

Ian walked away without looking back, without saying a word, as though Halsey no longer existed.

The English called such an action a *cut direct*. It meant that the person had done something unconscionable, deserving to be ignored and socially ruined.

While not as satisfying as strangling the man, Ian decided

that the cut direct had its merits. He could walk away from Lord Halsey and be done with him. Fellows would deal with Halsey, as would Hart, but Ian no longer had to think about him. His family was safe, and it was finished.

Ian walked through the house to the carriage and climbed inside to wait for Fellows, turning his thoughts squarely on Beth, and home.

Chapter 20

The arrival of Cameron and Ainsley, Mac and Isabella, Fellows's wife Louisa, Daniel and Violet, and all the Mackenzie children—not to mention the McBrides and their collective brood—pushed Ian's thoughts from the events of the previous days.

That was all over—*now* was a fine time to enjoy. The house filled with light, noise, and laughter. Ian reflected that before Beth, he had only been able to endure a few people at a time, and those his immediate family. Since then, his family had extended into many, a circle that grew each year, bringing friends along with them. These days, Ian found himself looking forward to being among them instead of dreading it as an ordeal. He still mostly listened instead of conversing, but he could be in the middle of them now, watching, observing, taking pleasure in their company.

Hart's birthday, a few days after the family's arrival, brought even more people to Kilmorgan. The doors between the huge formal drawing rooms on the ground floor had been flung open, combining several chambers into one. Family and guests swarmed them, talking and laughing, eating, drinking, while musicians filled the empty spaces with Scottish tunes.

So many colors, Ian thought as he stood holding a half-drunk glass of Mackenzie's finest malt. Blues and greens of Mackenzie and McBride plaids, plus the tartans of their neighbors and friends—red and black, yellow and green, red and blue. The ladies were in gowns of the plaid of their clans or popular hues of the day—bottle green, electric blue, silver gray, the palest pinks, yellows, and ivories on the youngest ladies.

Beth wore a gown of deep blue trimmed with silver braid—the skirt hung straight from her waist in front but gathered into a soft train behind her. Gloves covered her bare arms to the elbow, and the necklace of precious stones Ian had bought her in Edinburgh rested on her bosom.

Beth was animated as she moved among the guests, her cheeks flushed, her eyes as sparkling as the necklace. At one time, Beth had been shy but gracious—now she was a fine hostess, one of the brilliant Mackenzie women.

Ian enjoyed watching *her* most of all.

"Heard you tried to choke the Earl of Halsey to death." Mac Mackenzie, resplendent in Mackenzie plaid, formal coat, and watered silk waistcoat, stopped in front of his brother. His glass held lemonade, not whisky. "Damn, I wish I'd seen that."

Ian moved slightly so Mac did not block his view of Beth. "Halsey is finished."

"That he is. England will be too hot to hold him. His barrister might get him off on the charges Hart's laid against him for theft and kidnapping, but he'll have to flee the country, regardless. No one is happy with him." Mac grinned, his amber eyes glinting. "I think Old Malcolm would have toasted ye."

Mac lifted his glass and gazed up at the portrait of Malcolm and Mary Mackenzie that hung high on the wall, painted shortly after Malcolm had taken up the mantle of the dukedom. The pair looked down upon the assembled company with great dignity, but Ian swore he saw a twinkle in Malcolm's golden eyes.

"And, you got my bloody awful paintings back," Mac went on. "Thank you for that."

Ian shrugged. "They're not awful."

Mac looked pleased. "Kind of you to say so. I'll paint you much better daubs than those, though. I'll start tonight, in fact."

Mac toasted Ian with his lemonade, then turned and made his way toward the crowd around Hart. No matter how elegantly Mac dressed tonight, Ian knew he looked forward to throwing off everything but his kilt and tying a kerchief over his hair, ready to immerse himself in his art. As soon as Mac could politely escape, he'd be up in the studio in his wing of the house, busily painting away.

Cameron was the next Mackenzie to stop beside Ian. His suit and kilt were as formal as Mac's, but they hung negligently on his large frame. While Mac had been verbose about Halsey, Cam only pressed his big hand on Ian's shoulder.

"Well done, Ian."

Ian nodded, warming under his brother's praise.

Cameron stood with him a moment, the two of them studying the crowd. "Hart's in his element, isn't he?" Cam waved his whisky glass to where Hart stood quietly in the midst of a circle, all in that circle fixed avidly on him. Cam scoffed. "Hart hasn't changed. He loves to orchestrate everything, as usual."

"No, Eleanor does."

Cameron gave Ian a startled look, then laughed out loud. At that moment, the Duchess of Kilmorgan, cheeks pink, smile bright, glided unerringly to Hart, ending up at his side, her arm going through his. Deftly, she edged Hart from that group and took him to another.

As Hart glanced down at Eleanor, who was chattering,

as usual, his eyes took on a light of both hunger and deep happiness. Ian realized that Hart didn't give a damn where Eleanor was taking him, or whom she wanted him to speak to, as long as she was with him.

Another Mackenzie, a near mirror of Cameron, but twenty years younger, came at them. "Now then, Dad," Daniel said, giving his father a nod. "Ian, I believe that Ackerley fellow is looking for you. Although at the moment, he's listening to my wife explain to him the tricks of a fraudulent medium's trade. He's lapping it up."

Violet Mackenzie, her dark hair shining, was speaking to Ackerley, her expression amused. Ackerley looked poleaxed.

"Vi has that effect on men," Daniel said with pride. "Though I believe I'll go steer him away. He's a widower—he might get ideas. I don't care if he's a man of the cloth."

Daniel winked at them and moved purposefully toward Ackerley and Violet. Cameron boomed another laugh. "A man married to a beautiful woman can never relax his vigilance. Danny learned that soon enough." He rumbled in his throat. "Although if any man looks twice at my daughter-in-law, they'll not have only Danny to face."

Ainsley, Cameron's wife, her light blond hair dressed in a wonderfully complicated knot of ringlets, came to rest at Cameron's side. Cameron went from growling bear to human being in the space of an instant, his arm stealing around Ainsley's waist.

Ian started to move away from them, wanting to speak to Ackerley, then remembered the lessons in politeness he'd painstakingly learned from Beth. "Excuse me," he said to Ainsley. "I need . . ." He gestured with his glass to Ackerley.

Ainsley flashed her warm smile, looking pleased. "Of course, Ian."

Ian gave her and Cameron a nod, made brief eye contact with them both, then strode away. He fleetingly wondered if he'd performed the social niceties correctly, then forgot all about it as he reached Ackerley, Violet, and Daniel.

"Come and talk to me," he said to Ackerley.

Ackerley looked surprised, but Violet, who'd ceased her conversation the moment Ian arrived, gave Ackerley a soothing look. "Ian would not ask if it weren't important," she said. "We will speak later, Mr. Ackerley."

"Indeed," Ackerley said, somewhat breathlessly. "I look forward to it."

Ian again made himself remember to utter a polite leave-taking to Violet and Daniel, then led Ackerley out of the drawing rooms.

Guests roamed freely about the house, most congregating in the gallery, which had become a source of fascination now that it had been the scene of a crime. All the stolen art had been restored. Fellows had found the remaining paintings and bronzes in Halsey's cellars, shoved between racks of wine. Mac and several art historians had worked swiftly to repair the damaged artworks and return them to their places in the gallery.

Ian led Ackerley up the stairs to a sitting room in his wing of the house. He shut the door behind them, and the noise of the crowd below dimmed.

"Well?" Ackerley asked, sounding eager. "Are you ready to resume our sessions?"

"No." Ian set his whisky glass on a table. He hadn't spoken to Ackerley much since the night of Jamie's abduction, needing time to think things through. Ian had mulled and pondered the question in many different ways, always arriving at the same conclusion.

"I have decided," Ian said. "I no longer wish you to cure me."

Ackerley's face fell. "No? But we were making such progress. I planned to write up my notes and send them to the philosophers of science in Vienna—"

Ian held up his hand. "I don't wish to be cured."

Ackerley heaved a sigh, but he gave a resigned shrug. "I cannot force you, of course. That would be remiss. But may I ask why?"

Ian waited, then realized that Ackerley was, in fact, asking why.

"I am mad," Ian answered. "I always will be. But if I hadn't been mad, I wouldn't have found Jamie." And that would have been unthinkable. "I *work*. So, I want to stay mad."

"Ah." Ackerley gave Ian a thoughtful look. "That is true. I would say that you do, er . . . work."

They both fell silent. Ackerley chewed his lower lip over his neat beard while Ian stood motionless.

"One thing," Ackerley said after a time. "Do you mind if I continue asking you questions about your madness? To satisfy my curiosity. My besetting sin."

Ian shrugged, already finished with the topic and moving on to other matters in his head. With Halsey and danger out of the way, Ian could resume the fishing appointments with Jamie. The fish would be biting tomorrow; he was sure of it.

Ackerley was still talking. "Also—do you mind if I continue reading Lady Mary's journals you found in your attics? Perhaps with a thought to publishing them? Lady Mary's account of her elopement with Lord Malcolm makes an intriguing love story."

Ian could fish with Jamie, then later Ian would clean up with a bath, asking Beth in to wash his back. "As you like."

"Or, perhaps I should ask His Grace? It is his house, after all . . ."

"No." Ian's attention snapped to Ackerley. "The journals are mine. You take them and do as you wish."

Ackerley opened his mouth to continue speaking, but was interrupted by Beth's gentle voice. "Ah. I'd wondered what had become of you two."

The hum of the party below came to them, reality intruding into Ian's quiet sanctuary.

The next moment, Ian didn't care. His wife was here, with her blue eyes, her warm voice, her half smile. The noise beyond, the nervous throat-clearing of Ackerley—all faded before the joy that was Beth.

"Beg pardon, Beth. I didn't mean to be rude." Ackerley glanced at Ian, then he flushed. "Well, I'd best be getting back downstairs. Thank you, Beth, for allowing me the privilege of attending your gathering. Quite a regal crowd."

Beth shook her head. "Family and friends only. Hart insisted."

"Even so, I am quite the nobody, but I am enjoying myself immensely. Lord Ian, thank you for indulging me."

Ackerley was in front of Ian again, holding out his hand. He so enjoyed handshakes.

Ian stared at Ackerley's open palm. Ackerley, as the silence stretched, began to withdraw, but Ian shot his own hand forward and clasped Ackerley's in a firm grip. For the first time in Ian's life he *wanted* to shake another's hand, understood why it meant respect.

"Thank you," Ian said sincerely, "for all you've done."

"Oh, well, I . . ." Ackerley looked pleased. "I haven't done anything, really. I . . ." He cleared his throat as Ian released him. "I'll just go back downstairs now."

Ackerley gave Beth a bow and a wide smile, then he left the two alone, whistling a little tune as he went.

Beth watched Ian as he remained in the middle of the room, gazing down at his bare hand. To this day, Beth had not learned exactly what went through Ian's mind when he stood, unmoving, and went *away*. At the moment, she had no idea whether Ian pondered the nature of the universe or was simply fascinated by the lines on his own palm.

She'd concluded that the only way to find out was to ask him.

"Ian," she said. "Do you want to go back downstairs? We will soon all trudge to the ballroom for waltzing."

Ian continued to study his hand, making no acknowledgment that he had heard her. He did this sometimes, became so fascinated with the world inside his head that an hour could pass before he'd return.

"If you prefer to remain here, it is your choice," Beth continued. "I will make your excuses. Or perhaps I will not say anything—it is no one's business what you do."

When Ian didn't respond, Beth gathered her skirts and turned away. She'd go downstairs, continue helping Eleanor and her sisters-in-law hostess, and return to Ian later.

"Stay."

The one word brought Beth swiftly back. "Ian?"

Ian didn't answer. Beth halted beside him, the necklace he'd bought her cool and heavy on her chest.

Ian glanced at Beth from the corners of his eyes. "Love you, m' Beth."

Beth's heart swelled, overflowing with what she felt for this man. "I love you too, Ian." She slid her hand onto his large one, which had so captured his attention. "All of you, my darling. Just as you are."

Ian studied her satin glove, her fingers small against his, then lifted his gaze to fully meet Beth's. "Then that's what I'll be."

Beth tightened her hand around his. "It's all you ever need to be."

Ian's answering smile lit every fire inside her, banishing every fear, every trouble of the last terrible days. Her Ian had come back to her, stronger than ever.

And devastatingly handsome. The wicked look he turned on Beth burned her.

"My Beth." Ian traced the pattern of the necklace, then he leaned down and pressed a fiery kiss right over her heart.

"My Ian," Beth whispered.

His arms went around her, and Beth's hard, handsome Highlander scooped her against him for a long kiss.

The kiss opened her, heated her. Ian drew her close, folds of his kilt melding with those of her skirts. His hands skimmed up her back, and Beth felt her bodice loosening, cool air touching her skin.

"I don't want to go down to the ballroom," Ian said quietly. "I want t' stay here. With you."

"Yes." Beth's answer was breathless. "I think that situation will be perfect."

Ian Mackenzie turned in place with her as the music of a waltz began below. Her gown loosened more as they moved in their own dance, fabric sliding from her body, though the necklace remained.

Ian spun slowly around with Beth, supporting her in his strong arms, his golden eyes entirely on hers. Then they were falling to the carpet, Ian catching her, the lights and colors of the room whirling like the green and crimson glory of the auroras.

Ready to find
your next great read?

Let us help.

Visit prh.com/nextread

Penguin
Random
House

CITY

OF

GHOSTS

VICTORIA SCHWAB

SCHOLASTIC INC.

Text copyright © 2018 by Victoria Schwab
Map copyright © 2018 by Maxime Plasse

This book was originally published in hardcover by Scholastic Press in 2018.

All rights reserved. Published by Scholastic Inc., *Publishers since 1920*. SCHOLASTIC and associated logos are trademarks and/or registered trademarks of Scholastic Inc.

The publisher does not have any control over and does not assume any responsibility for author or third-party websites or their content.

No part of this publication may be reproduced, stored in a retrieval system, or transmitted in any form or by any means, electronic, mechanical, photocopying, recording, or otherwise, without written permission of the publisher. For information regarding permission, write to Scholastic Inc., Attention: Permissions Department, 557 Broadway, New York, NY 10012.

This book is a work of fiction. Names, characters, places, and incidents are either the product of the author's imagination or are used fictitiously, and any resemblance to actual persons, living or dead, business establishments, events, or locales is entirely coincidental.

ISBN 978-1-338-11102-6

10 9 8 7 6 5 4   19 20 21 22 23

Printed in the U.S.A.   40
This edition first printing 2019

Book design by Baily Crawford